Travels and Times of Five Generations

Prudence Backhouse

Published in 2022 by
Prudence Backhouse
in association with
Arthur H Stockwell Ltd
West Wing Studios
Unit 166, The Mall
Luton, Bedfordshire
ahstockwell.co.uk

British Library Cataloguing-in-Publication Data
A catalogue record for this book is available
from the British Library.
ISBN: 9781399918909

*The views and opinions expressed herein belong to the author
and do not necessarily reflect those of AH Stockwell*

Contents

Contents (cont.)

To the children, the grandchildren and the six little greats

The caravan, at the fruit farm, still in use at The Mill.

Introduction

Some thirty years before this book was written, I was given by an aunt some stories about her family, collected and written down while she was growing up in Alexandria. She was Christine, younger sister of Dorothy; and Dorothy became my mother-in-law. Those notes remained in a drawer until after the deaths of both of them, and they had probably assumed I was not interested. But the notes became the foundation of the first part of this book.

The story takes place over five generations – of setting forth and homing in, of disruptions and returning.

In 1864, George Alderson, from Suffolk, was given, by his company, the job of fitting a water pump in Egypt for a customer. He and his family expected he would be home in a few months. Instead, captivated by the city of Alexandria, he decided to stay there for his lifetime. With a partner, he established an engineering company; and with his English wife, a family of ten children.

The oldest was Alex, who grew up to take on the company. He and his wife Nellie had five children – the eldest was Dorothy who was adventurous and unconventional, as was the man she married.

He was Hugh Backhouse, from Yorkshire, and he had set off at the age of sixteen to pursue his dream of wildness and endeavour in the Argentine. It was the First World War that brought them together, Hugh, having dutifully enlisted, being sent to Alexandria for his military service. After the war, their ranching life in the Argentine began, and their two children spent their early years in the wide open spaces, often on horseback.

But, among other things, political and national disharmonies in the Argentine – part of the clouds gathering towards the Second World War, resulted in the family moving to Britain, taking away the hope and expectations of their son StJohn for his life on the ranch, which was later illicitly sold. Instead came years of being moved around, adjustment, education and decisions of his own. He joined the Royal Navy at sixteen.

While Alex and Nellie were coping with the War in Alexandria, I was growing up in a very British family through the war. StJohn and I met while he was on holiday from Montreal, where he had settled. He was staying with his mother, Dorothy, now caring for Alex and Nellie, ousted from their beloved Alexandria by political changes in Egypt.

We married and went to live in Montreal. But my roots in England drew us back, with our baby son, and over ten years we had three more children.

StJohn ran his own business successfully for several years – but then – there had to be space, and contact with growing things. After a long search and fraught start, we experienced thirty years of challenge and fulfilment.

Years later, three of the children, two grandchildren and little 'greats' had moved to Devon, where we were, and where had lived generations of my forbears.

Travels and Times of Five Generations

1: The First Tale

For Love of a City

I find the dates and places and peer through the words to visualise the families taking shape in their moments in history, circumstances and social settings. Some individuals cast themselves into foreign lands they planned for, fell in love with – or even refused. There was valour, persistence and hard work, the acceptance of foreign ways, the romance of wild spaces and traditions, narrowing sometimes to society's activities and means of affluence. Among all the branches I have glimpses of the children in the midst of their contrasting worlds of freedom or pampering, aspiration or limitations, and the impacts of social disruption or total war.

I never met my father-in-law, Hugh Salmon Backhouse. To me he was a shadowy presence behind my husband's life, to be admired for his art and the books he had written – *Among the Gauchos* and *Chief of the Arab Scouts*. But when our children and grandchildren became interested to find out more about him through the Internet, StJohn was not forthcoming. His hackles went up. Somewhere there was a hurt, or guilt, or something too precious to share, so I avoided the subject with him, and only became interested later. I only suppose that Hugh was aware of our marriage, though his letters did not mention it.

In order to tell our story I have drawn some facts from *Among the Gauchos*, combining them with stories StJohn told us. Hugh subtracted two years from his age on publication, for his own reasons. His wife and children are not mentioned in the book. He was writing from Stockholm, during and after the Second World War, where he was reputed to be working for the secret service. He was encouraged in his writing, and painting, by a Swedish publisher, and newspaper people, who gave him enormous help. Perhaps at that time it was thought that the inclusion of family would detract from the romantic independence of the stories, and perhaps the family was not the centre of his interest anyway. But in reading *Among the Gauchos* it is strange to come across places of which we have photos that include Hugh and the children, and names of ranches familiar to us. The security of his family could have been another reason.

StJohn's mother, Dorothy, the eldest of four daughters and a son, was born in Alexandria, Egypt, and I met her and her valiant parents, Nellie and Alex ,in 1953, knowing little of their story.

Dorothy's youngest sister, Christine, gathered and wrote down much of what she learnt about the family history, and I am indebted to her for the stories of the Aldersons from 1864. She gave the typescript to Dorothy, who gave it to me years later, and by the time it had lain in my desk drawer for another thirty years it had become history, and I am grateful to have a little of the human side of that period of British–Egyptian interaction, up towards the Suez Crisis. Christine was also good at telling stories to children, and it is as StJohn would have heard them when as a child he stayed with his grandparents in Alexandria that I have included them.

I was born in 1935, and for my family 'colonials' were slightly humorous. My father, W. Harvey Gervis, was a surgeon from a long line of medical men. He would lean back in his chair and say in gently mocking tones, "When I was in Poonah…" The worlds of polo and great estates and the hazards of governing other lands were remote. While StJohn's great-grandfather George was selling irrigation pumps to Egyptian landowners, my forbears were riding on horseback down Devon lanes, visiting their patients, or treating them in hospital or their own consulting rooms. Prudence Gervis was carved into a couple of Devon headstones.

But here was I marrying a colonial.

George – The Pioneer

Irrigation pumps were becoming popular with Egyptian landowners, and British engineering companies were successfully supplying the demand. In 1864, George Beeton Alderson, StJohn's great-grandfather, who had completed his apprenticeship with Ransome & Sims of Ipswich, had explained the merits of his company's machine to his Egyptian customer, who was well satisfied.

"I would like you to come to my estate and set it up for me," he said.

George tried to explain politely that the pumps could be delivered and set up without him. But the Pasha had decided he would only buy it if George came too.

After much discussion between the customer, George and his employer, it was decided that he would go out to Egypt, and do the job.

His father, George Frederick, and his mother, Marie, were no doubt surprised when he went home and told them what was being arranged. They thought their young son (he was twenty-one) was in a nice safe steady job, not going off into the world just to sell a pump. But George cheerfully packed up his clothes and made the arrangements, telling them he would be home when the job was done.

It was a similar beginning for Alfred Dale, another apprentice, from Whickham Market. He was from a farming family, one of nine brothers and one little sister called Mary Anne.

Alfred was adventurous and fond of doing experiments with electricity. He had persuaded his family to stand in a circle, hands joined, while he passed a mild current through their hands, which Mary Anne did not enjoy at all. But when Alfred told her he was going out to Egypt, she was very sad because he was her favourite brother, and she begged him to take her with him. He dried her tears, and told her that if he stayed (which he did not expect to do) he would come and fetch her. But her mother said to herself that it would be all right anyway, Mary Anne would meet someone suitable for her nearby, and settle down.

So the one, and then the other, sailed away to that very different country.

George was met by Ibrahim, an employee of the purchaser of the pump, which was laboriously transported across a strip of desert near Alexandria to the site. Amid the details of his care for the machine, George hardly noticed the shock of the different climate and scenery until it was safely in place, and he could change his clothes and begin to think of putting his training into practice and the pump into use. Over the top of the pump house, a room was to be built for George to live in during the time he must instruct Ibrahim and his team to work it, over the next few weeks. With help from them and the estate owner, he began to pick up the language, and establish working relationships. Then, as materials were supplied, they had to be built into a possible form of accommodation. He also had to adjust himself to the food supplied for him, and write letters to his parents, on notepaper he had included in his luggage, telling them of his progress. It was a gradual process of work and learning.

'There is an island in the surging sea which is called Pharos' – so runs Homer's *Iliad*, a copy of which Alexander of Macedon is reputed to have kept by him when he came and founded his city of Alexandria in 331 bc. Pharos is three-quarters of a mile offshore, forming a harbour that could hold 1,200 ships, and a freshwater lagoon, Lake Marcotis, lies to the south.

He brought teams of architects and builders, and the city planned on a grid system, developed into one of the loveliest in the world, and a centre of trade by land and sea.

He stayed only a year, and went off to continue fighting the Persians, who had ousted the Pharaoh ten years before. Then he died of a fever at the age of thirty-three, ruler of a large part of the world. His body was brought back to Alexandria for burial by one of his generals, Ptolemy, who may have been his half-brother, and all his generals began sharing out his land. Ptolemy, the first of a succession of Ptolemys with Cleopatra in its seventh generation, took a long swathe of Egypt, including the Nile Delta.

The Ptolemy's were respectful of the Egyptian gods and goddesses, and took part in the building and preservation of temples, so they were not resented as the Persians had been. Many Greek scholars came to live in Alexandria – Eratosthenes who measured the circumference of the earth; Hipparchus, who mapped the stars; Euclid, who formulated geometry. It was probably Sostratus who designed the lighthouse built on Pharos, one of the Seven Wonders of the World. It was over 120 metres high, and had a revolving mirror of polished bronze that reflected the glow of a furnace for thirty miles out to sea, to guide ships past the reefs and islands. It stood for over 1,000 years.

Legend has it that the seventy scholars from Jerusalem who translated the Old Testament books of the Torah into Greek worked on the Isle of Pharos.

When Napoleon arrived in 1798, the population was only about 5,000, compared to the half million in Cleopatra's time. Well aware of the great history of Alexandria, he came to reinstigate, bringing 200 learned advisors for astronomy, archaeology, literature and much more, founding the Institute of Egypt to record and document. He also brought two printing presses, one using Arabic letters he had obtained from the Vatican. At the time when George arrived it was the only city outside Europe to be publishing newspapers and journals in different languages (including English), and using that Arabic printing press.

An Anglo-Turkish force ousted Napoleon in 1881, but many of the advisors stayed on, and Muhammed Ali, in charge of Egypt under the Ottoman Empire, encouraged European development, education, culture and settlers. The city was rich in theatres, libraries and schools.

One of his successors, after long persuasion, had given permission to a French engineer, Ferdinand de Lesseps, to oversee the building of a canal that would link Europe to Asia – the Suez Canal. Britain was at first opposed to the idea, but was subsequently drawn into its benefits and catastrophes over the next seventy-five years. It was opened with great fanfare, including visits of European royalty (and performances of opera and music), in 1869, surely witnessed by George Alderson and Alfred Dale.

So this was the flourishing city that George walked round after he left his little dwelling over the pump, a city often at odds with its colonial power. George was captivated by it and remained a citizen and benefactor for the rest of his life.

In his exploration he came across another Englishman, called Stafford Allen, an engineer who was aiming to establish a business to work in the city. There were so many things that could be done, he told George, to improve facilities around the harbours and waterways. After many discussions, it was agreed between them that if George could procure some capital, they would work together.

So George arranged a return passage to England, his mind busy with plans. After visiting his family, he went to see an old family friend called Lancaster Webb, who had a tanning business and would be able to supply the special leather for the fan belts of the pumps. He explained the situation, and the possibilities in opening up business in Egypt. After much conversation, Lancaster Webb said he had faith in George's ability and enthusiasm, and that he would lend him the capital needed.

Then George caught the train to travel from Stowmarket to Lincoln, further north, and it was already dark when he got there. However, he hired a cab to take him to the suburbs where 'Old Man Proctor' lived – of Ransomes & Sims, where he had trained. By this time it was eleven at night. He rang the bell in the dark, silent house. No response. He rang again, and a head appeared from an upper window.

Proctor said, "What do you want at this time of night?"

George called out his name, and said he wanted the company's sole agency for Egypt, and to fix it all up now.

"Go away and come and see me in my office in the morning," growled Proctor.

"I can't do that, sir, as my boat leaves for Alexandria in the morning," George called.

There was a long pause, and George thought, 'Why did I spend so much time with my family?'

Then Proctor said "All right."

He admired enterprise. He came down and opened the door.

They sat around the table for several hours, Proctor wrapped in his dressing gown, discussing the various aspects of the business. Then they both signed a piece of paper, which was their sole contract.

When George returned to Alexandria, he went straight to Stafford Allen and gave him all his news. The company of Allen Alderson & Co. Ltd was soon afterwards set on its way.

As the business prospered, George was able to buy some land to the east of Alexandria on a part called Bulkeley, and he gradually had a house built in accordance with his aspirations and in the style current among the better-off of the city. He found five other bachelors to rent accommodation from him, and called it The Monastery. He built (or bought) a small house in the grounds, also for rent.

Alfred Dale, also working successfully in the city, had bought a house nearer to the delta; and after going on leave he brought Mary Anne to be with him, as she had long wanted. Before their return, he insisted on their both learning to speak French, and recruited the local schoolmistress to teach them, because, he said, French was the language spoken at parties.

Mr & Mrs Dale were not delighted at seeing their precious daughter going off to Egypt: "A Muslim country! What next? And what about the heat, and the flies?"

But Alfred assured them he could take good care of her. They sent her off with a trousseau of good clothes.

After the initial excitement, Mary Anne was often lonely among servants she found hard to understand, and after a while she became ill. Alfred consulted an English doctor, who diagnosed typhoid fever. They found nurses to care for her and she survived and began to recover, but the doctor felt she would benefit from a break away from the heat of the delta, nearer the sea breezes.

As it happened, he knew the couple who were renting George's cottage – they were kindly, he said, and would look after her well.

So this is what happened, and Mary Anne got to know the bachelors in the big house, including George. When they were free, they would come to the cottage to escort Mary Anne to the beach for her dose of sea air.

'Although she was not pretty,' wrote Christine, 'she had lovely eyes and an amusing way of saying things that attracted the lads' – especially one called Neville Bull, who worked for Allen Alderson's. He was good-looking and practical and they implemented what used to be called a 'sedan chair', which meant folding their hands across each other's to carry her safely to where she could watch them swimming. Gradually she became fit and strong again, and Neville proposed to her. After a while, she accepted. Though not an entrepreneur, he was kind and steady.

George was also interested in finding a wife, and he wanted someone from his own county of Suffolk, as was Mary Anne. Before he came to Egypt, he and his brother Frank had been frequent visitors to the house of Dr & Mrs Wells, in Stowmarket, who had a beautiful daughter called Ellen. They both fancied her, but Frank got in first, proposed, and was accepted. George was disappointed, but concentrated on his work instead.

Frank was training to be a doctor, and when Ellen had a bad cold he recommended a mustard plaster on her chest. Unfortunately he applied it too hot. Ellen had a hot temper – she flung it at him along with her engagement ring, and nothing would change her mind.

When George, in Egypt, heard the story, he sent a letter to Ellen by the next mailboat, saying that he had always been fond of her, and would she come out and marry him? Ellen being flattered and still in a fluster of pique, wrote back accepting his offer.

The bachelors were dispersed and the house made ready. In due course Dr Wells brought Ellen over, and she and Mary Anne, though very different characters, became friends. Ellen renamed the house Norland House in honour of her home in England. Mary Anne was not yet married, and Ellen asked her to be a bridesmaid. In 1870 they had a beautiful and fashionable wedding; and a little later, Mary Anne and Neville had their wedding as well.

For the next few years both ladies were occupied in coping with an environment and relationships neither had been born to. Mary Anne's requirements were more modest than those of Ellen, who, although she had all she needed (as they say), was not, according to Christine, a happy woman. They had to learn to cope with servants they might not easily understand, acquiring enough of what was known as 'kitchen Arabic' to communicate – all this, of course, in addition to having babies. Mary Anne had four, three girls and a boy; Ellen, over fifteen years, bore ten, the oldest of whom was called Alexander – always known as Alex.

So many untold stories behind those ten rather long solemn faces ranged round their parents, which do not reveal the reputed prettiness of some of the girls, or the conflicts between some of the boys. On one occasion Alex dumped his youngest sister in a pond, exasperated with her teasing; and he was strongly reprimanded by his mother, who tended to spoil him. In fact Ellen fussed over Alex, who was considered delicate. There were ups and downs and stormy times.

One morning, without looking first, Ellen emptied a basin of soapy water from her window over an acquaintance who happened to be walking below. Ellen claimed she should not have been there. George bought her a new dress.

It appears from photos that there were two nannies – one for the latest baby; another, with Egyptian helpers, for the rest. But Ellen was referred to as 'a bit of a Tartar' as she grew older.

George and Ellen.

George and family.

Cleopatra's Needle (one of four).

Cleopatra's Needle (two of four).

Cleopatra's Needle (three of four).

Cleopatra's Needle (four of four).

Sadly, Stafford Allen died, and his brother, another Frank, took his place. The company widened its scope and prospered. Many local industries which had been noted by Napoleon's team and centralised under Muhammed Ali, now benefited from the installation of pumping plants with condensing engines and boilers. Many tales were told about George (some of which are included later) and he gave much to the city. He bought an area of land to donate to the community as municipal gardens, and he founded the Seaman's Home for retired people. He was later awarded a knighthood for his services.

Many young Egyptians from the wealthier groups were returning from colleges in Europe to utilise their expertise. The Bourse, where cotton was traded (in particular by the Greeks), became an enormous centre. Theatre, music, literature and social occasions flourished.

In 1877 there was great excitement in Alexandria about the transportation to England of what had illogically been called Cleopatra's needle. The family kept several photos. This great granite pillar over twenty-one metres long was cut out in 1450 bc in honour of the victories of Pharaoh Thutmose II, near Aswan. It had been transported 950 kilometres on wooden sledges over log pavings lubricated by the pouring of mud and water, and floated in a boat down the Nile, which was a skilled job for a navigator. It was erected at Heliopolis, the Sun City. Then the Romans moved it to Alexandria, and set it up in honour of Caesar Augustus in the temple Cleopatra had dedicated to her Caesar, but seventy-five years after her death it had toppled on to the sands, so the inscriptions it bore had been preserved. It weighs 180 tons.

It had been offered to Britain in 1820, but nothing had been done until Prince Albert encouraged the idea and a retired surgeon offered £10,000 towards its transportation.

Whether the Mr Watson photographed in Alex, and involved with the operation, was part of Allen Alderson's or came from England is unclear, but certainly an engineer in England called John Dixon, presumably having received detailed measurements, designed a steel casing over twenty-seven metres long, and over four wide, with space for ballast and a cabin for a crew to steer and control lights. It was to be towed behind a steamship called the *Olga*. The casing, in nine watertight sections, was shipped out, and Allen Alderson's excavated the obelisk from the sand, so that it could be packed up and moved – hence the photos, not mentioned in the *Telegraph* (reprinted with permission).

By 1877, George's eldest son, Alex, would have been seven years old, and was probably taken to see the proceedings alongside other interested spectators, to recount his memories years later to StJohn, his grandson.

When it was within its casing, it was rolled into the water and towed to the harbour. The crew later boarded and it was secured on a steel cable of thirty-six metres, and was towed away.

Unfortunately, in the Bay of Biscay a gale blew up, the ballast shifted, and the Captain of the *Olga* decided, in chaotic waves, to take off Cleopatra's crew. In getting a boat alongside, six men died, and two more were injured on the second attempt. The *Olga* headed for home through the gale, and Cleopatra was left wallowing in the waves.

It was picked up by a Spanish boat and towed to Ferrol, and £5,000 was charged in salvage fees – paid by John Dixon. The Port of London's largest tug brought it to a buoy off Gravesend and, finally, round to the Embankment. In September 1878 an elaborate hoist was constructed and the obelisk was jacked up, and finally, slowly – slowly – Dixon engineered it into position. Queen Victoria sent a message that she was 'much gratified'.

The ruler of Egypt from 1863 under the nominal rule of the Ottoman Empire (with Britain in the wings) had been Khedive Ismail. He had been educated in Europe and encouraged European methods of agriculture, administration and architecture. The city of Ismailia, named after him, at the centre point of the canal, was laid out at his country's expense as a spacious French city, with squares and avenues and great stone houses. He founded more schools and colleges. All good, but he was also ambitious for his own power as against that of the Sultan. He made huge payments and bribes towards an imperial decree to secure more authority for himself, and by 1875 his exchequer was empty. He sold his £4 million worth of shares in the Suez Canal to Britain's prime minister, Disraeli. But the next few years were stormy ones in Egypt, with the British government endeavouring to keep a tight hold on both Egypt's finances and the canal itself, not always helped by unstable Egyptian governments. There was a large and unpopular garrison of British troops around the canal with barracks through the suburbs of Ismailia. Rising nationalism, both of the Islamic and political persuasions, jostled for power.

There was unrest in the Egyptian Army. As well as resenting the fact that senior positions went to Circassian (Turkish) officers, they wanted to exclude British influence in government and in 1881 the troops rioted in Alexandria. There were deaths and arrests. The army was headed by an Egyptian, Arabi, who appeared sword in hand outside the palace with his demands, and in 1882 the new British prime minister, Gladstone, with his French counterpart, Gambetta, composed a joint note to the government that managed to upset everybody.

They demanded that Arabi be exiled. Instead he was promoted to major general and Minister of War.

In an attempt to forestall chaos, Britain and France sent a naval squadron to Alexandria in support of Tawfiq, the son of Ismail, who had been elected in his place.

As riots and disturbances were continuing, George Alderson booked passage for Ellen and the children and nurses to England, to stay safely with her family. Alex was now nearly twelve. Ellen supposed that George would be coming with them, but he told her he had to stay and guard his business. For the next few weeks he slept in his warehouse on the pile of special leather that was used for the pumps' fan belts, a gun by his side. Many foreigners were leaving.

Neville booked a passage for Mary Anne and her children on a cargo boat to Malta, in which they travelled in the hold. In Malta they were placed with many others in an army barracks – full of lice, Mary Anne reported, which she tried to keep out of the hair of her little girls. Nellie's was especially beautiful. Mary Anne's baby son died while they were there.

There were more riots, and more killings. There were two governments, Arabi in Cairo, the Khedive Tawfiq in Alexandria. And Arabi's men were building fortifications on the shore. Seymour, Admiral of the Fleet, threatened to attack if the guns were not removed, and the Egyptian cabinet rejected the ultimatum.

A P&O boat took businessmen and traders, including George and Neville, three miles out to sea, and the British fleet shelled the city. Leaning on the rail, they wondered at each explosion if it was their house or premises being destroyed. Gladstone, the British prime minister, had hoped that the Sultan would send troops to quieten Arabi's army, but he refused unless all British troops withdrew, which, for the sake of the canal, Britain was unwilling to do. When the minister returned from the embassy at 3 a.m., he was handed a telegram, in code, informing him that a force of 20,000 troops had overcome Arabi's men at the battle of Tel el Khebir, out in the desert. Arabi and his two leading men were exiled to Ceylon.

A government of Egyptian politicians was formed, but under British advisors, and the army was put under British control. In January 1883 a circular was issued by Britain to the European powers;

> Although a British force remains in Egypt for the preservation of public tranquillity, H. M. Government is desirous of withdrawing it as soon as the state of the country and the organisation of proper means for the maintenance of the Khedive's authority will permit it.

After several weeks, Ellen and the children returned, and social life resumed. Mary Anne came back from Malta with her three little girls (minus her baby son) and found all was not well with Neville. He had quarrelled with one of George's employees and left the company, so he had no job and was in a low state of mind and finances. He then tried another job and could not settle to it. Things were so difficult that Mary Anne decided she wanted to take the girls to England, where one of her brothers, who was married, had offered to care for them. And then Neville was offered a job that he felt was acceptable, in a factory, towards the south.

But how was it all to be accomplished? Mary Anne turned to George, their oldest friend but it must have been a hard decision for her.

She gathered together her bits and pieces of jewellery (including a beautiful little gold watch and chain that Alfred had given her as a present) as a surety, and went to see George to ask for a loan to take the girls to England, and for herself and Neville to pack up and travel to Kaffe Zayat.

Norland House, where Ellen and George lived, was large and imposing and Ellen had a carriage and pair with a Sudanese coachman to drive her around. George was very kind. He told her he did not need her jewellery – her word was good enough – and he asked how much did she need?

Mary Anne had it all worked out, and insisted he keep the jewellery – which he said he would keep in his safe for her – and she received the money, in tears.

She paid off her husband's debts and booked passages to England, and the girls' stay turned out to be a happy time for everyone (except Mary Anne).

She returned, packed up all they had, and set off for the factory, where they were offered a small flat over it. Mary Anne worked very hard to make their life acceptable. One thing that Neville was really good at was carpentry, and he made them some useful furniture. He also built a trellised verandah, enhanced with climbing plants, on which they could sit out in the evenings and catch the breezes. Mary Anne wrote cheerful letters to the girls, without mentioning any difficulties. She deeply missed them, and managed to send a little money each month to her brother and sister-in-law.

George was determined that Alex should be educated in England, and when he was thirteen he was put in the care of the captain of a Moss Line steamship, to be met by his uncle now a doctor in Hampstead, and taken to school at Cheltenham, where later he was joined by his brother Bertie. It was reported that Alex was more enthusiastic about rugger than lessons, but was lively and popular. He spent his holidays with his uncle and aunt and afterwards served four years' apprenticeship with his father's old firm, Ransomes & Sims. Frank bore no ill-will to George for taking Ellen – he was very happy with his wife Eliza.

In 1891 Mary Anne decided that Neville was settled enough for her to leave him for a short while to go and visit her children. She could only do it if she worked her passage, as it were, and through George she heard of someone who required a nurse for her baby while travelling to England. She kept a diary of her trip, and in front of the book Bella (Mary Anne's eldest daughter) later wrote 'Mrs Bull's Adventures on her Way to England'.

This diary came to me through Christine. It is not easy to read every word – the ink is faded and the writing close – but I typed a transcript of it some years ago because it is interesting in many ways, although also rather sad, and a reflection of the attitudes of the time. I have included it here, a little shortened.

***

April 17th

I received a telegram from Mr Alderson at 1pm asking if I would nurse a sick child going to England. Answered at 2pm that I would, at 5pm came another telegram saying I must be ready to start at once, tonight, for I ought to catch the morning train to Ismailia and then on to where I would get all instructions. So I began packing at once, and was ready by 10.30. Slept a few hours and then up and ready for start. Neville will go with me to Suez. Left at 8.41, arrived 10.30 where we met Alfred [her brother]. We arrived at 12.30 midnight at Ismailia, then left for Suez, arriving there at 6.30 where an Arab met us and took us to a hotel where we washed and had breakfast and then we went into town to see Bayts & Co., who told us the lady needing a nurse had telegraphed from Aden. While I was eating dinner the boat came in and we had to start at once. Bayts took us on the steam launch, then we found the boat would go into quarantine for 24 hours. Neville left me and I went up onto the steamer to find quite a young lady looking out. I found such a little delicate baby in their cabin, my heart fell, for I saw it was all a job. How shall I manage – and there is no place for me to sleep in, no privacy, sleep in one place, to wash in another, to dress in another, how I wish I had never heard of the offer. What a night it was and to think how many more there will be before it is all over. Next day was trying beyond bearing. I prayed to God to help me bear it as I wanted to see my children. Nothing else would have tempted me to start upon such a job, especially after finding such a selfish set of people in that cabin. Oh it was horrid, horrid, horrid. I feel miserable beyond anything, the baby so unwell and cross too. At noon Neville came on board, but I could see so little of him, the child required so much attention – how bitter all is but only for the children would I bear it.

April 21st

I was up early after a wretched night, walked with Neville who says unless I get good pay and my passage to England and back I should not go further than Port Said and I am willing to throw up the chance only it looks mean to back out of anything. If these people are just and pay what we ask I will go but I will grit my teeth to all feelings and just bear all. Neville came on board and we passed through the Canal, Ismailia at midnight – I made up my mind to do it, Neville thought I could and perhaps it would be better afterwards.

Well the days and nights have gone by somehow and I have not been able to take accounts, it has been such hard sleepless work and with no sympathy from anyone. Such a cold selfish set I never had the fortune to meet in my life before.

April 25th

We arrived at Naples, stayed in the Bay all night. Early morning I went on deck after dressing and bought a few things. There were so many seeing, nearly everyone bought something. Mrs Parry went ashore the night before at 10pm to go to the opera but she said they were cheated and went to a cafe, they came back about 1am. We left Naples at about 4pm and the boat began rolling about, it was rather a rough night and I was up and down all night. Early next morning the sea was very choppy, ship pitching a good bit and I came over sick. After being sick felt better and kept pretty well all day. Baby very troublesome, continually fretting at night. They had dancing as the sea was calm one night before reaching Naples. I went up on deck after the child was off to sleep and saw a little bit towards the end. There are Indian servants on board, 4 Ayahs belonging to different ladies. The one with us is not half bad, will do anything I tell her, but it is difficult to please all people as this poor girl finds, I see more than ever that it is better to follow Christ's law and to love one another, to do to others as you would have others do to you. This horrid way they have of looking down on anyone who does any kind of work as dirt beneath their feet – but I must not judge them they may be better than I think only I see them with my poor weak eyes. How I wish it was all over. I wonder what Neville is doing. God keep my dear husband in safety from all sins and harms… I wonder if he misses me.

April 29th

Took baby on deck after asking the Doctor's permission, we stayed rather more than an hour, the child takes his food very well, 6 teaspoons of Extract of Brands Essence of Beef, 15 drops glycerine and a pinch of salt in one cup of pearl barley every 3 hours.

Finished off socks and one flannel dress for baby, began 2nd dress also mended another. Tonight there were games on deck after dinner, great shouting, laughing and clapping. I could hear from down in our cabin but I was so tired I went to bed at 9.30. Up again at 12 and 3 am and 5.15, a better night, and as soon as it was light enough dressed myself then baby and let the girl go and tidy herself up. [Did 'the girl' wash nappies?] After which I wanted to bath baby but could get no hot water so went on deck where we saw Gibraltar with the morning sun shining full upon it, it looked very grand. Sister Gertrude lent me her glasses to look through at both sides, the African and the Spanish coasts, the sea is just lovely, the air warm, it has been a lovely time, nothing very much rough so far…

April 30th

Baby rather better during the night, took him up on deck at noon, the day was fine but nothing of note except for a restless fit of Mrs P but it passed. Baby slept till 12.30 then bottle. I was up at 5, went to dress, baby cried all the time, it is still cold and the ship rolling very much.

May 1st

We came close to the coast of Portugal, saw Lisbon and passed quite close to the mouth of the Tagus, just stayed to look a little time and came down and found baby awake crying, got him off and had a little peace. The child is bathed twice in the day, has bottle every 3 hours...

I went on deck, the ship had a heavy roll on, it was difficult to sit on chairs, sliding about. It was difficult to get down the ship lurched so much, and what a night it was, everything rushing from one place to another, at noon went on deck again with Baby but how rough it was, I could scarcely keep my feet. We stayed about 3 hours. I can eat fairly well now, such food as it is, but I am not treated nicely. The Ayahs get better, nicer food as they look after it or their mistresses for them, but I will ask no favour from anyone, horrid set that they are, a purse-proud vulgar novel-reading set. Oh God make me thankful and humble, I see so much of the pride that is hateful in thy sight, give me a loving true heart to do my duty. These people look down upon me with such contempt because I am doing the work of a nurse to a sick child, and how they can fault-find, what miserable back-biting, there is no friendship. How thankful I should be to go from here, how dearly I have paid for my voyage home, but it will soon be over, look nothing when it has passed. [Here there is a list of people, including nuns, that she has seen about the deck.]

Left the Bay of Biscay at sunset and at 5.30 on May 4th the Pilot came on board. At 6.30 we entered Plymouth. I had got Baby off so went on deck to see old England. At first sight how pretty the hills looked covered with green, trees and fields in the distance. These people all received letters and have friends awaiting them in London – it is well to be rich, how many friends one has. Well I must continue as best I can for more than a week, came into the Royal Albert Docks.

Mrs Parry's father-in-law, such a very nice gentleman took them to the Langham hotel, where she tried to get the things she wanted. There we waited, Ayah and I, with a crying baby, til I got quite furious with them for not bringing up the child's food. I rang and rang til they brought it and gave them a good talking to. Then my tea was brought and child had a little sleep. The nurse arrived from Cheshire, but her head ached so I looked after the baby through the night. Mrs Parry had gone shopping, had her hair done and gone to the Opera. I stayed in next morning til Mrs Parry came up, when I said I would like to go. She gave me a cheque for £14 on Royal Bank of Scotland, and thanked me very much.

***

Then Mary Anne had her boxes put in a cab and set off to find her eldest daughter, Bella, at the School of Telegraphy. They did not recognise each other at first 'Til I saw a look of Neville in her eyes, then I felt she was mine'. She talked to teachers who gave her an excellent report of Bella, which made her very proud, and the two of them talked for hours. After sending telegrams and letters to Neville and George they travelled on the train to Wickham Market, and then walked over the fields.

Bella said, "There they are," and she could see Nellie and Muriel running towards them.

> How pleased I am to see my dear ones once more, I cannot tell it, my heart is so full – we all slept in one bed, for I could not be parted from them for one hour.

There is no record of how long she stayed, but in due course – probably not long – she took the ship again and travelled back to rejoin Neville.

Mary Anne's eldest daughter, Bella, had completed her shorthand-and-typing course (very modern) in London, and a job was to be arranged for her in Alex. Later Nellie wrote to her parents asking if she and Bella could come out and see them, and they agreed. Neville made more furniture, Mary Anne new curtains, and the girls made their way to their parents' house, until Bella left for Alex.

But Nellie realised that her mother's life was not easy and with the help of George she was offered a job as a governess – or nurse. The child, Kathleen, was eight and she quickly grew fond of Nellie. Mr Charteris was head of the post office and they had a nice house in which Mrs Charteris did a great deal of entertaining. She taught Nellie about catering and parties and organising events, which was very useful to her later on. Nellie was able to send a little money to her mother. She enjoyed her days off in the city, meeting families they had known as children.

A little later, the youngest sister, Muriel, became anxious to come out as well, and arrangements were made for her to stay with relations in Alex. Perhaps Mary Anne thought this was best. Perhaps she was content with her lot – one hopes so. When next the Charterises were going on leave to England, Nellie travelled with them to pick up her little sister.

On the return trip she found that Alex was also on board, going back from his apprenticeship to join his father's business, and they found they enjoyed each other's company.

Alex became a popular young man about town and perhaps, after his training, was also contributing to keeping the company, which was very busy, up to date with new ideas.

He also enjoyed a game of golf and would sometimes come and collect Nellie to play with him. She wore a long full skirt, a blouse and always a large hat. Kathleen was possessive of Nellie and resisted her going – she said she hated Alex.

George had in mind a certain young lady for Alex. She was fashionable and rich and he did business with her brother. It looked to Nellie as if she might lose Alex. When next the Charterises went on leave, taking Kathleen, they arranged for Nellie to act as companion for those few months to a rich widow who would be going to Switzerland. This was exciting and interesting, and Nellie loved the scenery and the beautiful hotels. She was sitting outside one morning waiting for her employer, feeling just a little sad, when a letter was brought to her. Alex's writing. It was a proposal of marriage.

So there were (after all) excellent communications before e-mails.

During their engagement, Nellie was often invited to meals with Alex's family, which she found an ordeal, being rather shy. She was fair and coloured easily, and his three brothers delighted in teasing her and making her blush, until Ellen would intervene. Also they would fight and scuffle with each other – as boys do. Having had only sisters she was unfamiliar with the behaviour and found it worrying.

The five sisters were 'loud and un-shy', as Christine put it. Ellen had always considered Alex to be delicate and had fussed over him. The girls would lecture Nellie on how she was to look after him – she would listen and say little, but was glad when the visit was over. She was sure she would make Alex happy, and she did.

They were married early in 1898. Two of Alex's sisters were bridesmaids, as well as her own sister Muriel. Nellie had orange blossom on the lace veil over her head. Her dress was white satin, ruched with chiffon and ribbon, with a long satin train. The bridesmaids wore elaborate dresses and cartwheel hats with lots of trimmings. Bella was already married, so no longer eligible as a bridesmaid. Mary Anne's brother Alfred and his daughter were there as well as the rest of Ellen's family and many friends.

Aware of the incipient insecurity in the city, and perhaps also to try and please his wife, George purchased a ship that had been used in the Crimean War. He had it towed round to Aboukir Bay, several miles beyond the city, and moored it a little out to sea, accessible by a small sailing ship. He had it fitted up to be convenient for several families to swim from. He also wanted to build a holiday house on the shore. The owner of the land (Prince Toussoum, a Circassian) never sold his land, but he granted George (with whom he did business) a ninety-nine-year lease "which will last your time." This became a meeting place for the ever expanding family. I was told it survived until 1939, when it sank in a storm. He called it *The Ark*.

Tales of George

Stories about George were told to the following generation of children, both by himself and, later, by his children (in particular Alex) to his grandchildren.

When George was first employed in Egypt to look after the pump, he lived very simply over the pump house. He got on well with the people and picked up the language quite quickly. After work and their meal they liked to crowd into his room and talk. George found it difficult to send them away, and they sometimes stayed so late he was tired in the morning. So he made a plan.

He went to bed very early, turned out his lamp and pretended to be asleep, but his revolver was in his hand. Hearing a step on the stair he sat up and fired the gun into the air. The fellow ran quickly away.

In the morning the fellow said to George, "What a welcome you gave me – a gun fired at my head!"

George said, "I'm really sorry. You know I wouldn't hurt you, but if I'm asleep and hear a sound I fire off my gun without thinking."

After that his evenings were peaceful.

***

One summer, a European circus came to the town and went bankrupt, so they could neither pay their fares to get home nor pay for the land they were on. Their plight was put to George, and he offered them a site in the garden he had made for the public. They were all very pleased.

The manager thanked him and asked for a favour: "Will you appear in the lion's cage for a few minutes?"

George was surprised, but didn't want to refuse. Large posters were put up round the town with pictures of George's head in a lion's mouth. On the day, it seemed the whole population had turned up. George was nervous, and asked if he might smoke his cigar for comfort, but the keeper said his lion didn't like smoke.

When he actually went into the cage, and the door clanged behind him, the lion took no notice, and after a few minutes he was allowed out.

But the turnout had been so great that the circus could afford to go home.

***

The residents of Bulkeley (the area on the edge of Alex where George lived) formed a committee with the idea of building a church for themselves, and a certain Edmund Carver had donated land. They asked George to help. He became enthusiastic and enjoyed discussing the plans, but felt it was all moving too slowly. Money had been subscribed, which George was in charge of, but there was still wrangling at meetings and he became impatient.

He found out that all the members of the committee were going on leave.

"Aren't you going, George?" they asked.

"No," he said, "I have work to do."

He sent for the building contractors and told them they had three months to build the church.

"That is impossible," they said.

George told them to employ more men, and get to work at once. His enthusiasm fired the men, particularly as he was always there to smooth out problems and encourage them. Towards the end of the three months he placed acetylene lamps around the site, so they could work later in the evenings, and the great project was completed on time.

When the committee members returned they were surprised to receive invitations to the inaugural service, and even more surprised to see the little church in all its beauty.

In a book called *Alexandria, City of Memory* by Michael Haag, the author wonders why, among other surprising things in Alexandria, there was a Protestant church in Bulkeley. That is why, and how. And being fair-minded, George also sponsored the building of a mosque, by Stanley Bay.

After Ellen died, George married his Greek secretary, Helen Ponzetti, who looked after him devotedly until he died in 1926. She then moved to Switzerland, where StJohn visited her after the Second World War.

Dorothy and sister Christine.

Sailing to The Ark.

The Ark.

Bathers.

Alex and Nellie.

The Cloisters.

Playtime.

Dorothy with Family.

2: The Second Tale

Part I of Alex and Nellie with Gallipoli, the First World War and, Far Away, Henry

Railways had come in the 1850s, the telephone in 1884, tramlines and modern banking in 1897, cinema in 1906. Alexandria was the first city outside Europe to have its own municipal government (several years ahead of Cairo) and it was prosperous. In 1901 George Alderson was one of the founders of the Victoria College, which catered for both day and boarding pupils of many races. It was run on English lines, many of the teachers being recruited from Britain. Several of George's grandchildren, and even great- grandchildren, were to attend it. Cultural life was rich, with societies and lectures, music, debates and theatre, which bloomed over the top of often chaotic politics.

The work of Allen Alderson's continued and diversified. They supplied machinery for factories, including for sugar production, excavated a canal, and undertook work for the building of the mixed courts, which sorted out land disputes and were conducted in Arabic. They also worked on the reinforcement of the Corniche in the harbour – not popular with bathers.

When Alex and Nellie were married, his health was always considered a major concern, and he was subject to a variety of health theories, pills and potions. Someone brought Christian Science literature to the city, and Alex gradually became deeply interested. Over time he discarded all the medicines and remained free of them, and healthy, throughout his life, which Nellie fully acknowledged, though she did not receive or benefit from it as deeply as he did. Christian Science was shared with the children – Dorothy, the eldest, in particular embraced it.

Coincidentally, my maternal grandfather visited Boston at the time of one of the early Christian Science gatherings – either an inauguration or an annual meeting. He was a solicitor and was attending an unrelated legal conference in the city. He was very impressed with the calm and happiness that he felt radiated from the crowds of Christian Scientists, and spoke of it for days after his return home – the name of the founder was made familiar to my mother. I suspect that the heavy cloak of convention (along with gentle mockery), fear for his reputation if he stepped out of line against the social and religious norms, was hung about his shoulders. He was a gentle, humorous man, but in his last years the twinkle had gone and there was a streak of bitterness.

Dorothy was born in 1899, then a boy, Neville, and three more girls, Irene, Christine and Vivian. In their large house, called The Cloisters, built for them by George, they employed a team which included English nurses with supporting local staff – and the employment in the city was welcomed.

Laurence Grafftey Smith worked for the Foreign Office in Alexandria for many years, first as 'acting consul-general' and years later as vice consul and consul. He wrote a book called *Bright Levant*, in which he describes his life from the First World War through to the Second and the processes, personalities and hierarchies of politics and administration. He remarked that the 'Peels, Aldersons and Carvers etc. displayed more rugged British virtues in almost uncomfortable manifestations'. Alexandrian girls were closely chaperoned. But perhaps their reserve was a form of insulation against the fairly frequent and sometimes serious disruptions around the streets, either between restless soldiers or between individuals of conflicting ideologies. He says little of the war – nothing of the disastrous Gallipoli campaign.

He describes the city as a 'large sprawling Egyptian town, whose labyrinth of tangled streets swarm with hundreds of thousands of half-submerged Egyptians, living in poverty and ribald gaiety, alongside the white highlands of society and commerce'. Here there was beautiful china, piano playing and visiting singers, French paintings and Persian carpets. French chefs might have a staff of fifteen, and conversation among guests and residents would be far-ranging – among diplomats and politicians, visiting judges and the current representatives of Egyptian royalty. In contrast was the downtown house of the poet Cafavey. He worked in the irrigation department, but hosted visiting poets, artists and writers, who had to ignore (or not) the blandishments from the windows of the brothel on the ground floor of the big house in which he lived. Grafftey Smith expressed his appreciation of talking with Cafavey.

He also wrote of the pleasures of swimming from George's old boat, *The Ark*. He referred to it as having been a hospital ship, and romantically suggested that Florence Nightingale might have trodden its boards while caring for the wounded on the way back from the Crimea. He said it was an ideal place from which to 'dive and dive again, especially when the sea was phosphorescent after an influx of silt, – every swimmer cut himself a golden silhouette of glow-worm spray as he moved against the darkness.'

Far away in England, by a very different sea soon to be touched by the same dark tide of war as Alexandria, my grandfather Henry Gervis was peacefully running his private medical practice in Brighton. He was offered a commission in 1915 as 'Captain a la Suite' at the general hospital. A small book that he wrote after the war has remained in the family. The following is from that source.

In 1914 he was given a khaki uniform to wear, which he was a little shy of going out in; but when he did, a passing child said, "Look, Mother, a soldier!" and he swelled with pride.

At one o'clock one morning he had a message that a convoy of wounded had been sent to a nearby school that had been converted to a hospital. Two other schools, two and two and a half miles away, had also been commandeered and became part of his responsibility. He had to inspect food preparation and the meals, and remarked that the same meals were served to every man regardless of their digestive states. He spent every morning on these wards and, when needed, the afternoons as well, leaving two afternoons a week for his own practice.

He was given 15/6d. (reckoned now at £26) a day, no allowances, his own car and petrol. He said there were 'forms, forms, forms', and he was often told to go somewhere and arrive to find no one had heard of him, and he would be sent elsewhere.

He was sent to a transit camp in France in 1918, and given a gas mask. It was his first time in a tent. His clothes were damp, his tobacco went mouldy and his envelopes stuck. He remarked that for twenty-five years he had been warning his patients of the dangers of 'damp' – but he never suffered any ill effects.

Then he was told they were going to Eat Apples (Étaples), so he undid and packed up his bed, with difficulty, and with several men was driven there in a lorry. When they got there they were told they should be at Carmières, through which they had passed, so they drove back, to a large site of huts and tents.

There were officers from England, Scotland, Ireland, the Netherlands, Canada, South Africa and America. After his years of married life it was like being back at college, and there were many interesting debates and discussions – and always cheerfulness. Convoys of wounded men were frequently coming in to be sorted. Those who could walk were grateful to be sent back to Blighty (England) for treatment. Blighty (as the Oxford Dictionary informs me) was a term used by soldiers – an 'Anglo-Indian' corruption of Hindi *bibyatt* – Europeans). The 'liers' were piled into ambulances for return if fit to do so.

He noted that on stations soldiers smoked all the time. He rolled his own cigarettes simply because when he had started to smoke, they were not manufactured.

He was very impressed with the nurses employed, who would, as well as treat, advise, care and comfort. Not so with the occasional padre, who often got sick and were difficult and demanding patients. Leave was officially every six months, but you would only be told the day before and trains were always hours late.

In November, right at the end of the war, there were terrible epidemics of flu and pneumonia, and as many died of these diseases as had been lost in the fighting – including one of the doctors, who had given up his practice to join up. Walking back on a moonlit night to his tent, Henry reflected about how hard it was for parents to lose sons or husbands in this way when, with the war coming to an end, they had hoped to see them home soon.

As he walked, another bombing raid began, and more men were brought in, terrified and wounded.

He wrote, 'Let me express my deep thankfulness, that I have been able to play a small part in the work of alleviating the suffering of those who have sacrificed so much for their country.'

Back to Alexandria and the Aldersons

Dorothy had been sent to England to Cheltenham Ladies' College in 1912, when she was thirteen, and remained a pupil until April 1915 (a disastrous year for Britain and Alexandria). She was always very proud to have been a pupil there, and I think considered herself more ladylike than me. Whether she would have stayed on longer if the circumstances in Alex had not been as they were I do not know. Christine followed her for two years, from 1920.

With the growth of prosperity, many more young Egyptians were being educated, either at home or abroad, and managing new industries. Women's voices were beginning to be heard in places where they formerly had not.

But Egypt lost £20 million of its capital in the first two years of the war.

Alex's younger brother Roy had taken an engineering course in England, and married while he was there. He returned with his wife, and opened an office in Cairo for the company. When war was declared he enlisted, but he was killed a year later, a few months before his son, also Roy, was born. He had become a favourite with the Alderson children. Another brother, Reggie, emigrated to Canada.

In August 1914, Germans in Cairo and Alexandria were interned, and sent to camps outside the cities. Britain had declared Egypt a British Protectorate, partly in order to keep some sort of grip on the finances, and on the Suez Canal, around which were army barracks. But apart from occasional arguments the relationship remained reasonably smooth. The commander of the British troops in Egypt had said that they would not call on the Egyptian people for aid in the war. Nevertheless they soon did, under what they called 'compulsory volunteering' – the same system that had been implemented in Africa.

Grafftey Smith knew the Egyptians well, and the way the village systems worked. By 1917, 125,000 men had been drawn into the recruitment to assist the army with transport and whatever else. The officers who came to the villages requesting men, or fodder, or animals, were not always Arabic speakers, so they applied to the village headmen, who sometimes asked people for more than had been requested and kept the difference, blaming Britain for the amount; or they sometimes volunteered individuals who they themselves would prefer out of the way. Although the pay for goods and services was reasonable, the atmosphere in some villages soured. It was not, after all, their war, and stirrings towards independence grew stronger.

Another cause of resentment was that areas of cotton grown around the villages began to be restricted in favour of food crops. Cotton was a lucrative crop from even a small acreage, and the Bourse, the cotton-trading centre in the city, was the largest hub of the export trade, which had made many families rich. (In England, when I was a child, items marked 'Egyptian cotton' were part of the household goods.) But the system meant that sons and breadwinners disappeared and work was neglected.

In 1915, the prime minister of Greece visited Alexandria to drum up patriotic support. The city was dressed in blue and white, and 20,000 citizens, many of them Greek, turned out to cheer him all the way from the port to the sports club, where he was entertained.

The Disaster of Gallipoli

Turkey, which had been part of the now-crumbling Ottoman Empire, had remained neutral. They had ordered two battleships to be built for them in British yards, and paid for them by public subscription.

Meanwhile the war against Germany was not going well. There were endless lines of trenches and a stalemate in France. Good news was needed.

In October 1914 the Ottoman Empire along with Turkey entered the war as an ally of Germany. Many Turkish units would now be in the charge of German leaders. Winston Churchill, as First Lord of the Admiralty, saw an opportunity for a success. He commandeered for British use the two boats ordered by Turkey, and planned a campaign in which the Royal Navy would be key: cross the Mediterranean with a fleet of warships, sail through the Dardanelles straits to the Sea of Marmara, then confront and subdue Istanbul, to get Turkey out of the war.

It sounded simple. But it was not simple. Every snag and set-back one could possibly imagine would assail it, and every cruel circumstance for the men involved. The reason I include it is because of the impact its various sequences had on Alexandria, and the Aldersons and many other families, who lent rooms and staff to help with the wounded.

Thousands of troops were already being recruited in Britain, and the response in Australia and New Zealand had been tremendous – 'Australia will be there.' So the Anzacs (Australian and New Zealand Army Corps) had been formed – 2,000 men came to Alexandria from the navy, 20,000 from the Imperial Royal Force. They came with thousands of horses. Many went to the camp at Mina, near the Libyan border with Egypt, where they learnt to parade, crawl with a rifle, and shoot, throw mines and bayonet people. The city was overflowing with troops – the red-light downtown districts increased.

Grafftey Smith remarked that the Germans, and to a lesser degree the French, provided for 'female requirements' for their troops, but this was not a fit subject for discussion for the British, and he probably would not have wanted it to be. But he was saddened over the months by seeing some of the splendid young volunteers struck by disease in the cities. The Australians were paid six shillings a day; the Tommies one shilling.

A fleet that included French and British troops, battleships and minesweepers set out from the harbour.

As they approached they were watched by the Turkish troops camped around the straits and on the surrounding hills, who laid mines around the coast. British guns were fired towards the forts on the lower levels, but firing was returned and six British ships were put out of action (either by the firing or by mines) and some sank. Many men were wounded or drowned. Attempts at minesweeping were thwarted by the firing. Twenty-two marines were killed, and the French lost 600 men in the first few minutes. The remaining ships withdrew on 18 March and the damaged ones limped back to port. The wounded men were taken into Alexandria to hospital, and the Victoria College was commandeered as further hospital space. Over the following weeks several of the big houses, including The Cloisters, opened rooms and volunteered staff to help with those more lightly hurt, in shock or exhausted.

A re-formed, restocked Mediterranean Expeditionary Force, formed by Churchill's continued enthusiasm, steamed out again in early April.

Admiral of the Fleet Lord Fisher, who felt that Churchill was obsessed with a hopeless enterprise, said, "Damn the Dardanelles."

From the start, leadership was divided, and the established system of promoting leaders in order of seniority often resulted in older, less determined men taking over where those next in line might have done better. There were fairly frequent deaths from disease. For example, Rupert Brooke, the poet, died from septicaemia while aboard ship – not quite the 'corner of a foreign field' he had envisaged.

Equipped with maps that were not always accurate, landings were planned on the various promontories. Gunboats fired towards the fortifications on the shore, but their range was limited by being under fire themselves. Included within the fleet was the 'Trojan horse of Gallipoli', a 4,000-ton coal ship concealing 2,000 troops. Landing orders were imprecise, and the intricacies of the terrain rendered planning impossible. Also, the currents at the top of the peninsula were strong, so some of the landing craft were overturned, or men drowned on flooded craft or in the sea, being also weighed down by heavy packs.

On 25 April – a beautiful morning – at 2 a.m., watched by the Turkish troops on the hills, 2,500 men were landed and began scrambling up the scrubby rocky slopes. They encountered Turks in trenches, firing and being fired on, killed and wounded. There was confusion in the gullies of the hills, with regiments in divided disorder. Turks ran ahead, firing back at them. This continued, with short breaks, over three days, with wounded men trying to get down, falling and being stepped over. Three to four thousand men were taken back to the hospital ships.

The Anzacs were set to go up a further hill, along with Indian army units and Sikhs, and they and the Turks fought step by step for control of this hill. Almost all the Anzac leaders were killed in the advance, and, the ground being hard and stony, digging trenches, for burials or sleeping, was almost impossible. They were dragging heavy guns up, taking three or four men, as they climbed. The Turks, moving ahead and shooting back, were in equally desperate straits.

Impossible orders kept coming. Out of 1,000 men, 715 continued to struggle up the hill. The Turks had lost 2,000.

The campaign was publicised as a success, but details of all of it were never fully released. General Hamilton admitted the failure to Kitchener around the 8 May. Ammunition was low, he was promised more. An armistice was arranged for burials to take place. A Turkish officer was taken blindfold to confer with General Hamilton. There were thousands of rotting bodies from both sides. Spirits and strength were low. But at the meeting there were friendly exchanges: the Turks were given cigarettes, and they gave uniform buttons as souvenirs. A Turkish member of the delegation pointed to some graves and said, "That's politics," and to some bodies and said, "There's diplomacy." At the end of the arranged time limit, the firing began again.

The Red Cross and Red Crescent were in operation, but walking carrying stretchers was hazardous. There were nurses on board the hospital ships, but medical supplies were low and men would awake screaming. The rest of the supplies were 1,000 kilometres away in Alexandria.

Summer was approaching, with heat, flies, maggots and disease all increasing. Their bully beef was served almost liquid, with hard biscuits and limited water. An attempt to advance half a mile up a hill was an enormous undertaking, with both sides throwing bombs containing ball bearings, bits of exploded shells and wire. There was sometimes only a few metres between the opposing trenches, and sometimes individuals were seized with a kind of blood lust – kill, kill, kill. Bombs were being picked up and thrown back. The thousands killed and wounded on both sides are beyond imagining.

August passed in another confused standstill. Again orders were given to advance, but experience caused the troops to doubt the sense of it. Admiral Fisher (on his boat) resigned, and Churchill, now discredited, was ousted. (Perhaps the humiliation strengthened him, and by the Second World War he had been forgiven). He was replaced by Balfour, who held out (knowing so little) against evacuation, which Kitchener was, inwardly, now in favour of. Army unit after army unit was being decimated.

The raw recruits of Kitchener's New Army of 600,000 were landed, under fire, and waded back up to their necks in water, and in the dark. At their arrival the Turks had been ordered to run down the hill, falling over the dead and wounded, to attack on the beaches.

There were now hospitals on the islands of Imros and Lemnos, and in Heliopolis, as well as the ever overflowing ones in Alexandria. French resolve for the campaign was waning, but no ending was being formalised.

Keith Murdoch, (father of Rupert), a journalist, played a part in the campaign to evacuate. He agreed to take a letter from another British journalist, Ashmead Bartlett, to Prime Minister Asquith – this letter was a chronicle of catastrophe. Murdoch wrote to the Prime Minister of Australia. This letter was suppressed, but he decided to reveal all to the British and Australian Governments, describing the campaign as 'one of the most terrible chapters of our history', and blaming the general staff for 'stubborn persistence in the face of hopeless schemes'. Kitchener finally declared for evacuation.

By November the winter storms had arrived. Rain poured down the hills, flooding trenches, washing men down and out to sea. Frostbite then became the new hazard. Some of the Indian troops who went barefoot lost their feet and hundreds of all races were afflicted. Fifteen thousand more men were evacuated.

The new general, Munroe, laid plans, which included the attempt not to alert the enemy to an imminent departure. He had the men muffle their boots (or what was left of them) to march down to and across the bay, and set timed explosions on the hills as they were evacuated. Thousands of horses were shot and left on the beaches, and stores were shelled.

At 4 a.m. on 8 January 1916 the last boat left the shores. Many had come across for the purpose.

Lord Kitchener was drowned when his cruiser was torpedoed in the North Sea as he was returning to face the Commission of Enquiry. This subsequently held eighty-nine meetings, but the Australian were too disillusioned even to attend. Whether they reclaimed the kangaroo mascots they had left in Cairo Zoo is unclear.

Some of the survivors from this awfulness came to be cared for in Alexandria by the likes of Alex and Nellie Alderson, their staff and family, including Dorothy.

The whole operation had been as callous to those employed to perform it as to those it was intended to vanquish. The fact that it was not published might indicate its place in the centuries-long awakening to the inadequacy of brute force as a solution.

3: Hugh and Hugh's Story

Hugh Salmon Backhouse was born in Collingham, Yorkshire, in 1891, son of Marie, formerly Bailey, and stockbroker John Robert. He was the youngest of a large family. At the age of sixteen, after three years at Lancing College, with a short while in the cadet corps there, he left England for the Argentine. He declined the offer of an allowance from his father. He took £50 and letters of recommendation to several Argentine businesses 'interested in camp affairs'. Perhaps it was the 'camp affairs' that appealed to him, for his aim was to work on a ranch. He took one of the letters to its address in Buenos Aires, but, after awaiting attention for half an hour, he tore up the letter, dropped the pieces and left. So much for that.

Among the other visitors in his hotel was one who would be travelling to a ranch further south – one near Bahia Blanca – and in conversation this person kindly offered to enquire whether they might consider employing Hugh. He would find out, he said, and let Hugh know. Hugh waited with trepidation for several days, trying to plan what he would do if nothing came of it. Then a letter came: they would be willing to take him on.

∗∗∗

His funds just allowing, Hugh took the train south as instructed,

> which rolled and lumbered across the Pampas lands. I could see great herds of cattle grazing, with an occasional Gaucho riding. Wild horses with tails up and manes flowing dashed off in clouds of dust.'

This from his book *Among the Gauchos*, which he wrote more than thirty years later. It was published in England by Jarrolds and translated into several languages, including Spanish.

He was met at the appointed station, kindly received, and given a room for the night. Then he was driven another eight miles south to the camp beyond the ranch, and put to work.

For a week he pulled nails out of boxes, then was set to tar gates, wondering where was all the romance he had been looking for? Then it was loading bales of wool, then dipping sheep, which he thought were utterly stupid, and his feet were sore from getting trodden on. Next there was a drought, followed by a blizzard. They were ordered, in pitch darkness, to saddle up and take the shorn sheep to shelter. They were huddled in a scarcely penetrable circle, and hundreds died. So it was skinning the drought-afflicted animals, and finally burning the carcasses.

All this time he had been learning to ride as the gauchos did, often bareback.

Over the years, he worked his way up to being the manager of the ranch, Las Tassis.

During this time he was probably corresponding with his family, for in 1909 his brother, StJohn, who had taken a four-year course in engineering, came out to the Argentine, and obtained a job first with the Central Argentine Railway, and then as a draughtsman with the Leibig Meat Extract Co. a booming section of the meat trade at the time. But when war was declared in 1914 StJohn and Hugh returned to England to enlist, where their brother Rawel had already joined the Royal Army Service Corps. StJohn trained as a pilot, and Hugh was sent to Alexandria in the Dorset Yeomanry, in September 1915, as a second lieutenant.

Three strands present themselves for Hugh's story – his military record from the Archive Department, the historical record and his own book, which is without any dates. He omitted two quite lengthy episodes in hospital, but included the last. Many of the details slot into history.

When he arrived, he was sent to the training camp at Mina. After his experience in the Argentine he must have been interested in the variety of the horses and their mounts – farmers, landowners and soldiers from Britain; Australians and New Zealanders (the Anzacs); and horses from America, whose training methods were different from those of the gauchos.

Out to the west of the Suez Canal was the Senussi tribe, initially hostile only to unbelievers. Two British steamers had been torpedoed by the Germans, who handed any surviving crew over to the Senussi, who subsequently denied all knowledge of them. This triggered the British into retaliation, further provoking the Senussi, who were being encouraged by the Turks. The Dorset Yeomanry were among those delegated to confront them. They were later joined by the Western Frontier Force, which included vehicle-mounted guns and both horse- and camel-mounted troops, introducing them, Hugh included, to working alongside camels. The fact that horses needed about nine kilos of hay, four of corn and twenty litres of water a day made desert conditions for them problematic, while camels could survive on thorn bushes and water at five-day intervals (though a drinking sequence could take two and a half hours).

Men and beasts had to learn to tolerate the heat and flies, huge contrasts in day and night temperatures, and sometimes blowing sand that could unmake trenches and clog their rifles, or their breathing. The valiant survivors of the Gallipoli campaign, having recuperated, were aligning with new recruits in campaigns to drive the Senussi back into the desert, but there were several unsuccessful and costly attempts, as lessons and methods were learnt.

On Christmas morning, 1915, they rode for six hours across the desert, and paused for bully beef and biscuits for lunch. The Australians encircled the Senussi, and guns were blazing in both directions. By the end of the day 200 of the yeomanry had lost their lives.

Heavy rainfall intervened through January, and Hugh, according to his record, went down with jaundice. He did not rejoin his unit until March, when the battle took place. It involved a half-mile gallop into a group of Senussi, who fired back as they retreated. The yeomanry pursued with slashing swords – one of the last such charges of the war. But it was still several months before the Turkish general leading the tribe surrendered.

With this threat past, the bars and cafés of Cairo and Alexandria became popular along with sightseeing trips to the countryside. But their leaders had other ideas. General Murray planned for deployment to the east, to drive Turkish forces out of Sinai. It would be necessary to continue the railway along the Mediterranean coast, towards Gaza, and to build alongside it a waterpipe to supply men, animals and steam engines. This was all set in motion, with the help of Egyptian recruited forces, and the importation and movement of thousands of tons of material.

A cavalry course and a Grenadiers course were added to Hugh's record – both of which he passed. He put it a little differently – as a series of competitions and a race, all of which he won.

He was told to go and speak to a Colonel Butler, in the Shephard's Hotel, Cairo. Butler had been in charge of small troops of riders known as the Arab Scouts, tasked with tracking groups involved with smuggling arms or goods to the Turkish forts or garrisons. He was feeling he would like to retire from quite such an active life, and had heard of Hugh's ability with horses. He invited Hugh to meet him for dinner at the hotel (which Hugh greatly enjoyed), questioned him about his experience and put the matter before him. Hugh was delighted.

Hugh on a camel.

Hugh.

The picture was not straightforward. Some tribes remained loyal to Turkey because of the ancient affiliation to the Ottoman Empire, now crumbling, and the Germans were allying with the Turks. But many of the Arabs, including Sharif Hussein ibn Ali of Mena, and his sons, wished to throw off the old Turkish yoke and unite the Arabs in a revolt against it. His son Abdullah Hussein had secretly visited Cairo for talks with Kitchener and other military leaders, with a view to allying Arab forces with the British against the Turks. The British were not interested in the Arab cause, but willingly accepted any help.

Hugh was deeply interested in all that Colonel Butler told him of the different tribes, their traditions and affiliations. A day was arranged when he would go to meet some representatives, including Abdullah Hussein himself, at a place called Karnusos in Sinai.

Here he was given a tent and an Arab servant, and the groups of fighters were on parade for him, some on horseback and some on camels. The most spectacular were the Bisharini from Sudan, all tall and of great dignity, their camels more splendid than any he had previously seen. Their riders wore blood-red turbans and carried knives tied on their arms with a leather strap, in addition to carrying their guns. They all made up four groups with a leader for each. The Colonel made a short speech, naming Hugh as his successor, with the finances as well as the leadership in his hands. He was shortly promoted to lieutenant.

He chose for himself a particularly swift camel, which he trained with gaucho methods – exhaustive swift running, followed by food and fondness. He called him Nemo, and rode him for all his time in the Arab Scouts. He and his men lived mainly on dried rations, with some tinned food, and occasional fruit, or a sheep cooked over a fire.

Colonel Butler's attitude to Abdullah Hussein was in accord with the current British political aims, which were to keep the lands on the Mediterranean for the Allies' subsequent dispensation. Ideas of self-rule for those whose homelands they were had no part in the agenda. Butler said he tried to let Hussein relate to 'the puppet position he has', within the system.

As Hugh was to find, the problem lay in trying to ascertain the loyalties of either settled groups or a travelling few, before either attacking or being attacked.

Turkish supplies also travelled north along the Hejaz Railway from Mecca towards the north of the Arabian Peninsula, and there T. E. Lawrence was operating with his Arab troops, blowing up sections of it wherever he could, along with its passengers and cargo. Lawrence had chosen Hussein's brother Faisal to work in partnership with him. Collectively the battles of the Arabs from 1916–1918 became known as the Arab Revolt, and Lawrence was to share the Arab's bitterness at Britain's disregard at the end of the fighting.

The Arab Scouts were perfectly willing to attack those who, generally through bribery, would aid the Turkish garrisons – because they were traitors to the Arab cause.

At about the time when Lawrence trekked northward to surprise and capture the town of Aquaba (as he thought, for the Arabs), Hugh was admitted to hospital with tonsillitis. He was not finally discharged to Alexandria until August 1916. It was perhaps in this interval, convalescing, that he met Dorothy, who was doing her bit with the rest of the collective help in Alexandria

He returned to his men, and made his base near a station called Kossima abandoned by the Turks, in the desert south of Beersheba, he chose a man to be his special aide, others he could delegate as scouts, and he sent patrols daily north and south to spot groups in transit.

One day the south weekly patrol returned to say they had crossed the trail of about forty camels heading north-west, fifty miles south, the trails fresh. Hugh reckoned that with their faster camels they would catch up to them – and shoot to deter them.

His Arabs were tense with excitement as they covered the ground – such forays were their lifeblood. They rested only briefly overnight and continued to where a small hill would conceal them. As the sun rose Hugh ventured to the top with his binoculars, and spotted the dots moving towards them. Lying low, they waited again, and then fired.

Confusion reigned. Camels tumbled. The aim was to persuade them to retreat – he did not yet wish to take prisoners. A few raced northwards and were pursued by some of his men, but the rest turned back to the south.

Hugh had become suspicious of a tribe headed by Sheik Yussef. Being uncertain of his reception, he sent his trusted man, Mohammed, to explain that his proposed visit was a friendly one, and later he himself was welcomed, a little cautiously, into Yussef's tent, with its thickly carpeted floor and fine hangings. He was given a meal (as were his men), and coffee served by his wife.

His object was to dissuade Yussef from being involved with smuggling, if that was what he was doing, and there followed several hours of conversation. At the end of it the atmosphere was cordial, and Yussef remained an ally, and a guide in the desert, tracing maps in the sand to explain the terrain.

When they returned to their base Hugh was asked to take over the old fort of Nekhl and be ready there to meet engineers who would come to repair walls that had been damaged. So after some rest they began preparing for the journey, distributing food bags to the 100 men he chose, and filling water tanks for their transport. He left a man in command to continue patrols, Nekhl being a three-day journey.

His foregoing scout reported that the fort was manned, but there was no knowing whether they would retaliate. He planned to offer warning fire before dawn. There was no sound but the swish of the camels' feet through the sand, as, divided into three groups, they approached from different directions. Then they dismounted, hobbled the camels, crept forward and lay on the ground. At daybreak, one of the groups fired, resulting in sounds of panic and some return of fire. They then remounted and all stormed towards the fort, from which firing ceased. Their tactics involved speed and surprise, to compensate for their relatively small numbers. Those in the fort left, and they took it over.

They explored, finding no water, and no engineers arrived that day or the next. Their water was running short. Hugh slept under the moon in the ruins, keeping his anxiety back from his men, who remained trustingly calm.

Another sleepless night, praying for some miracle. Eventuality Hugh felt heavy rain on his face, and in the next few hours they were able to refill their containers. His men accepted all this as normal, but were relieved when he announced his decision to return to base and wait no longer for the engineers.

On 18 March 1918, in the middle of his time with the Arab Scouts, Hugh and Dorothy were married. The ceremony took place in the British Consulate in Cairo, Hugh being released by special permission of a secretary of state 'from active service in Sinai'. The two witnesses were Dorothy's father, Alex Alderson, and James Mantantelli, acting consul. I would guess that Dorothy might have preferred this simplicity to the busy weddings of other times. Perhaps as Hugh returned to his troops she quietly returned with her father to her brother and sisters, and began to sort out her belongings with a view to sometime, and to somewhere, moving on. She was dedicated, and remained so.

Naturally there is no mention of the marriage in the military record; neither does Hugh refer to it in his book, which continues with his various exploits.

Yussef, in conversation, had hinted that his northern neighbour, a sheik named Mahmoud, might not be so friendly to the British. Hugh decided to visit him. On the way they encountered a fierce storm, which crashed around them. It was the end of a long drought. His two scouts returned with an Arab walking between them – and reported that this was one of Mahmoud's scouts. They had found him hiding behind a rock preparing to shoot at them.

Hugh's chief man, Mohammed, commanded him to lead the way to Mahmoud's camp, which he did, at speed, on foot, and several Bedouins mounted their camels and approached them as the camp with its low tan tents appeared spread out in front of them.

The Sheik came out, in silk robes and a silver-and-leather belt. After the formal greeting he invited Hugh into his tent.

The man looked shifty and uneasy. Hugh felt he was hoping for a bribe, and that whatever his activity, nothing would change him. However, in case he could find out more about him, he requested a nearby site in which he and his men could spend the night.

Mahmoud ordered a man to lead them to a certain sheltered ravine with tall cliffs on three sides. Hugh told his men he was suspicious of some plot. They made their campfire, had their meal and let the camels eat. When it was quite dark, they tied the camels' mouths to keep them silent, then moved out into the valley and waited.

Towards midnight, Mohammed whispered that he'd heard something from the top of the cliffs. A few seconds later there was a thunderous noise as rocks and pebbles poured down on what had been their campsite, and would have been themselves.

The next day they saw a camel caravan approaching – the reason for Mahmoud's attempted killing. One of Hugh's scouts followed the group, and when the caravan stopped for the night he returned to report its position. The Arab Scouts would be outnumbered, so needed a plan. They waited until dark, and silently moved close by, but spread out.

At a fox-scream signal given by Mohammed they all fired towards the group repeatedly, as if they were many. Screams and shouts and some harmless fire ensued. Then Mohammed, who had a powerful voice, ordered all firing to stop or they would all be shot. After repeating the threat several times there was silence – and then surrender.

He then commanded a fire to be built and all weapons to be collected and piled at a distance, and all to sit round the fire. They were resigned to the situation, unaware how few their captors were. Two of them went in to collect all the weapons, and then, guns still at the ready, the rest entered the camp and surrounded the seated prisoners.

At daylight, Hugh inspected the package bales that were to be transported, glad their delivery had been prevented, for the Turkish goods and weapons would have greatly aided the remaining groups still challenging the British settlements and the building of the railway.

The next challenge was to transport both loads and prisoners to El Arish, the headquarters, tying the transport camels in strings by their tails, and with the prisoners on foot between their captors.

They moved off in an arc to avoid Mahmoud's camp, and it was a long, weary trek with only short breaks. Three of the prisoners were evidently eminent men unused to submitting to orders, or walking.

He learnt later that these men had been leading bands to descend on British outposts, damage the water pipe and attack the builders.

They slept little through another night, and, with few supplies remaining, travelled on at the monotonously slow speed, almost exhausted. At last, with some of the camels as sore as themselves, they could breathe the sea air, and were met by the governor. The prisoners were locked up, the camels stabled and tended, and his men treated as heroes. After giving his story, Hugh slept for fifteen hours and stayed for three days.

This long story had several side shoots in Hugh's account. But even without them – it is a good story.

Meanwhile (among other things) Gaza had been overcome and wrecked, the city of Maen had been besieged, and the Balfour Declaration had announced the establishment of a Jewish homeland. General Allenby entered Jerusalem, and Lawrence was awarded the DSO for his hard-won victory in Tafila.

During their return to Kossima, they encountered six Bedouin on a hunting trip after gazelles. They had two saluki dogs, and two of the men carried a hooded falcon on the leather glove of their wrist. Hugh decided to travel a short distance with them, to learn the method of hunting gazelles with falcons.

The two falconers were in the lead, the other four men, dismounted, followed with the linked dogs. As they came to a small herd of gazelles, the falcons were released and rose high into the sky over the herd. As Hugh watched the leading pair of gazelles, they seemed to merge into one as the falcons whirled about their heads, confusing and blinding them. The dogs were released and threw the gazelles down, and they were quickly killed with a knife. Hot meat in his hand brought the falcons down to eat, and afterwards to be re-hooded.

In Kossima Hugh's party were welcomed back to tell their story, and Hugh was warmed by the loyalty and interest of these seemingly wild men.

The next duty was to capture Mahmoud, and using their tactics of speed and surprise they overran his camp, gathering the Bedouin in tight groups; and keeping the abject Mahmoud under the close surveillance of the powerful Mohammed, he was taken into his tent for questioning.

First, why had he tried to kill them? The answer was as he had thought: Mahmoud had been anxious that the smugglers should reach their destination, which was the still-beseiged city of Ma'an, in urgent need of food. He had been paid to provide supplies. He only wanted to live in peace. He would swap sides and serve them instead. Hugh chose escorts to take him and ten of his men to headquarters.

Hugh had been enjoying the violet-and-purple sunset, and the light over the desert spaces. But as they travelled back the heat became unbearable. The camels seemed worried – a storm was on its way. A rolling sound came from the hills as a thick yellow mist approached them and was blown into fantastic shapes. Then came an icy wind, blowing up the sand, and the camels were gathered tightly, backs to the wind. They themselves huddled together with blankets to protect their heads and breathing. They had to hold the blankets tightly as a sandstorm can result in suffocation. The fifteen-minute hurricane was a veritable hell. The only consolation was that they were on flat ground – not sand dunes, which would have blown upwards around them.

In July 1918 Hugh's service with the Arab Scouts officially ended, and he was directed to Kantara – a place which had grown from an Arab village to a town, with blockhouses, a cinema and shops, a centre for huge railway yards and warehouses along the railway line. It seems strange in a way, as the work he had been doing had been effective in hindering the smugglers, but the Arab cause was subsumed below the British aims to the north, now concentrated on the occupation of Beersheba. The Turks left it heavily mined, and the engineers were set to work to get the water running again. Hugh was there to help clear up and keep hostile forces at bay.

After witnessing explosions, they moved inside with extreme caution, and learnt to very gently attach a long line to a suspicious object and move to a safe distance before pulling it. Sometimes an explosion occurred – with no loss of life or limb. He stopped one of his men about to open a door, and tried this line method first – resulting in a huge blast.

When the city was considered cleared, he was instructed to continue to thwart smugglers journeying to Turkish outposts, but some problems emerged. While it was necessary to maintain enough troops to undertake such operations as surrounding and controlling groups of smugglers, there might be intervals of time between such events. Men left at the base, or those sent on their own to scout, had begun to forcibly help themselves to supplies from other passing (and often innocent) Bedouin. It was sometimes considered a means of making a living.

Hugh was aware that what might be called lawlessness lay deep in tradition, and in the blood. Individuals, or whole tribes, could fight to the death, or surrender, slinging stones first piled, wearing a shield on one arm and standing within a circle. The mastered accuracy of throwing (used effectively to kill an ibex) was an art, and could be a murderous one. It could lead to endless feuding, unless settled by surrender or blood money.

Many tribes who had remained loyal to the Ottoman Empire were hostile to the Allies for religious reasons, and often hostile to each other.

In returning from a scouting trip Hugh and a large group of riders passed through a rocky valley, and Mohammed alerted him to a sound from higher up. A second later, rifle fire echoed down among the rocks. Some of the camels were hit, though not seriously, and after some fierce riding and skirmishing they managed to surround their attackers, though a few escaped. Those they had overpowered (some of whom were wounded) they escorted closely guarded back to their camp, to hold overnight.

The next day they travelled with them to El Arish, where Hugh was called to see the governor. He told Hugh that headquarters had been receiving almost daily complaints from Bedouins reporting that members of the Arab Scouts had been forcing them to hand over money or goods.

Hugh explained his problems of supervision, while his prisoners were interrogated and afterwards released. He spent two days in discussion and returned to continue the patrols, warning that the taking of goods from others was a punishable offence.

Then he received a message he did not like: Captain Peake of the Egyptian Army would come to take control of the Arab Scouts, who would shortly transfer to Lawrence's forces.

Two days later his four head scouts, with Mohammed, asked to speak to him freely.

"You were appointed to us and have cared for us," they said. "We would prefer to go back to our villages rather than be transferred."

Hugh knew that his privilege of leadership had come through the choice of Colonel Butler. But he would have been willing to work with Captain Peake, within the Arab Scouts. His record notes a transfer back to the Dorset Yeomanry. But he put his men on parade for Captain Peake, who was duly impressed, not least by the Bisharini and their superb camels.

But the impasse remained, and it was decided that Hugh with a selected troop would travel to Cairo to consult, and hopefully solve the problem.

They reached Cairo, where the Egyptian Army would care for the camels. He was asked to disarm the Bisharini, but he said there was no need to do so. They would not be disorderly.

The troop met him the next morning outside the Shepheards' Hotel, causing a stir of interest in the streets. Talks lasted for several hours. In the end he retained his leadership, but a sergeant from the yeomanry, who had become a friend during campaigns against the Senussi, would join to assist him. His name was Pedley.

Hugh asked permission for three days' leave in Alexandria, to visit friends.

The friends, of course, were his wife and family, though he did not say this in his story.

He took his special aide, Mohammed, four scouts and his troop of Bisharini along to The Cloisters. Dorothy, Alex, and perhaps her brother and sisters, and even Nellie, came out to see them.

Later, leaving the camels stabled, he took his men to the market and made purchases with them. They were like children seeing things for the first time, for these were desert, not city, Arabs. Then he stayed at The Cloisters. When they returned to Kossima his men told the others of their experiences, and the evening campfires were joyous.

Pedley had not ridden a camel before, and had a tumble the first time. But he took to it, and said it was more comfortable than a horse. Hugh was able to continue his work without anxiety. He covered hundreds of miles, deterred various potential smugglers, and encountered bands of friendly Bedouin.

They also located a huge cave which was being used for the storage of goods for smuggling to the scattered and diminishing Turkish outposts and garrisons. They had been told of it, and discovered it, in a narrow ravine in the hills. He and Mohammed, after cautiously pausing outside the dark entrance, moved quietly inside; and after pausing again to listen, Mohammed struck a match – and several more – to show them what was there. They moved carefully around huge bags of cereals and many other supplies, which they gradually set ablaze. As they left they heard explosions from deeper within, when ammunition must have blown up. They were satisfied their work had been well done – for all the waste it would not have been possible to carry the goods away. A little distance on they were fired at, the explosions having alerted those who perhaps should have been on guard. They retreated at speed, rejoining the rest of the troop.

On their return, Hugh received another message: "Gather the entire scouts and wait for instructions."

Obeying further orders which seemed to him ridiculous, he travelled to Northern Palestine, where it was raining, wet and slippery – hateful to the camels, some of which fell. He made an angry protest and was detained for three weeks without occupation. Perhaps it was then that his reposting to the Dorset Yeomanry, which he had received, was cancelled.

He was still with his Arab Scouts when a large part of the yeomanry forces had regretfully to give up their horses to the Remount Service, and sign on with a machine-gun battalion, to be sent to France.

There is no way of knowing whether the visit to The Cloisters actually took place, or whether the display of his men, and the picturesque Bisharini, on the lawn, was a romantic story he would have liked to be true. There were those like Laurence Grafftey Smith who developed an affection for the Arabs whatever their shortcomings, as Hugh had, though many British people, including some members of the army, did not; and the treatment of them was not always good. Families like the Aldersons showed care and warmth for their staff, but the lines were clearly drawn, as in Britain itself. The admiration Hugh felt might not have been shared even though he wrote of their having been greeted with great respect and goodwill.

The yeomanry had sometimes been fighting in terrible conditions over the months, sometimes in desert dress in freezing rain. Their riding boots wore out on occasions they had to dismount and fight as infantry. The Turks always fought bravely, but they too had lost thousands of men and their mounts, and were often near-starving. The British horses were sometimes hungry and in poor condition, as they were themselves at several times of the hardest fighting.

As Hugh had expressed perhaps over-forcefully, it was not feasible to use camels in the north, on wet grass or during wet seasons, where many of the current battles would be.

Although smugglers and raiders were still having to be repulsed, it was decided to demobilise the Arab Scouts. More mechanical and motorised units were coming into use.

Some camels were handed to T. E. Lawrence, and some would be used along the drier coastal strip. These included his own mount, Nemo, which he said, he handed to an old friend, Colonel Whylie, and not without regret. Perhaps it was felt the Arab Scouts were more trouble than they were worth, and of course they all had to be paid (it was a little while before the finances were tidied up), and the men were not suitable to use as infantry.

It was not easy to explain to his men why they were being released, but they were returning to what they knew, and where they had been at home. There were scenes of separation, and hopes to meet again. But to watch them travelling away from him must have been hard (in spite of the problems they'd given him) after all the expeditions, their bravery and co-operation, and the successes they'd all experienced. Hugh seemed to have become as immune as they were to the various woundings and suffering inflicted along the way, but he wrote of feeling lonely and sad. He realised that something about the wild expanses of this desert country, for all its hostilities of blowing sand, aridity and storms, had become dear to him. It was partly the knowledge of its ancient and also biblical history, always underfoot. Perhaps when he was sent to Beersheba something echoed to him from his brief schooldays, of Abraham planting a grove in Beersheba or poor ousted Hagar wandering from it into the desert with her bottle of water and her baby (Genesis Chapter 16).

It was leaving an impression on him deeper, he said, than anywhere else. His affection for and interest in the different tribes he had worked with were as strong as his relationship with the gauchos. 'The Bedouin', he said, 'feel at one with the air, the wind and the sun, and the wide expanses.' He respected their sense of Allah's nearness. The Bisharini from Sudan were harder, more wild, more feared, but they had all served him well.

The last few pages of his story are a little hazy; as ever, they are dateless and incomplete of some facts.

He wrote of taking a post as a cavalry instructor (not on his record) and then receiving a heavy hoof kick on his knee that disabled him for some time – the first time he mentions (he calls it the first of experiencing) a physical misfortune. He was treated at a station hospital in Gaza (the record states 'injury', 'Adm. Gaza' and then 'Adm. Alex'), and he said he regretted being unable to take part in the last victories of the war.

In October 1918 he was posted to work in the prisoner-of-war camp at Maadi, outside Cairo. He found it interesting though monotonous after his life in the desert, but he served there for almost a year.

And during that time there occurred the Egyptian Revolution.

Hugh must have been aware of the chaotic and brutal events unfolding around the cities – he mentions being told that the Egyptians were terrorising the city with murder and fire. Certainly the Cloisters family would have been aware of it, whether there or in their holiday home.

There were many causes for it: the 'voluntary recruitment', the inequality of landownership, the presence of thousands of foreign troops not always civil to Egyptians… The immediate trigger was the refusal to allow a delegation of Egyptian politicians to attend the coming Paris Peace Conference to put their case, as had been recommended by Reginald Wingate, the High Commissioner. This had been refused by Curzon at the British Foreign Office, who had no sympathy whatever for ideas about independence. The recently elected Lloyd George government in London had little experience of Egypt. A telegram was sent ordering that the delegation should instead be exiled to Malta.

This telegram Grafftey Smith delivered with a heavy heart, anticipating the result. But the exile took place. Wingate was withdrawn (to be replaced by General Allenby) and the riot began, on 18 March 1919.

The older students were first on the streets, followed by the schools, including the girls' schools, marching and chanting names and slogans, and then the cities were seething with angry citizens. Foreign passengers arriving on trains, including British servicemen returning from leave, were hauled off and killed. Many large properties, military and civilian installations, villages and stations, were burnt. There were strikes at all levels. The Chancery was spat at – but not torched. Hundreds of foreigners and Egyptians lost their lives over the next two weeks, until General Bulfin exerted military control. The British government was 'shocked'.

Allenby recommended that the exiled politicians should be given a hearing (which appeared to some as succumbing to violence). But a limited independence was arranged. Hugh must have returned to The Cloisters, for at 27 September 1919 we have 'Embarked for UK'. And Dorothy was with him, aboard the *Highland Piper*. His repatriation certificate from Winchester of 1 January 1920 refers to him as 'married'. Only a week later, they were off again: a second honeymoon, aboard the same ship.

I have in my cabinet a tiny brass cannon on a wooden stand, and a little brass tray with miniature brass cups. The story is that these were made for Hugh by some in the prisoner-of-war camp.

From one world war and through the next, The Cloisters, with Alex and Nellie, their gradually marrying family and their business, survived amid a fragmenting society and changing city.

The vast empty spaces appeared very differently to the eyes of Richard St Barbe Baker, founder of Men of the Trees in several countries (which became the International Tree Foundation). He features a little later in this story. To him it was a devastated land destroyed by man over centuries of invasion and neglect, resulting in the washing-away of hill soils to rivers and the sea – 'the land of milk and honey' now a barren waste. During the First World War, General Allenby, also recognising this loss, instigated the work of tree planting even amidst the rigours of his campaigns.

St Barbe Baker had come to Egypt on the invitation of the High Commissioner, Sir John Chancellor. They had met in London, where Chancellor had heard of the forestry work he had been doing in Kenya. Here the practice of nomadic farming, with areas of forest cleared often annually, and the larger trees burnt, left behind impoverished soil – potential desert. St Barbe Baker had encouraged them to plant trees on the plots they left, so that the roots would hold the soil together, the leaf litter form fresh soil, and the trees hold the moisture in the air.

St Barbe Baker arrived in Kantara in 1929, and travelled up to Jerusalem, where he had been invited to stay in Government House. His aim was to assemble a group from among as many facets as possible, and open a new band of Men of the Trees.

He visited first Shogi Effendi in the Persian Gardens. He was the grandson of the founder of the Baha'i faith, to which St Barbe Baker belonged. There were still Arab landowners, and he visited several to discuss the need and possibility of refreshing the land with tree-planting, and found accord on this among them. He felt strongly the need and the justice, as he saw it, of the return of the Jewish nation, being in awe of the biblical history. He seemed unaware of the possibility of conflict, believing that so great a project as healing the land through tree planting would draw the races together.

In his view, Islam had welded the desert tribes into a nation, and he enlisted the support of the President of the Supreme Muslim Council. Also, the Mayor and the Bishop of Jerusalem, and Latin Church, the Chancellor of the Hebrew University, representatives of several government departments and heads of educational centres. A date was set for a gathering three weeks ahead.

He made a reasoned but impassioned speech which held all sides of the audience. The founding of his group was proposed and supported, and subsequently went into action.

The Feast of the Trees was an ancient Jewish celebration that had been marked throughout the Diaspora. But in 1929 there were events of tree planting on a grand scale by settlers around Jerusalem and elsewhere in the country. He witnessed long avenues being planted by hundreds of schoolchildren, who afterwards picnicked with their parents and relatives, including on bags of fruit and nuts that had been presented to them. It was a day all unknowing of the subsequent evictions, desperation and killing.

The road to San Miguel (one of three).

The road to San Miguel (two of three).

The road to San Miguel (three of three).

Hugh, Dorothy and Joy.

San Miguel.

Joy and Johnnie at Las Tassis.

On the Estancia.

The end product – polo ponies.

Polo.

Johnnie on Toviano.

The swimming lake.

Locusts destroying tree.

Dead locusts pile.

Maté pots, Gaucho knife and bombilla.

Johnnie, Alex, Dorothy, Nellie and Joy.

4: The Third Tale

Dorothy and Hugh

They left London for Buenos Aires on 8 January 1920, aboard the *Highland Piper*, and travelled to Los Tassis, which was the ranch Hugh had managed before the war.

San Miguel, Las Barancas. La Chiltonia Chica – names familiar to us.

Dorothy said, "Every time we had a place nicely fixed, someone would come and offer for it, and he would sell."

He wrote himself, "The most interesting part is the building-up of things, and once completed, to move on to new places."

The narrative of 'The Ranch' that StJohn conveyed to our children was seamless – perhaps a combination of the last two.

Hugh cannot have been easy. In his book *Among the Gauchos* he wrote,

> It is always a nice feeling to get back home to the Estancia again after days of travel; and the somewhat monotonous routine that goes on there is for the moment forgotten. Back home, and within a week, one is ready and eager to face the hardships of the trail once more. It beats me to know why, but there it is! Routine does not agree with some people and I'm afraid I am one of them.

Among the Gauchos is full of fascinating incidents, character studies and deep breaths of the essences of life for and with the gauchos, the landscape of the Argentine and stories of horses and other animals. But it is not the story of his family life. They are not mentioned, and it is only by piecing bits of it together with the photos Dorothy had, that one can form any kind of timeline.

Hugh had given his address as 'The London and River Plate Bank, Buenos Aires', and the army had not quite forgotten him in his first year back in the Argentine. He was the subject of at least six letters between various financial/ military headquarters in Egypt, requesting that he should be contacted and should reply. The finances of the Arab Scouts were finally sorted, apart from the ongoing question of a matter of £20 that had been dispensed to him (just before his marriage). They asked him to write and account for it. It was questioned between the Office Commanding the Egyptian Expeditionary Forces, the Frontier District Administration, the Bucks Yeomanry Accounts Department – and the War Office in London. The correspondence lasted throughout 1920. Finally, on 1 January 1921, he replied to the War Office in a manner which might have caused exasperation. But a form with his name at the top of it, which contained a long list of scribbles, headed with 'money adjustments' ended with a faint stamp saying 'closed', and dated 7 June 1921.

His letter directed to 'Secretary Finances, War Office', read:

Sir,

I am in receipt of your favour dated 6 December 1920.

I answered a previous letter addressed to me here. I answered all questions and explained as much as possible for the advance of £20 which is said to have been made.

I must remind you that I got a Clearance Certificate from the Command Paymaster E.E.F. [Egypt Expeditionary Forces] Cairo, and St. Munro would be witness that I had done my utmost to clear the mess that was made of the Arab Scouts account, I having handed over in proper order the Arab Scouts and receiving a clearance certificate. I cannot be expected to carry in my mind after two years what may be a mistake of some young clerk and I should therefore recommend that this [illegible word] unaccounted for £20 should be paid by the public.

I have the honour to be
    Your obedient servant.

H Salmon Backhouse

How much of the 'tidying-up' might have been done or not done by Hugh, whose brief education might not have equipped him for it, one cannot tell, though he had been made responsible for the finances of the Arab Scouts.

On 8 January 1921 they travelled from Buenos Aires to Los Tassis (the ranch Hugh had managed before the war) on horseback, with pack animals, sleeping in a tent – a new experience for Dorothy.

Hugh was longing to establish himself, and the opportunity came through an offer from the owner of Los Tassis. His son, who had owned a ranch near Cordoba up in the Sierras, had died, and he offered Hugh a partnership in the estate. Hugh was delighted, and began his preparations. He purchased a large Ford car, which became his hobby as he added extra gears and gadgets. Small cars were not suitable for rough ways or hill-climbing, and San Miguel was 4,000 feet up. They set off again with an accompaniment of laden pack animals and experienced many difficult moments. But it was worth every mile.

The ranch had been built by the Jesuits of adobe (mud) brick, with white pillars holding up the verandah that went all round the house. The garden was full of fruit and flowers, which must have delighted Dorothy. It had recently been under the management of a young cousin, who became a close friend. There were wide views across woods to the hills beyond, and the river, clear and with deep pools, ran close by. Over the next months they established themselves, with occasional visits to Cordoba.

It was here that Hugh began his business of breeding and training horses for polo, inspired by the speed and agility of the wild horses, and amazing abilities of the gauchos, which he had always watched and emulated. If tossed by a newly mounted bucking horse, they would slip a leg across to land on their feet, and hanging on, remount, and travel on and on until the horse tired. Then repeat, the next day, and the next.

He had space enough to grow maize and alfalfa, room for corrals and barns. There were gauchos always travelling and looking for work. A visiting man would be given a drink of maté and a conversation would follow. There would be a discussion of possible work, and a lengthy estimation on both sides of their ability to work well together, and it could be he was sent on his way. Otherwise there would be a process of bargaining. In this way, as the property itself evolved, a workforce gradually built up.

The military in Cordoba already had a polo club, and while at San Miguel Hugh organised others, so that he had places to try his horses out and sell them. When there were matches, smallholders from miles around and owners of other estancias, some of whom played polo, came to watch, and friendships were formed.

Dorothy lost her first child, a daughter, at birth, in Cordoba – she told me that the midwife kept her walking and walking when she wanted to rest. There was always an echo of regret. But then her daughter Joy was born in 1923, and two years later a son. Perhaps Hugh wanted to call him StJohn in memory of his own brother (the pilot who had been shot down and killed) but he was always called Johnnie (StJohn became his business name many years later!).

When Sir George Alderson died in 1926, Hugh and Dorothy were in the midst of their few Argentine years that formed the cherished idyll of StJohn's life. Dorothy might have been relieved not to have taken part in what would have been solemn celebrations in the city George had loved and chosen all those years ago.

Dorothy and Hugh entertained for a meal the son of the Governor of Cordoba, who was looking for a ranch that would please his artistic and demanding wife. Hugh accompanied them on several rides round the area to locate a suitable place, but after a few weeks they decided it was San Miguel that they wanted. And Hugh was ready to move on.

He had seen from a hill above the ranch a valley that was part of San Miguel property. He trekked down to it, and found a mud hut and a stretch of land that excited him enough to buy it. The river flowed past it, and there was wind enough to turn mills for lifting the water.

So they set about creating a new home, which took many months, and he called it Las Barrancas – The Cliffs. There was no road – stones and boulders had to be moved, and his loaded vehicle was drawn down the slope by mules, with its wheels tied. The mules were almost run down – the vehicle tipped and pots and pans and furniture were scattered.

Pigs and chickens had been taken to San Miguel, and when they moved to Las Barrancas the pigs migrated there to greet them. A piglet he gave in a bag to a friend ran back to rejoin the family the following morning.

So they settled into their new home, which StJohn dimly remembered, and perhaps it was here and in the subsequent ranch that was Dorothy's happiest time, when the children were under her wing.

As time went on, Hugh was more and more frequently away, at first playing in polo matches around the country, and then going by ship with his trained ponies to sell them in America and Britain. There would be a manager living in his own house nearby, in charge, but Dorothy would keep closely responsible and aware of the running and maintenance. There would be a head gaucho, and a team of peons, or workers. Many of his ponies were played in international matches.

Perhaps it was the access to Las Barrancas that became a drawback, or perhaps, having made it comfortable and profitable, someone offered to buy it and Hugh was again ready to move. Dorothy remembered being told suddenly out of the blue that they were leaving. But the next ranch, La Chiltonia Chica, photographed but not mentioned in his book, became the most developed, with its own polo ground, a fenced tennis court, and a large lake with a diving board, all achieved under their care. By that time StJohn was old enough to be about and useful – for example, in helping to make bricks from mud drawn from the lake, with chopped straw, moulded and dried – good small-boy work, if monotonous.

With the bricks was built a changing room and kitchen by the lake, for visitors. The diving board was built from sleepers, and there was a little boat. StJohn spoke of hunting and killing frogs, whose legs, he said, were good food. It was a relief to Joy when he was out and about, and no longer, as she saw it, being a nuisance to her.

For they quarrelled fiercely, as dear little siblings do. Joy attacked him with a knife and cut his nose (when for some reason he couldn't explain he dropped the kittens in the soup). StJohn hit Joy with a large stick when she interfered with his building of a moat, and he was beaten by his father, who happened to be there. He had not beaten Joy for cutting him – which he considered was unfair.

Joy was usually with her mother, who began teaching her to read. She had had some books sent to her for the purpose by her parents. When she felt StJohn was ready she began to encourage him both to read and to use a pencil. He was interested, but when he realised this was going to be frequent, and definite, and demanding, he became less keen, and sometimes had to be tied to the chair or he would scamper off. But she persevered.

Uncle Reggie, who had emigrated to Canada and become both a pilot and a wanderer, visited the family in a small plane – a visit StJohn remembered as an exciting event. Perhaps it was his stories of Canada that StJohn recalled later.

There were two windmills. One fetched up water from the pure stream for the house, where there was a bath and – a notable asset at the time – a flush lavatory. The other was for the animals and irrigation. There was a large kitchen range burning logs. Two girls helped in the house, and StJohn would listen to the creaking of the mill in the wind at night.

Hugh was not the kind of father to play games with his children, though he was very proud of them. One day he tied a long rope to StJohn and, handing him a brush, lowered him down the path that ran down the edge of the well, so that he could brush the sides. A snake came out of a hole and hissed at him – Hugh lifted him away, moved him on, and told him to continue brushing.

The dusty area in front of the kitchen door was swept daily, so any trail made by a visiting snake would be seen. But one morning, as Dorothy was about to step into the room where Joy was sitting on the floor playing, she saw a snake, up-ended, swaying for a strike, behind her. When on her own, she carried a revolver, and very slowly, and half behind the door, she raised it, and shot the snake over her daughter's head.

Another day, when she had let them go for a short walk and was looking out for their return, she saw that a puma was following a little distance behind. She had to watch and wait until it was near enough for a shot to scare it away.

When he was at home, his father's revolver lived on the bedside table, and Hugh gave his son the job of unloading it each morning. One day Dorothy was turning the mattress, and StJohn, half playing but thinking he had done the job, aimed it at the mattress. The trigger clicked and shockingly it went off. They looked at each other over the mattress – for a moment he had thought he had killed her.

For a small boy trotting here and there, there were always interesting things to watch – natural things or human activity. The ornero birds made their cone-shaped nests on the top of fence posts, and he would stand fascinated as the cones developed. He discovered that if he walked quietly round and round an owl sitting on a post a little distance away, it would twist its head this way and that to watch him – until it got giddy and fell off. He stood under trees and watched birds building nests above him. He always carried a knife, and when a wild turkey walked by he managed to grab it and grapple with it. He cut its head (almost) off and took it proudly to the kitchen.

There would be creative activities to watch. In a big barn leather goods were made from the cured skins of their own cattle and horses: bridles and straps, saddles of the gaucho kind and the very different saddles for polo. Teams of men would be cutting, shaping and oiling to produce decorative as well as useful things, such as belts with burnt-in patterns, and thin strips of leather were used to bind tufts of dyed horse-hair into decorations for festive days. Boots were made from the skin of a freshly-killed foal fitted and dried around the foot, as StJohn's were.

They used to hunt ostriches out on the pampas. They would circle above their heads the *bolliodoros* – heavy balls on the end of long, long strings, thrown to encircle the birds' feet. From the soft skin of the ostrich's neck they made pouches to hold tobacco or money; they ate the eggs and the best parts of the meat.

A short distance from the ranch was a wooded area holding the enormous cesspit. Here lived a race of large toads which could spit poison, and StJohn took a great dislike to them. He set out with the revolver to destroy them. He fired several shots, killed some and managed to avoid the poison, falling over backwards at the recoil from each shot. He returned feeling triumphant, and replaced the revolver. Perhaps a child's take on imperialism?

The gauchos lived chiefly on meat with bread. Sometimes they would have a stew (*pucchero*), mainly made from joints of animals roasted over large fires. Meals were always accompanied by maté (tea) drunk from gourds (sometimes trimmed with silver or inscribed) through a silver straw called a *bombilla*. Any visitor would be offered maté on arrival. StJohn liked to eat outside with them, and they would offer him tasty bits of meat on the ends of their long knives. Nothing could ever surpass for him the taste of that meat.

The engine of one of the vehicles made a strange noise when it was started. When the driver opened the bonnet he found a cat inside, cut almost in half by the fan belt. He dropped the apparently lifeless and bloody body into the stream, from which StJohn drew it out, because this particular cat, which had always been wild and apparently untameable, was one he particularly wanted to befriend. He made splints to keep it straight and still, binding its body round with cloths he requested from his mother. He stayed in a barn with it almost continuously for three days and nights, turning it over frequently, and feeding it with little pieces of meat – for its eyes had opened and its jaws worked.

It gradually recovered and became his companion, sleeping on the pillow above his head at night, following him about during the day.

Years later, StJohn himself would write about some of the incidents he remembered.

> Sometimes we went to the village called "Venardo Tuerto" some miles away [this in the ancient Ford his father kept going by diverse means]. And I would slip away and seek out the local lads. We would play marbles, or take fruit off a passing cart. There was a nasty man that no-one liked. One time we crept into his patio and put a large banger – firework packed with mud in front of his door. Just as I was lighting the banger he came out with a large cow-whip, just as the banger went off. We were lucky to escape.

There were two gangs always fighting each other (will it ever end?).

> Once we were going down a street dodging stones being thrown at us, and as I passed a large tree a man came out and hit me across the back with a chair. We used to put caps on the tram-tracks, and wait til the cars came over them and made a huge bang. Once I crept to a private swimming pool and was swimming about when three or four chaps came and tried to push me under. But I had good breath.

The ranch was not always a safe place for a child – particularly one who liked to be in the midst of things. When fencing was being erected, the ends were stretched from one place to another, and on one occasion an end sprang back and wrapped around him. He was brought in to Dorothy unconscious (they thought he was dead) and so covered in blood she could scarcely sort him out, but she did, with help and love and patience, and eventually he was released back to freedom – having learnt one thing to avoid.

These memories were clear, but he also remembered small things from before – for example, of himself and Joy running round the verandah of San Miguel with fireflies glowing in jars.

He once noticed several vultures gathering low in the sky, and walked across to investigate. He saw a horse struggling frantically with its legs caught in the fence – something must have frightened it into a gallop. Realising it was trapped, he ran to fetch his father, who brought his gun. Feeling very important, StJohn led him to the place, and they watched the plunging animal together. Then they drew a little nearer, and, realising it was seriously injured Hugh raised his gun and killed it with one shot.

To see an animal killed was nothing new, but he remembered a bull so large and stubborn that it took many men a long while to fight with it and goad it into position. Then, with one shot between the ears, it dropped straight down, all the huge brown mass of it, in one second.

He came across a can beside a vehicle one day and dipped a stick in it. He found it dripped colours. He knew it was oil – but this was irresistible. He carried the stick to a stream, and the colours were magical. Tired of repeated tipping, he took the can, and slowly, slowly poured the oil into the flowing water, completely enchanted by the rainbows, forgetting any other thought.

He was found out, severely reprimanded, and beaten. Oil had to be fetched from far away.

His father noticed that the milk yield was down on one of the cows, and the calf was not thriving. He watched her, quietly, before milking time. One day he saw on the ground under the cow a snake stand up on its tail and suck a teat. The cow and Hugh stood stock-still – until he shot the snake. The other teats were sore and wrinkled. He shot the cow, and gave the calf to another to rear.

There was great excitement when his grandparents, with one of Dorothy's sisters, visited the ranch, the train being stopped, as it were, in the middle of nowhere so that they could descend. Their luggage was lowered and they were all met by a fleet of vehicles. They brought dolls and a doll's pram for Joy, a teddy bear and tricycle for StJohn. It was nine years since Dorothy had left.

When his fifth birthday came, StJohn was told that his present was outside. And out there for him was a little piebald pony that had belonged to the Indian post boy – a pony StJohn had long loved and coveted. Hugh had exchanged him for a trained pony of his own. His name was Toviano.

Now StJohn's happiness was complete and his freedom extended.

Although trained to be ridden, Toviano would sometimes play hard to get in the enclosure where he grazed. Carrying a small bucket of grain to tempt him, StJohn would slowly and repeatedly approach, only to have him whirl away as he touched him. After a particularly lengthy session, having finally caught him but feeling very cross, StJohn determined to teach him a lesson by riding him for an extremely long way, forgetting that he was not supposed to go beyond the bounds of the ranch. He knew the owners of the neighbouring ranch, and decided to visit them.

When he arrived, they were surprised to see him, but kind, and gave him something to eat. They suggested he should quickly return home. He was still a long way away when it began to grow dark.

The pony plodded on, and he saw firelight ahead. A group of gauchos were around a campfire eating and drinking, and at their invitation he dismounted and joined them. Meanwhile his father had set out with a couple of men to search for him. He too was attracted by the fire, and so found him.

When StJohn was set ignominiously on the front of his father's saddle, with Toviano tied to trail behind, he realised he was in disgrace. The ride home was not cheerful. (It was not Hugh's choice to welcome the Prodigal.) At least on that occasion he was not beaten (perhaps that was vetoed by his mother), but to him the punishment was worse. For days he lived under the threat that Toviano was to be turned loose on the pampas, never again to be his own; and he was forbidden not only to ride him, but to care for him.

But he surreptitiously watched the man in charge. And when he judged the job was not being done properly, he reported the details to his father. Finally Hugh relented, and Toviano became his own again.

Locusts

A great black cloud on the horizon was moving towards them. Locusts, he was told, and while he was trying to ask questions his father was giving orders to everyone – the two girls who worked in the house, the peons and the gauchos – sending them in different directions. Smoking fires were to be lit around the ranch house.

"Why smokey fires?"

"To drive the locusts away."

Men were gathering together metal sheets and metal cans, and anything that would clash noisily together, and fanning out across the property. The cloud approached, and before it was overhead, blotting out the daylight, came the clash and clatter of everything being banged, in all directions, StJohn with his contribution working as hard as anyone. It all went on and on for minutes, for an hour, as the cloud, still airborne, gradually disappeared towards the horizon. It had worked – the locusts had been driven away.

But about five weeks later, news came again of locusts. The eggs of those fliers, laid several kilometres away, had now hatched into *saltomas* or hoppers, and they were an even worse menace than the adults. They travelled as a huge army along the ground, destroying every green thing in their path, falling into wells and utterly polluting them, and destroying trees, including their bark. There was only one weapon of defence and killing, which involved the use of more metal sheets than Hugh had on the property. He sent a wire to a friend on the railway to send as many and as fast as possible. The station was six miles away.

In the meantime all available sheets were positioned across his cultivated fields in lines, with a trench alongside, and at each end deep pits were dug. Coming up against the sheets, the hoppers would move along to the end and fall into the pits. Carts trundled to the station, and after twenty-four hours the loads of metal sheets arrived.

Hugh summoned help from any neighbour who was available, and every man worked flat out, finishing their task when the swarm was about eighteen metres from his property. A group of pine trees he had planted and cherished was destroyed. The pits, as they filled with the suffocated insects, had to be dug out about every half-hour, and the rotting insects produced a nauseating smell. Eggs laid by hens who picked up stray insects were tainted and inedible, and horses eating grass over which they had passed became sickly. All this is told in *Among the Gauchos*, but it was also told me by StJohn as a time of the most horror he had ever experienced.

***

There was another disaster to come; but though StJohn witnessed and remembered the after-effects, I think Dorothy kept the children occupied inside when the strangeness of the morning began, and the horror of it did not enter him as the horror of the locusts had done.

In 1932 the volcano called Cerro Azul in the Andes erupted, but on that morning no one knew why it remained dark when the clocks said it should be morning. Hugh found his men all inside talking, some afraid the world was about to end. He noticed a pall of dust on the grass, and was puzzled himself. Then he decided to drive the nine miles to town and gather news. He learnt of the volcano – some said several volcanoes. The dust in the air was getting thicker as he drove back to tell his family, and to get the men out to care for the animals as best they could.

The fact that he then decided to drive 200 miles south to visit a friend he thought might be in need of help seems strange, but it left Dorothy and the children in the peace she utilised to keep them from being afraid. It was a dangerous journey through mounting dust and confusion, but he managed it safely.

The dust was ploughed in the following year, but the damage to crops and pasture was extensive.

***

In addition to all this, the stability of the country was being shaken by the rise of Germany. There were many German immigrants, mostly smallholders and traders. The German Embassy founded a paper called *El Pampero*, which extolled Hitler, and in addition there was resentment among some Argentinians at the large areas of land enclosed by ranchers, mostly British. Government policies oscillated. The atmosphere began to change, and some ranchers were selling up.

Hugh's world, and all that he had built up, seemed under threat – the world of polo, and of shipping ponies, was uncertain. But the captain who had wooed the young Dorothy away from the comfort of colonial Egypt (and also given her the children she cared for more than anything in the world) was not the same as the man who had become so popular among the rich, particularly in America. Spoilt, she said. To her, he had changed 'from cowboy to playboy'.

StJohn knew nothing of this. He was well aware that his father travelled constantly to England, and to America, selling ponies and playing polo. But to leave? They were all going to leave? But the ponies came from here – why should we leave? When will we come back? But no one seemed to know.

"The country has changed," his father said.

"But I want to be here, on our ranch. What about Toviano?"

"He'll be looked after," his father said. And his mother: "You must say goodbye to him."

He went out and rode Toviano as though he was punishing him, so that Toviano would not miss him. He rode him hard across the ranch, off the ranch and back again. He rode him to exhaustion, and came back to the packing of cases.

"We're going on a big boat," Joy told him. "It will be lovely."

In March 1933 the family travelled on the *Avila Star* of the Blue Star Line Ltd, to England, leaving Hugh's manager to cope with the ash-ridden ranch, and problems with the cattle and horses. A happy coincidence in the sadness was that among the passengers was Johnny Weissmuller, a famous swimmer and Tarzan of the films. He took a liking to StJohn, and coached him in the ship's swimming pool, improving his diving, which was of benefit to him later on.

Their destination was given as Rugby, and StJohn, then eight, remembered a castle with enormous fireplaces and sofas, tiger-skin rugs, extremely kind hosts, and polo (attended by many smart people in many splendid cars) played in the grounds. Hugh had been captain of the Argentine polo team, and played with other teams around the country over the next few months and years, and the family moved with him. In one of the houses StJohn became friendly with the son of the cook; and seeing him going out, asked where he was going.

"To school."

"Can I come with you?"

"I expect so."

And he was welcomed in. He enjoyed this spell at a small country primary school – no red tape as far as he was aware – and he was sad when his mother, who had not known where he had been going told him they were moving on.

I never heard from StJohn that they visited the ranch again after the 1933 move away. But there is a record that they sailed again, also on the *Avila Star*, from London back to the Argentine in September 1934, probably because Hugh was rejoining his polo team and they went with him. Then, however they travelled there, Dorothy and the children were in Alexandria at The Cloisters in 1935. Her youngest sister Vivian, married to Laurence Grafftey Smith in 1929, now had two sons, and probably Vivian brought them to The Cloisters, and all the cousins met.

Vivian was held to be the naughty member of the family, and some years later she was obliged to hand her sons over to their father, who had divorced her, she being the 'guilty party'. He had married again (an American called Jane), who made him very happy, and the boys came back to him in the embassy. Vivian and Grafftey Smith had been married in the little Church in Bulkeley that George had built. She was eighteen; he was thirty-seven.

"A pretty child," he said.

Hugh went back to New York, then Mexico, and back again to London. He may have picked up more of his ponies to ship and sell.

StJohn kept several newspaper clippings about Johnny Weissmuller. He also kept a magazine article from America about his father, who was sometimes referred to in polo literature as 'the quaint Hugo Backhouse', because on occasions he preferred to wear loose gaucho trousers (*bombachas*) rather than British breeches. But the following article, under a photo of him mounted on a careering pony, gives a different view.

> Life begins at 8 a.m. for Hugh Salmon Backhouse, the five-goal Argentinian poloist, known on three continents as Baccusi. He rounds up high-class polo mounts in South America, plays them in England, and this year invaded Long Island Fields. Here he puts the finishing touches to a famous pony. Baccusi remained after the matches to study the horse show with a view to returning in the spring with new brands of Argentinian horse-flesh, suitable for steeple-chasing et. al.

After the difficult but purposeful years of ranch life, it was hard for Dorothy to adjust back to the social life of Alexandria. She told me she found it 'piffling'. Perhaps Joy enjoyed it the most. She was very pretty, and sociable, and after the isolation of the ranch, though alleviated by visitors by the time they had developed La Chiltonia Chica, it was different to find herself with interested uncles, aunts and cousins.

Many other things were of interest to StJohn. He sat with his grandfather at the enormous desk that had belonged to George, while Alex told him about the company, showed him diagrams and pictures, and gave him a penknife which StJohn kept in his pocket for the rest of his life.

One of Allen Aldersons' activities that Alex told him about was one that had been introduced after George died. This concerned the caterpillar tractor for ploughing – a lot less trouble than either with an animal or the wheeled tractors otherwise in use. The company had become the representative of the Caterpillar Tractor Co. of California. Wheels tended to mire in some of the sticky soils and with caterpillar tractors food production was benefited. The first one had come in 1929. Ploughing demonstrations had taken place in the next and subsequent years, watched by hundreds of interested spectators – the general public and landowners.

Alex took his grandson round the market, pointing things out, giving him sugar cane to suck, and speaking Arabic – which impressed StJohn (finding his proud use of Spanish impotent).

At night he thought of his lost wide open spaces, and of Toviano. He and Joy went to the Victoria College. Joy enjoyed the companionship, but StJohn, realising everyone else knew more than he did, saw everyone as a challenge. But gradually his natural friendliness prevailed.

It was a few months before Hugh wrote to say he had rented a home for them in Brighton – 27 Braemar Road.

Brighton – where my father had grown up with his older brother and sister, where his father, Henry, had walked in his khaki uniform, and from where he had gone to serve in France. I remember visiting my grandparents in their large rather dark house – the big black and white tiles in the porch, and walking under a rose arch in the garden. They had been Mayor and Mayoress of Brighton earlier, amidst all the splendour of robes and chains and speeches. Sometimes we had visited Brighton Beach to trawl the pools with nets.

My mother had taken me there several times (with a fluttering heart) to receive certificates for poem writing or reciting at the Dome at festival time. (By this time, StJohn, ten years older than me, was far away.) StJohn used to skate at the ice rink, and met Jean Simmons, the film star, whose prettiness he never forgot, and he used to cycle up the hill behind the town to fly a kite and watch buzzards over the Devil's Dyke.

When they arrived in Brighton, Dorothy's mind was divided between her parents in a none too settled Egypt and her desire to give her children some stability. She found each of them a school, where they had to struggle with lessons. They were eleven and thirteen.

Hugh was involved not only with polo, but with other plans of his own. It was not always peaceful when he visited. Sometimes there were arguments in the evenings after the children were in bed. They would run into the room – Joy to her mother, StJohn to his father – 'to mend them'.

StJohn gathered a small gang of boys from his school, sworn to loyalty and secrecy. They used to meet – by whose dispensation I do not know – in the crypt of a church, which must have enhanced the clandestine atmosphere. There they would plot the kinds of things – sometimes destructive – that gangs of small boys tend to do, sometimes getting into trouble, wearing their caps and blazers inside out. But beyond all these excitements, his focus was on getting back to claim his ranch. He persuaded a friend to go with him.

They made their way by bus to Southampton, possibly with money pilfered from their parents. There they managed to find out where were the cars going to Buenos Aires – and perhaps he remembered. There were traits I knew in him that would have enabled him to find out: asking different people small questions, casually, as if it was just chit-chat, his patience and his long habit of observation. The cars were left unlocked by the ship's side before being manoeuvred on to a net to be lifted by crane. Each boy nipped into a car and lay down behind the front seat.

Whether it was her instinct, her prayers, or something he had taken with him (perhaps all three), but teamwork between his mother and the police paid off.

"Out you come, sonny!" (He would never forget that.)

And they were delivered home.

He was taken on as a boarder at his school in Brighton, and stayed there until he left, prematurely.

During one holiday they moved to London, to a little house Hugh had been preparing for them in Cadogan Lane. It seemed illogical, with war clouds gathering, but Hugh liked to be in the centre of things. And perhaps there was a kind of truce, based on parting, for StJohn's memories of the years there were mainly of things enjoyed – apart from the Blitz.

Next door was another rancher they had known in the Argentine – StJohn saw him as compressed and deflated in the smaller space.

American tractors come to Alexandria.

In Alexandria with grandparents.

In England.

They had many acquaintances and visitors, mainly polo friends. One was a Member of Parliament. One day, when talking to his father, he invited StJohn to tea, and he went round to his house the following afternoon. Lavish spreads of food were becoming rarer, and StJohn tucked in merrily.

Then the 'gentleman' said, "I've a collection that might interest you."

Stamps? Guns? Butterflies?

He took StJohn's hand to lead him into another room, but a deep instinct of self-protection rose in StJohn. As a bedroom door was opened he drew his hand away with quick strength – and ran out of the house.

Perhaps he missed a prize collection. Perhaps he did not. Somehow, even though not understanding, he was shocked – he knew something had been wrong. He despised all politicians from then on.

It would have been interesting to know what Hugh's response to this would have been. It is likely that StJohn told his mother, and that it had been her nurturing of his awareness that had alerted him. If it was discussed between Hugh and Dorothy it would not have brightened the relationship.

During a conversation, their neighbour mentioned having heard that the Brazilian Embassy was looking for someone who could speak Spanish (as StJohn could) and take down letters. Perhaps StJohn should try for it? He was a presentable youth. He was sure they would accept him.

'This is it,' he thought, 'heaven sent.'

He walked into the huge office with pad, pencil and plenty of confidence, which, after much conversation in Spanish, they were prepared to share. They began dictating a letter to him, but he had never written in Spanish. His scribbles were indecipherable to him, or anyone else. Sad and humiliated, he left.

However, after a few days casting about the area, he got himself employed part-time as a carpenter's mate, and became an interested and willing pupil. Over subsequent holiday months he worked with a plumber, an electrician and then a builder, in each session learning skills useful for ever after.

The builder was the son of Argentinian parents, and he invited StJohn to visit.

There were some strange, sad—happy occasions. He remembered their flat as rather dark, and he found himself surrounded by familiar but faraway objects. They all spoke Spanish, and drank maté as of old through a silver *bombilla*, from maté pots, and mourned their lost land. They had come to England with their English employer, who found he could no longer make use of the father, and they were now kept, meagrely, by their son's employment.

StJohn remembered a day when they were all to go to the station to see his father off on a train. He did not remember where his father was set to go

– only that, as he was about to step on the train he turned back, paused, and said, "I can't go." (His son's face?)

Dorothy said, "You must go."

The door slammed shut. There was no meeting with him, and, as far as StJohn knew, no correspondence, for thirteen years.

This could have been because he actually was, as the story went afterwards, in the secret service in Stockholm. It is likely that the divorce had already taken place, but in any case it would be safer for the family if there was no correspondence. In Stockholm interesting events took place, and after a while a new career. But the fact that his ponies were bought by kings, princes, and maharajas was no substitute for a father.

Joy was now an attractive teenager, often invited out on dates. Sometimes she took her brother along as her escort – if she felt the need. But he was away at boarding school when the bombs started falling.

He had a letter from his mother, telling him that for his own safety he would be staying in Brighton with friends for the holidays. This was too much for him. With his father now away, he felt he should look after his family. He used his end-of-term train ticket to come back to London. He arrived late one night as Dorothy was writing him another letter. She thought she was seeing a ghost. He did not go back to school.

One evening StJohn came home to find Cadogan Lane roped off because a bomb had fallen a few doors down from their home. It had not exploded, but Joy and Dorothy, among others, had been evacuated, and had to find somewhere else to sleep while the bomb was being dealt with.

StJohn did stints of fire-watching on the roof of his local church. One day, after a nearby house had been flattened by a bomb, he saw a screaming baby on the pavement. Unable to leave it, he picked it up and took it to a hospital, but was suspected of being its errant father – which was embarrassing.

Joy at seventeen joined the WRNS, and at fifteen StJohn joined the Royal Navy Cadet Corps, where he was given a training in engineering. At just sixteen he joined the Royal Navy. Dorothy had been offered a job elsewhere in the country.

In order for there to be somewhere for Joy and StJohn to go, and perhaps meet, when they came on leave, they found a two-bedroom basement flat for rent, paid for by Dorothy, and put some clothes and essentials into it. All the rest of their furniture, china and ornaments, mementoes of the Argentine and of Hugh, they loaded successively on to a borrowed builder's cart, and after work, in the blackout with one minimal red light, they pushed it round London, selling the contents to shops, market stalls, the King's Road, anywhere, for very little. Then StJohn went to his barracks.

Sybil Chadwick Prue's mother a masseuse standing third from the right.

Sailor boy.

Gervis family.

St John's Navy Days.

Banjo songs, Harvey Gervis.

A visit to Tunbridge Wells.

5: A Childhood in Wartime

StJohn, exploring, crawled along a tunnel in the undergrowth and came face-to-face, in an unforgettable pause, with a creature he thought was a wolf. They stared at each other for several unfrightened moments, until the animal wriggled around and walked back the way it had come.

I crawled, exploring, through the bracken on Tunbridge Wells Common, and came upon a plant rising from the ground, its arching stems holding pearly-white bells – and stayed still to remember for ever that first sight of Solomon's Seal (*Polygonatum multiflorum*).

My mother, Sibyl, never really stopped being angry at having to give up her job as a masseuse at the hospital (now she would have been a physiotherapist). She and Harvey Gervis had met as professionals at St Thomas's Hospital, he on his way to becoming a surgeon. He was considered aloof and difficult to approach. Sibyl realised he was shy, and gently teased him.

When they were to be married, she was up against the assumptions not only of her parents and society's 'norms', but Harvey himself, who enforced her leaving her job with a kind of rigid gentleness – it would look as though he couldn't 'keep her'. It was years before I realised, on account of some of her remarks and a few conversations, that the seed of bitterness sown sent disruptive shoots into her life, and later life. There were always nannies who saw more of the children than their parents did – she could have returned at a suitable time after the births without much change in the routines.

She embarked on all available activities with great energy and enjoyment – but even then there were limits. She and a friend enjoyed following a pack of beagles on a Saturday morning – until both husbands decided Saturday mornings should be for them, and stopped it. She attended WEA (Workers' Educational Association) classes on literature, and others on cordon bleu cookery and flower arranging. She gardened beautifully, and had one or two professionals advising her among their friends and acquaintances, and she enjoyed social life and entertaining good friends and enjoyed doing things with us.

But there was always a sore spot. Her sister-in-law Ruth Gervis, wife of Harvey's brother Shor, had managed to remain an artist and teacher and have nothing whatsoever to do with her own housework and cooking. Sometimes, the sore spot showed up.

Yet, in wartime, everyone was losing out in some way – everyone had to pull together.

The Hug That Taught Me

I was used to seeing different people in the house in different places, working at various things. Sometimes Cornford was outside, but today he was in the basement, tidying. He was a tall roundy man with a big smile. I suppose I was three or four, I liked everybody, trotted about and was always talking. I don't remember what I had said that he found funny, but he bent down laughing and gave me a hug – as we do when a child seems enchanting and our arms spontaneously go round them, as we laugh.

I straightened up as I was moving away, and I saw his face. I wouldn't have known what the word 'drawn' meant. He was also going crimson. The encounter was over. I was momentarily glad he had laughed, but I was going somewhere else now.

But I remembered his face as clearly as a picture, and thought about it later. There was so much suffering in it that only getting older could translate for me. As I grew up to understand the social dividing lines that existed in our house, and others like it, I think I understand what had drained his face: he thought he had gone over a line. It was a different line from the one that would outlaw cruelty, or lust – it was only an overview on the quality of human standing – it was in fact an irrelevance, a false construction, that is only now more generally passed by.

Other criteria emerge to influence and cloud clarity. But I grew up uncircumscribed by that line. He was a person; I was a person.

***

The war, which started when I was four, was some kind of dark presence going on both somewhere else and around us. We were on holiday in Saundersfoot when it was declared; and my father, a surgeon, was summoned straight back to his hospital and we returned at the end of the holiday in a hired car. My mother was in anguish when we heard the news. She told me and my brothers to kneel down and pray.

In retrospect, thinking how I would have felt about a war when my children were small, I find it amazing how our parents kept feelings of dread and horror under cover. I think parents just did things – all sorts of things – to make it all as good as possible.

My mother kept rabbits – because of the war – in a shed at the bottom of the garden, which merged with the garden of the next-door-but-one house that came to be inhabited by the army (more of that later). She didn't like the rabbits, and we were not encouraged to like them – she cleaned them out and used the waste on the garden. My parents had a friend who was in the tinning business, and we would either have rabbit stew or very nice rabbit meat from a tin. When I was old enough I would be sent out to pick baskets of weeds for the rabbits from the common – plantains and dandelions, groundsel and juicy grass, but not buttercups (they are poisonous).

Our house was one of a greystone terrace at the top of Tunbridge Wells Common: 71 Mount Ephraim. It had been bought by my grandparents for my parents. This is the letter my grandfather wrote about it. The coincidence of place was to be repeated in 1953. Boarding school in the 1890s is interesting.

19th September 1931
(3 years before I was born)

Sibyl Darling,

On this very Saturday forty five years ago, I met at some Bicycle Races in Kennington Oval a lovely girl on leave from Boarding School at Tunbridge Wells. That lovely girl, now the grandmother of your children, is with me now at Tunbridge Wells, full of joy in the prospect of your happiness in the place where hers began!

She has accompanied me on my mission to settle the purchase of your home – it is done and we have walked over the house to leave a blessing for you and yours in every room.

It would seem that all the previous occupants of the house have lived there long and have prospered. I trust that those conditions may repeat themselves with you and Harvey and that you may long abide in fruitfulness.

I am, dear girl, with just a speck of pride in your projects.

Your ever loving father

Walter Chadwick

All the food was carried up the first flight of stairs from the kitchen to the dining room – hot water for my father to shave with was carried up two flights in a lidded green-enamel jug. The scuttles of coal for the nursery fire had to go up three flights, and we would run in from the next-door bathroom to dry in front of the fireguard with its shiny brass rail.

From the landing outside the nursery door you could look through or over the banisters (according to your time of life) down to the hall, and see the patients, leaning on sticks or swathed in plaster of Paris, going to the consulting room accompanied by the deep soothing tones of my father's voice. But the nursery doors – there were two (it was a long room) – were to be shut.

"Daddy's got a patient."

Sometimes my elder brother John would chase Guy, two years younger, round and round the doors. Guy might be crying, even bleeding, and I would shout over the banisters for help and not love my older brother. He would say that Guy deserved it.

When the big brass gong in the hall was rung to say lunch was ready, the boys would race to get astride the banisters and slide – one slither to the bedroom landing, another to the ground floor and dining room. I never grew quite as bold, but did learn to run down taking two stairs at a time.

The house was complemented by Virginia creeper, which has suckers like little frogs' legs, houses money spiders and turns scarlet in autumn. There used to be something called Empire Day (which had been celebrated in 1904, and probably other years, by George Alderson in Alexandria, with a crowd of different uniforms, speeches and dressed-up children). We used to crowd on to the little balcony on the second floor for a grandstand view of the procession that took place along the Top past our house. There were bands with enormous drums, Scouts and soldiers in smart uniforms and a great many flags, and it would occur on the birthday of my brother Guy, 24 May.

My father acquired an allotment – because of the war – "So that you children will not starve."

The practice of vegetable growing continued through the next three generations. We were always urged to finish all the food on our plates – even things I hated, like bits of fat, "because of the poor starving children of Europe", though what difference it made to them I never questioned. My father used to bicycle to the allotment before breakfast on his tall bicycle, bringing back any ready for the day in the basket.

The allotments were on a sunny slope of orderly green rows worked by all manner of men – no women worked there seriously, though they may have been allowed to weed. The organiser, dispensing advice and good cheer, was called Mr Bombanard – how could anyone forget that? Runner-bean flowers were so beautifully scarlet, and carrots so beautifully orange, drawn from the mysterious and interesting earth. Sometimes (reluctantly because my father had so little time) if I implored him, he would take me there on the carrier of the bike, and I was probably a nuisance. He would cycle home, have a cold bath, shave and change into a sober suit and sober working mood.

We had a lady billeted on us by the War Office. This meant she shared our meals, which inhibited our conversation. She wore a navy-blue uniform, and was the first person I ever heard use the word 'stink', which was considered a rude word.

One day she asked each of us, "What force would you like to join for the war effort?"

"The air force," said John.

"The navy," said Guy (who later became a proficient sailor of small craft).

"The Land Army," I said, which provoked hoots of laughter I found inexplicable and rather hurtful though my answer was prophetic.

The basement of the house held a scullery and large kitchen at the back; and in front was my father's workshop, where he boiled smelly glue over a gas ring, made bookshelves and anything else necessary, such as stands for patients which had a mirror underneath in which he could see soles of their feet reflected. Guy made model yachts there. It became our air-raid shelter. My father put up several strong beams, which were to support the ceiling if the house was bombed. Guy was given the job of painting the beams – I was told afterwards that this was a distraction because he used to get frightened at the bangs and rattles that sometimes shook the whole house. He painted fishes and twining weeds in beautiful colours. I had a small bed in one corner, and can remember being carried down the three flights of stairs and laid in it if there was a raid in the middle of the night. The boys had hammocks slung between the beams. My parents had a bed just outside, by the store cupboard. I never saw my father in it – I think he stayed out watching the searchlights.

By the time they moved into their final house, my father had become a craftsman, making little scale models of Georgian furniture he loved and always collected.

There was a round black mark in the centre of the nursery ceiling which remained, I think, until the end of the war. The mark had been begun one morning when I was peacefully playing in the nursery. Down in the town, my father had been visiting a patient in the Lonsdale Nursing Home, which faced up across the common to where he could see the tall grey silhouette of our terrace, up at the Top. He looked, paused, and looked again – there was a thread of smoke rising from our roof. In a few minutes he had reached his car, driven up the hill, thundered up the two flights of stairs and raced along the landing outside the nursery, startling me. He shot out of the loft window and I heard the clang of the sand bucket that stood there – an incendiary bomb had landed and was slowly gnawing through the roof. But now the ceiling would not fall down – there would be a repair, and only the black mark remained.

When my friend Jane came, if we went back up to the nursery to play after tea, and it wasn't raining, we would sometimes very, very quietly walk along the landing, out of the window and on to the roof. It was amazingly exciting. We could tiptoe the whole length of the terrace. And we could go cautiously to the wall along the front and look right over the common and down on to the town, with the big green dome of the Assembly Hall in the middle. But we did not look down to the ground below – that was frightening.

There were the flying bombs – doodlebugs. They travelled with a characteristic insistent drone across the sky. When the drone stopped, there would be a silence – then the explosion.

I was looking out of a front window one morning and heard one – the explosion came from the common.

My brothers and I went out later to investigate. Everyone seemed to be out. There was a crowd around what had been one of the Shelters. These were not shelters in the sense we had come to understand the word, but rather beautifully constructed public seating, with shiny solid seats on four sides and a thatched roof. The Shelter lay in shards among metal, and we learned that the old tramp who lived on the common and slept on a seat had been in residence that night and had been killed. I remember the jumble of material, the sense of confusion, intrusion on our space, and the crowd looking on silently.

Because our house was high up and fairly near the hospital, the blackout was very important – no chink of light must escape through the sides of the blinds that covered the windows under the curtains. One evening a stranger in black came quickly up the stairs to the nursery followed by my mother – we were guilty of the terrible offence, and this ARP (air-raid precautions) man had seen it from outside. I remember the seriousness of that moment as he looked at all the blinds – from then on, after drawing them, they would be checked and rechecked.

The Common opposite our terrace was one huge playground. In winter we had only to cross the road with our toboggans to be at the top of the best slopes. The boys ran down the hill to their school in the town in the few years before they went to boarding school. At first I walked with Nanny, sometimes with a doll's pram, and in summer we would have picnics under a birch tree or among the bracken – the doll would be taken out and offered a honey sandwich.

On the cricket ground, boys would be flying their balsa-wood-and-tissue paper planes, as Guy did, with a propeller they wound with their finger. They set it free in front of the wind and ran below to retrieve it. Occasionally, tragically, it crashed and was beyond repair, but the next plane would be even better.

There would be wounded soldiers in their bright-blue uniforms, arms or legs in plaster, exercising from the hospital, and I would proudly think it might have been my father who had tended them.

And there were The Rocks – an outgrowth of smooth grey sandstone – which included all kinds of challenges. There were ravines to slither through (perhaps inaccessible to today's less thin children), and cliffs large and small we could jump down or leave till another time. There was the Top Rock – the triumph when we could get up there on our own and look out over the whole common, and more triumph when we found we could get up or down really fast.

The huge exercise of evacuating city children was under way, and it was decided that Guy and I with my nanny would go to Dorset, where my father's brother Shor lived and our Aunty Ruth and their two children, Nicolette and Paul. Shor and Ruth were both artists and teachers – they also painted pictures and Ruth illustrated books for her sister, Noel Streatfield. We stayed only two months although it felt a long time, and were brought back because of the fear of invasion – it was decided we would be back together. I think I was tiresome – I can remember crying very loudly for a long time after having a measles vaccination in my bottom. Nicolette didn't cry, although she was miserable. Shor and Ruth were a little more strict than our parents, but they were very kind. I don't remember them getting cross.

While we were there Ruth taught me to read, and to copy lines of letters in a copybook, and this was very exciting. She also taught me to draw rabbits and overlapping hills (which are still about the only things I can draw just recognisably, and use to decorate letters to grandchildren, and great-grandchildren after them).

When we came back I started at a little school held in the Spa Hotel along the road (next to the house in which we later lived, though of course we didn't know that then). Our house had sash windows, and one day a maid trapped her fingers where the bars joined in the middle. When I was taken to school, crying, I could see the squashed white fingers when I looked up to where she stood fainting. I believe they had to get the fire brigade to release her.

The only trouble with having already learnt to read was that I got bored at school, behaved badly and spent a lot of time in disgrace in the corner.

The next school was a PNEU (Parents' National Education Union) school held in the house of friends of my parents. I can remember us all lined round the schoolroom chanting, "I am, I can, I ought, I will," which can still sometimes be useful.

I don't know why that changed, but the next school was across the common, and I ran down a different path from my brothers.

Sometimes my mother would say, "If there's a bang, lie down in a ditch."

I don't think I ever did, but it was nice to know what to do.

Nanny had gone – which was sad at the time, but now there was freedom. Sometimes I would go early on to the common, loving the dew and the fresh outdoors.

It was at this little school that I fell in love with poetry for ever. We had to learn a chosen poem by heart to recite in class, as one did then, and I should hope is still done now. One of mine was:

> When I set out for Lyonnesse,
> A hundred miles away,
> The rime was on the spray,
> And starlight lit my lonesomeness
> When I set out for Lyonnesse
> A hundred miles away.

This was the first verse of three. It is by Thomas Hardy. When I came to the end I was in an enchanted world, and there was a silence. As I surfaced I was given ten out of ten, which didn't normally happen. Perhaps it was not so much because I'd recited wonderfully, but because the teacher (whom I can also remember) recognised that I'd fallen in love, which shows you what a good teacher in an obscure little school can do for you.

Meanwhile, Guy was at a boarding school in Kent, and John in one that was evacuated to Lynton, in Devon. While there he fell off a roof that most likely he should not have been on, and broke his arm, so having it in plaster of Paris he was unable to go swimming with the others. Shortly after the school arrived at this supposedly safer place, there was an aerial battle overhead, after which, he told us with relish, some of the masters came inside carrying bloodied cords from the parachutes of the downed German pilots.

Shor and Ruth kept bees, and in addition to the hives in the garden there was a kind of flat hive that fitted on a window, and you could see the bees crawling about the comb and flying in and out. My mother read a lot about bees, and learnt from Shor, and my parents acquired two hives for our garden. All went well for a while – my mother tended them in her bee veil – but then I saw her one day lying on the couch looking very ill and was told she had had an allergic reaction from a lot of stings. My father took over and became a bee man. My mother tended to push things in his direction – she decided quite quickly that he would be better at managing the washing machine, and much later the washing-up machine.

Our garden was narrow, and quite often the bees if they swarmed would fly over the hedge and settle in a bush next door. Looking out of the window I would see my father sitting by the bush, gently brushing the swarm into a skep (straw bee basket). If he could see the queen he might put her in a matchbox. Then he'd gently deposit the swarm on the front of the hive and encourage the queen to walk back inside. And they would, gradually, follow.

Late in the summer he would bring the full waxed combs inside, and skim off the wax with a long sharp knife, the wax being deliciously covered with honey we would eat on our bread. The combs would be slid into the extractor – a bin with a handle on top that you turned so that the combs would spin round – and the honey was thrown out by centrifugal force (which was a good term to know). It ran down to the bottom, where there was a tap, from which we filled the jars one by one. The room would be filled with the scents of summer – different scents according to the time of the honey flow: clover or heather, or every summer flower. And when I saw hive bees on a flower, it was a kind of magic that they could make honey and spare enough for us to eat. It was all a manifestation of the skill of man and bee. And my father continued to supply us into the time of his grandchildren.

On Christmas Eve my father would be dressed up as Father Christmas to hand out parcels to occupants of the children's ward in the hospital. On one occasion he was wheeled (perhaps by the junior doctors) quite vigorously into the ward in a wheelbarrow, which I thought was unkind (he was holding tightly to the sides). My brothers and I had to hand out the parcels as directed. My mother each week gave out library books in the women's wards, and sometimes she would invite me to come and help her.

"Light love?" she would say – as it usually was.

She also did meals on wheels in the town with the WRVS (Women's Royal Voluntary Service) and occasionally shared that as well.

We would go into the little mostly terraced houses in roads I never otherwise walked, into rooms sometimes shabby, sometimes spotless, occasionally smelly. Plates were usually laid out ready on the table, and we would carry in the dishes. My mother would ask each person how they were feeling and getting on, as she put the food out.

Petrol was available for work only, and we cycled as a family at weekends. At first I rode behind my father – until old enough for my own bike. The picnic basket would be behind my mother. We went to Broadwater Forest and collected fir cones for the fire; we visited woods for bunches of primroses, and we gathered baskets of blackberries for jelly. If it was warm enough we might go to the outdoor swimming baths at Pembury. There was a slide, and fountains, and we would swim and then have our picnic there.

We also used to go to a particular stretch of the River Medway, near Fordcombe. Perhaps Guy would have his latest model boat on the back of his bike. We walked down the field past the willows and quickly changed. Guy used to set his sails to the wind as someone swam to the other side. He would place the boat slightly upstream, then came that beautiful swift moment of reality as it swept across the water.

Then we would swim. There would be the scent of water mint. There were kingcups and loosestrife. We might come across areas of cold water in bays and swim back to the warmer centre.

There were many occasions when my father would be called out to an emergency. Meals or events might be called off or delayed. He would also be called out at night. I once learnt that a farmer had sleepwalked off a barn roof and broken his neck. But I don't think my father would have taken kindly to the idea of shifts at weekends. I have a letter he wrote to his prospective mother-in-law – a bit of swank from a young man proud of his performance when on a temporary placement in Ipswich.

Dear Mrs Chadwick

I am writing to thank you so much for the delightful weekend I have just spent with you. I arrived here safely thanks to Sibyl putting me on the right train, and am now installed as a GP (temporarily thank goodness). I find it a great a change being a pauper doctor after being Lord High Everything at the hospital, it's quite amusing for a bit however. Again, thank you so much.

Yours very sincerely,
W. Harvey Gervis

My father was always congenial in his relationships, interested to listen and learn from anyone. It was only in the rigour of a long appointments list that his personal attention might flag. When my nanny with a bad foot was booked to see him, he did his part but did not acknowledge her in the long string of faces. He apologised profusely afterwards, but she never quite forgave him.

There was a Mam'selle who used to come and teach French to me and my friend Judith. She was a little lady with the sweetest smile, but sometimes she would become impatient if she thought we were not trying hard enough, and she would start to get cross and talk very fast. Then Judith would begin to giggle. Mam'selle would talk ever faster, spitting a little, and Judith would giggle harder. I would catch the giggles, and Mam'selle would stand up and collect her books, saying we were umpossible, and trot away down the stairs, leaving us rolling about in naughty delicious laughter. But I'm sure in the end our French accents were much improved.

The house at one end of the terrace, leaving one in between, had been the home of a family who were great friends of ours. Their garden was dominated by a large cedar tree, from which hung a swing, a trapeze and a rope for climbing. We had spent a lot of time there with them and I remember the sense of triumph when I first plucked up courage enough to hang upside down by my knees from the trapeze without holding on.

The two flower beds that had belonged to the girls had been given to my brothers. Guy grew some flowers and there was a notice on John's that said, 'Here lieth the innards of a bat' – or maybe a mouse or frog – that he had found dead and dissected under my father's instructions. (There was never any doubt that he would be a doctor – it had happened for generations.) He dissected everything – including old clocks and any kind of gadget.

The house had been requisitioned by the army and was full of soldiers. I was told I must no longer go there, which was frustrating. One day I ventured in – no one was about. I began swinging happily.

The houses had a small, square, flat roof accessible from a first- floor window, and suddenly a voice called "Can you give me a hand?"

Being naturally helpful – and foolish – I went across. He said he had his foot caught in the creeper. As I tried to undo the probably faked tangle, he seized me, said I reminded him of his little Mary, and squashed my face against his. I struggled free and ran home.

My mother was upstairs ironing – a job that exuded calm. She asked what I had been doing, and I told her (truthfully) that I had been playing in the garden. I had no wish to break the atmosphere of peace.

Our parents played all kinds of games with us – table croquet, Pit, Monopoly and Pounce, which some people called Racing Demon. During Pounce Guy would recite poetry to put us off our concentration ("Once upon a midnight dreary while I pondered weak and weary," and on and on). My father and I played 'pencilly-paper' games. My favourite was 'little words out of big words'.

Our absorption would sometimes annoy my mother, particularly if I was on a day out from my boarding prep school and the hours were few. She would come into the room huffing. And I knew that if I did not look up, favouring the game instead of her, I was doing something dangerous. I knew, subconsciously, that at those moments, at my fingertips, there was fire between them. I half played with it, yet knew it was a nightmare. Reality was their usual conversation, and their permanent presence.

My mother used to play the piano for us all to sing songs – lively rhythmical songs we could belt out, including a lot of folk songs and carols in season. And a great pleasure was enjoying my father playing his banjo. He had a rich bass voice, and a huge enjoyment of rhythms and rhyme. One we dearly loved was about Jonah and the whale, and there was 'The Smuggler's Song' ('Four and twenty ponies, trotting through the dark') and 'Bees, bees, talk to your bees – hide it from your neighbours –as much as you please'. When the Tolkein books came out, my father composed new and lovely tunes, and added them to his repertoire to play to his grandchildren.

He also played the concertina in a folk dance band and at other times a double bass, which was a glorious instrument to have in the house. The band, and the lady who ran the folk club, greatly enjoyed themselves.

I went a few times, but will not forget the savagery in the voice of one of her children, saying under his breath, "You don't know what it's like to have to do this all the time."

Revolt was not far off.

There were many shelves of books in our home, and as my reading widened I would sometimes take one out at random, just for the fun of reading, even if not understanding. I came across one called, I think, *Ghost Stories from an Antiquary*, which I read in small doses, growing more and more horrified, and more and more fascinated, until I knew it had to go – to put it back would not be enough. I took it down to a second-hand bookshop that had become a browsing place (filling my room with books costing a lot less than a penny, with a lot of poetry) and offered it for sale. I expect they made some money on it – it was a very special-looking book.

The instinct for self-preservation acted on spontaneously even when scarcely understood – StJohn from abuse, myself from fascination – is surely a given asset as valuable as speed. I wonder if the constant exposure to outside influences (Facebook, etc.) erodes and blurs it, giving rise to much of the anguish and mental stress that seems so prevalent.

My action was totally unprincipled – I had no right to sell my father's book, but that fact did not enter my head. No more right was StJohn's subsequent assumption that all MPs were probably villainous. Perhaps in some vague way I learnt that it is yourself you have to protect yourself from.

Perhaps another cause of stress and anxiety among children is that they are so much more alone – with their phones, of course, which come to take the place of 'background'. The money you can save by preparing your own and perhaps better meals – and even the enjoyment – is now underrated (even not considered); and a stressed and distracted child meeting a stressed and distracted parent is not mutually beneficial. In some cases the overall financial and/or emotional advantage can be minimal (and it is unfashionable to evaluate them) – of course not in all cases.

I remember my father coming in the front door strangely grey-faced and stumbling, and learning afterwards that he was not ill or wounded, as I feared, but only exhausted. He had been operating almost non-stop for three days on men soaked in oil, shattered or burnt, brought back even as far inland as this hospital. I afterwards had a nightmare that he had lost both his legs and was walking in the hall on the stumps, and he was crying – the pain and horror of this nightmare persisted for years. This was the awfulness of Dunkirk.

Jane and I were sent away to boarding school at the age of nine, which was before the war ended. We became convinced that there were Germans lurking in the laurels in the front garden of the school. We watched, and we made notes in special notebooks of times of 'sightings', sounds, evidences. If ever there was a case of seeing what you believe, this was it, for among the leaves we glimpsed the dreaded grey uniforms and black boots – though why 'the enemy' should be interested in a small prep school for girls we never even wondered. In the end we became so certain, and so troubled, leaning out of the window after lights-out, straining our eyes in the twilight, that we plucked up our courage and told our whole story to our headmistress, who was wise, and strong, and always courteous. She listened to us with quiet respect and we were young enough to feel that somehow the weight was lifted from our shoulders.

Whether or not the ending, which was strange and rather shocking to us, was deliberately engineered by her, we never knew or wondered. Jane and I were in our dormitory, and we heard the matron talking to 'the big girls' in the room next to us. (The school had a few pupils up to school-leaving age.) After a few moments we realised she was telling them some tale that interested them and that they found amusing. They were laughing, asking questions, exclaiming. As we listened, we gradually flushed, grew angry, then curled up within ourselves – for we were listening to the story of how two of the 'little ones' had frightened themselves with ideas about Germans in the bushes.

The spell of our myth, painfully, was broken.

Then the war ended, but my friend was told that her father would never come home, for he was a sailor and a torpedo had sunk his ship and he was drowned. Almost every night for weeks she cried, his photograph against her face.

Later on, Jane's mother, Joan, being on her own and a good sailor, came with us on the Norfolk Broads in their own slightly smaller hired boat, I think, a couple of times. In our spare time when we were not sailing, Jane and I explored round the nearby riverbanks. One day we came across an empty building with a rickety staircase inside, which we climbed. On the next floor, by a big open window space, were some very curious little white creatures on the floor, upright, hobbling and wobbling about, looking at us quite fiercely with black eyes. A variety of gnome? We stayed staring for some time.

When our mothers suggested we might have been looking at baby barn owls, we scarcely believed them. We were perhaps fortunate that a parent bird had not sailed in and attacked us – we were not very large. I believe the building used to be called St Bennet's Abbey.

Jane was very shy, and found social interaction difficult. The person she came to love and respect – and marry – happened to be a railway porter, and they realised that social life in England was going to be a problem, so they emigrated to Newfoundland (sadly for Joan).

Jane could do cartwheels and handstands as I never could – she was a brilliant swimmer and became a coach. She also had four children and we corresponded for some years.

Another contrast with today's methods is the freedom I had to wander, either with a friend or on my own. I remember going into my parents' bedroom while they were having their early morning tea, in a state of great excitement because I'd discovered a little wood, full of flowers, not far away. I'd slipped out at about 6 a.m. and walked, not far, but a new way. If I hadn't come back, no one would have known where I was, but that wasn't a worry.

After their long engagement, during which my father became a qualified surgeon – and after they were married (my mother, flapper-style, in a fashionable short wedding dress and short hair, which she always regretted when looking at photos) they went to live in the Isle of Wight. My father had always loved sailing and took every opportunity to sail, taking part in the races at Cowes. Subsequently he would put us into boats whenever possible, including dinghies on lakes and rivers; and we went on the Norfolk Broads also with Ruth and Shor and their children, Nicolette and Paul (who could both enviably draw), on two boats.

As Ruth didn't cook and my mother declined, and it would not have occurred to the fathers to do so, the two eldest, John and Nicolette, were given the job. There were nine of us, and it must have ruined their holiday. I remember John glumly slicing up an entire loaf of bread while they talked about the next meal – I think my mother gave advice.

There were moments of drama. I remember my father at the tiller tacking against a strong wind and yelling "Haul in that starboard jib sheet!" just before we might hit the bank. (Starboard, right; sheet, rope.)

My mother, soothing; "Don't worry – men just shout. They're like that."

And next day he was calmly punting us up a gentle river, the long pole sliding down between his hands.

One very still, sunny morning, early, Guy quietly suggested to me that we should take the dinghy out for a row. We gently boarded, untied, and rowed across the open expanse of water (I think it was called Hickling Broad), boats moored at its edges. At that time motor boats were no more than an intrusive nuisance. Everything was embraced in the quiet of the morning, the freshness of the water and the still bright air. We didn't talk much. I rowed (still learning); he rowed. Across and across we went. We simply imbibed. And when sounds began to come from our two boats, we went back for breakfast, taking a treasured memory priceless beyond any photo.

We were on the Broads when part of the war ended.

As we walked back from a shop, a man ran from a cottage and told us in great joy, "Italy surrendered at half past five last night."

We knew something good and enormous had happened, and like everyone else we were all singing songs on our boats late into that evening as the river rippled past our boat – and that was VE (Victory in Europe) Day.

In their turns, my brothers did their national service: John in Malta, Guy in Singapore. On at least one occasion for each son my mother sent anxious telegrams.

John replied, 'Sorry. Run over by a battleship'; and Guy, 'You really must be more careful. The telegraph boy's autocycle disturbed the bandit I was stalking.'

While on holiday in Italy, we were due to meet John returning, at Genoa. But he did not get off the train. There were several frantic telephone calls, and it transpired that he had been asleep, and carried on to Allessandria. After taking me and my mother back to the hotel, my father and Guy went back to await his return.

Early in the morning I softly opened the door of his room and saw him lying asleep, deeply suntanned. I closed the door and went back to my room content – we were five again.

In another year, on holiday in Scotland, we drove to Aberdeen in pouring rain to meet Guy. He walked towards us in his light-brown army macintosh and I realised he was no longer a boy, but a young man.

So what was the effect of the war on us? We, of course, had it easy – our house wasn't smashed or close relations killed – and I deeply felt Jane's grief for the loss of her father. Mine was precious to me, and was with us. There is no way of knowing if I would have been subject to nightmares, as I was, if the war had not been there in the background. After rather frequently shouting for them at night, they did the sensible thing and brought my bed into their room.

Then, if I woke up frightened by some ghastly vision, I would chant "Mummy, Daddy, could you put the light on cos I've had a nasty dream?" until the light went on. When the horror had receded, I'd say, "All right now." And the light went off.

Guy also had fears, but he did not shout at night.

We sometimes used to watch the squadrons of bombers flying out at night, and in the morning see them coming back in the same formation, with spaces where some had been shot down.

"Somebody's son or father," my mother once said.

There was, just beyond us, an enormity of horror, a pervading wrongness.

But somehow we knew, or were taught, that some things we did were standing up against that wrongness: the rabbits, the allotment, the bicycling – even my mother parting, a little regretfully, with the dresses she made for me, with deep smocking, in exchange for fabric coupons from the mother of a younger child, when I grew out of them. Not that keeping them would have made much sense! It wasn't that we understood how any of it meant anything, only that somehow it did, even when it didn't work – as when my mother cooked us whale meat, which we found revolting and wouldn't eat.

There were moments of deeper realisation, like the doodlebug on The common, knowing the familiar old tramp had been murdered by it – the silent crowd. And my father's exhaustion at the door.

My father loved his work, though it often saddened him. I remember deep down a conversation in which he cursed the stupidity of the ruination of young bodies of either race, through failures by politicians. Yet he despised the weakness of any surrender.

After the war (I was ten) we moved house because my father wanted a room (in addition to the consulting room) where he could apply plaster of paris to patients' broken limbs. The house my mother fell for he considered too far from the centre of town, and we moved instead to a rather curious house with a suitable downstairs room accessible from the driveway with a wheelchair. The house was decorated mainly in brown and orange. My mother worked hard to make it light and habitable – it was a struggle she won in the end. The practice (our bread and butter) must always come first.

In my teens I enjoyed my boarding school. In my form we all expected to try for university and we worked hard. I used to revise by torchlight under the bedclothes, anxious before exams. There was the marvellous library, music, the grounds, friends… We liked most of the staff. It was called Benenden.

I was one among the monitors, which meant I might have to select lengths of poetry for younger people who misbehaved to learn by heart. I enjoyed the selections. It meant I had a bike – we used to go out in groups at weekends. I also used to go and visit a boyfriend who had taken me to dances and lived just near enough for me to cycle there and back – all quite innocent, but not strictly legal and I was quite unaware of my own hypocrisy.

I was told to go and see my housemistress (who was a distant relation). I wasn't worried – something interesting maybe? but she told me she had been informed by my parents that they had decided they didn't feel able to afford to send me to university. My brothers were both at Cambridge – one more would be too difficult. She thought to comfort me by saying I might only have got to St Andrews.

I would have been happy to do jobs in the holidays, as my brothers did (they worked for the post office sometimes), but the decision had been made. Their qualifications mattered. And she really believed that other things (abroad, good social opportunities) would be as good for me.

So I was to be moved out of my form, into what was called the Modern Course, for people not aiming at university.

In the Modern Course we learnt cookery (which was interesting), how to mend a fuse, first aid, home nursing (which I failed) and hygiene – how many bacteria would be in your vest after three days. It was a two-year course. I had thought of teaching, but assumed I would need a degree.

There were some other interesting items. When the school had been a large private house there had been a butler, and the school had kept him on. He took the tea trays to the staffroom. He was asked to give the Modern Course a talk about what it all used to be like, and he was very interesting. We were surprised to hear of bullying that took place on younger people, not by employers but by the senior employees. He was called Busby.

Another lecture was given us by the head gardener, Mr Purvor. After the talk he took us round the large and immaculate walled garden, showing us how the bushes were trained, the beds cultivated, and the greenhouses kept productive. This privilege nurtured the tendency towards growing things planted by my father, and my mother's love for her garden.

Despite all that, I wrote and told my parents that it was all a waste of time and I might as well leave. And I did, at seventeen.

I found myself a part-time job in a second-hand bookshop that I'd frequented, and learnt a lot of interesting things; but a proper course of study was considered more progressive and practical, so I went to St James' to learn to be a secretary. This meant being a commuter, which enabled me to read *War and Peace* among other things, which was one advantage. And over the next two years I certainly cost a lot more than going to university would have done.

Although I didn't finish the course, the typing I did acquire was useful; and for a time I kept my diaries in shorthand, which I found indecipherable after a few months.

A like-minded friend and I walked about the streets at lunchtime smoking cigarettes (the only time I ever did) and feeling like femmes fatales (whatever they were).

Our new house.

Over the next few months I treated the boy I'd visited on my bike (who was a particularly fine person) very badly. He had lost part of one leg in the Korean War, and had a tin one that squeaked when he nobly danced with me. I was pleased to learn later that he had married someone kind and capable and worthy of him, and I still have Shelley's poems that he had given me.

We had another cousin, blond and beautiful, who was being hailed as a starlet for the stage. There were newspaper articles about her talent and likely future success, and we were all most excited for her. Then it seemed she was dropped, and all went quiet. Only later did I learn that she had not been willing to accept sexual suggestions made to her, and chose to take herself away from the situation. She married much later, a really worthwhile man from a different background, and had a happy family life and two little boys. Perhaps she had to absolve herself even of the accent and attitude that had disgusted her. She worked in the social services, on ascending levels, until she died.

Enter the Caravan

My father had gone into partnership with a couple my parents knew to buy a fruit farm. The husband had come out of the army, having carried his dream in his mind, and together they bought some beautiful orchards in the wilds of Kent, some distance from Maidstone near a village called Grafty Green. So my father moved his hives from the garden and bought a Romany caravan that had been altered inside to include the kind of conveniences supplied by modern caravans (or what was modern then), with bunks, a wooden table, good cupboards and a gas cooker, all decoratively painted. They collected attractive old plates and cups in keeping with it, and various ornaments. I found for them a group of shiny gourds, some with silver trimming, that hung just right, up in one corner.

My father found that wide hill with its views across the countryside, the fruit trees and the presence of his bees, a sheer delight. His idea was that he and my mother would go for weekends, and for a while it worked. He could be witty and funny and interesting, but he was not chatty.

I can remember his saying, in a kindly but puzzled way, while watching a group of women talking, "What do they find to talk about?"

He and I used to dry up into silence on the phone, which he tended to avoid, though at other times we might have interesting conversations. He thought a great deal, and would often come out with something really interesting after a long silence.

But it was the silences, during which he might be experiencing deep peace, that my mother ceased to tolerate. She grew bored. Could she not have read a book – anything? I could not forgive her. Gradually, he went more often on his own to see his bees, to keep the paintwork to perfection or – for heaven's sake – to relax. He could boil an egg, open sardines, make tea. I wrote out for him how to scramble eggs, for a change, but I don't think he ever bothered.

Groups of us would go there in the holidays, sometimes to help with the strawberry picking, sometimes just for picnics and walks.

One of John's best friends had a motorbike, which of course he learnt to ride. Richard used to bring it to a long straight road near our house, and one day John invited me outside to see it. He rode up and down a few times, and then Richard took me on the back, up and down several times, while I held on for dear life with the wind in my hair.

John so much wanted a motorbike, but it was no good – my father had attended to the smashed limbs of too many motorbike riders. Instead he bought both boys a car: Guy's was a BSA; John's a three-wheeler Morgan.

John and I went for a weekend at the caravan, well supplied with food and books, in his little car. In the early evening John asked me if I'd mind being left on my own, as he had planned to go to London. I didn't mind – I had plenty to read, comfort, and I could watch the twilight falling among the trees, stars pricking through. I didn't blame him, roaring off in his little car to do whatever he wanted. I hardly woke when he came back by torchlight in the small hours.

The caravan in the vicar's field.

Guy enjoyed school and rugby, and became head of his house, then an architect, taking part, among other things, in the building of the new city of Brasilia. He married and had three children, and, after moving to France with his second wife, became an artist, holding exhibitions and selling paintings.

John, who disliked rugby, was often miserable at school, and it seemed he was frequently beaten. After he married, he and his wife lived on a converted landing craft (known as *The Barge*) on the Thames, until after the first two babies. He made a beautiful wooden floor, among other things, for the boat. They had five children, and the practice of growing things passed down the generations. He became a much loved and respected GP.

6: StJohn's Navy Days, and After

There were the tales StJohn told me that I listened to wide-eyed. There are the lists of ships he was on through the years of the war, obtained from Navy Command, many years later. And there are the events of the war unfolding, experienced from our different worlds.

After enlisting at the age of sixteen, he was sent to the naval base at the Clyde for initial training. First he had to learn to sling a hammock, then it was group drills and exercises, learning to throw ropes for mooring, and the lowering of lifeboats, and an introduction to coastal navigation.

(Did he ever notice that a small town nearby was called Alexandria, like the great city in Egypt where his grandparents had lived?)

The barracks and other buildings used as shore bases were given shipss names, and HMS *Royal Arthur* at Skegness, on the east coast, was his next base – a holiday camp now taken over by the navy. Then it was HMS *Cabot* in Bristol, where he took an engineering course. For it would have been the engines that interested him, in spite of having to be down below when on duty.

By now it was June 1943, and he went to Portland in Dorset, based at HMS *Attack* and experienced service on an MGB (motor gunboat). These carried twelve men and were seventy feet (twenty-one metres) long. He was in the boiler room, as a second-class stoker. The power sources of the British ships were diverse and complex; attention to detail was vital. The brevity of his schooling would not have helped him – boys with higher qualifications were often creamed off on entry, for quicker advancement

It was while he was based at Portland that Italy surrendered. France had already fallen and was a sad and divided nation under occupation. As I mentioned earlier, I was on holiday with my parents on a boat on the Norfolk Broads at the time.

Equipped with tropical gear for an unknown destination (naval secrecy on all sides), it was March when they arrived in Freetown, Sierra Leone. Africa was a continent StJohn had never visited, arriving (as a first-class stoker) at a land base called HMS *Eland*. From there, there were exciting exercises on the

100-foot-long (thirty-three metres) MLs (motor launches).

And was there an explosion of weaponry on board ships in Freetown Harbour? Were the crew ordered to jump overboard and swim ashore? And was one of his mates clinging in fear to the anchor chain, and StJohn loosed his fingers and drew him to ashore? Or was this an exercise or a story?

Navy Command didn't know.

There was off-duty time on the beaches, to take photos of the various ships moored in the harbour, of the boys who did their washing for them, and of bare-breasted African ladies (as at that time and in that place it was the way of life – surprise, surprise) to fix in an album years later.

Different MLs took him to Takoradi in Ghana, and Lagos in Nigeria – so close together on a map, yet so many miles between – all part of what was then the South Atlantic Command, keeping watch on the coasts.

It was January 1945 when he returned to what must have seemed a cold and dreary Britain, and at some point he received a letter from his mother telling him that the manager of the ranch which was still owned by his father had sold it and disappeared with the money. Once Dorothy had caught sight of the man among the crowds on Oxford Street, and tried desperately, but hopelessly, to get him stopped. StJohn at first refused to believe it, then after a second letter was so miserable, and angry with his mother (quite unfairly), that he refused to write for several weeks.

The sense of it being there, to be his, had been his light at the end of the tunnel, his destination. Dorothy, anxious, contacted the navy; and his commanding officer, whether or not understanding, rebuked him for his lack of kindness, and for her sake StJohn squared up to the facts.

Then it was up to the even colder Aberdeen, to the jolly-sounding HMS *Bacchante*, then on up to the Shetlands, where the first night they huddled round the boiler in the base. StJohn told me of walking round the island in his free time, lying on the clifftop watching the gulls below.

And if from there navy ships had been clandestinely supplying fuel to ships of occupied Norway, to a Norwegian island swathed in camouflage, it would have been among the last exercises of the war, for there came the surrender and Armistice on 8 May 1945.

The vast war machines, the millions of pounds of investment and training, the millions of lives lost on land, sea and air, for an ideology that still sparks – but which had crumbled.

And after years of wondering, and enquiring, it no longer bothers me that the tales might have been youthful bravado. He never mentioned the words 'stoker' or 'boiler'. But he was there for me, and ours, for the next seventy years of his life. That is enough.

After being demobbed from the WRNS in London, Joy went to Alexandria, which she had visited during the war, and stayed for several months with her aunt, Irene Bernachi. It was there she met Major John Bellamy, who had joined the cotton trade and become successful. He waited for several months, having fallen for her, until she finally decided to marry him. They had two children, David and Angela (later Scott) of wildlife-TV fame.

Dorothy heard that a certain Richard St Barbe Baker was looking for someone to help him on his farm in Dorset, that he would instruct a suitable young man in forestry and supply bed and board in exchange for the fulfilling of the work offered.

The situation and possibility suggested her son to Dorothy, and she put the idea to him when they met after his time in the navy. The idea of countryside after the stresses of the war seemed perfect to StJohn as well. He had always loved trees, and although he was attracted to engineering after his Navy training, he felt that to access further training in engineering would not be easy. Forestry was nearer to something he could get to know and love. He was offered an interview, and was accepted. He was given a caravan, a pony and a little dog. He would have his meals in the farmhouse. He was delighted.

Richard St Barbe Baker was becoming well known as the founder of Men of the Trees (later to become the International Tree Foundation), the main aim being to encourage tree planting worldwide. He wrote for one of his lectures:

> Before any great progress can be made in combating the demon of destruction now rampaging the earth in the form of desertification, erosion and soil impoverishment, it is necessary to devise intelligent and scientific methods so that the tide of destruction may be turned. Extensive research over wide areas of the world will be necessary as a first step towards effectively combating the forces which have been let loose and which if allowed to continue their ravages will eventually threaten the existence of man upon the earth.

This prophecy is only now accepted by many.

He gave StJohn transcripts of twelve of his lectures – which, though interesting and inspiring, were not easy reading after years away from any study and after a hard day's work, but StJohn appreciated them and was inspired by them. He kept his copies, and I still have them.

Later St Barbe Baker toured Europe and travelled to many countries. He went to India and advised Nehru, and he toured 1,500 kilometres round the Sahara, planning reclamation, and wrote a book about the journey. He also carried out on horseback the Cobbett Ride – a trek of 330 miles through England, lecturing to schools as he went.

But this was all later; StJohn was with him in the earlier days. He had a friend/advisor who was often with him in deep consultation – perhaps his teacher and inspiration – and StJohn got to know him better than St Barbe Baker. He was a quiet, kindly man who over the months would take StJohn for walks in the evenings – perhaps a father figure, providing an element of companionship that meant a great deal to him. The Dorset History Centre, with much information on St Barbe Baker, was unable to find out more about this man.

StJohn's work involved bringing in the cows for milking and helping with the calves. He would be told "Trim that hedge" or "Erect that garage" and be left to get on with it. But it suited him to use his initiative. He used to ride the pony down to Chesil Beach, tie it to the 'No Bathing' sign, and swim out beyond the current.

Richard, probably in the midst of a divorce, was not quite taciturn, but he was severe. You did not talk at mealtimes unless you had 'something significant' to say – so meals were usually eaten in silence. There was only one occasion on which StJohn could remember him actually giving a smile. He was looking for Richard one morning, going round the house and barn, cheerfully singing (not loudly) a popular song – "Open the door, Richard, Richard why don't you open that door?" – and met him round a corner. He actually smiled.

He was a vegetarian, and in the larder were sacks of shelled nuts from which StJohn was sometimes allowed to fill his pockets. When he wanted a bath, he pumped up water from the copper down in the kitchen – it came up brown and gloriously hot.

One problem was the horse – not the pony, but the big grey cob with which StJohn often had to work, pulling tree trunks out of the wood and taking them elsewhere. This horse had no idea how to stand still. StJohn felt he had probably been bought cheap because he was so badly trained. He was told to plough the field in front of the house, but the ground was full of

Richard St Barbe Baker.

large stones. He had to keep trying to stop the horse in order to get down and carry them off. Despite all his efforts, the animal would keep careering on, sometimes pinning him against the fence. The job was done, and the next year he planted and harvested potatoes. But it was not a lovable animal.

Visiting Auntie Helen (second wife of George Alderson) in Lausanne.

Horse and dog.

To the backwoods.

Off for the stores.

His little house in Montreal.

On his pride and joy.

StJohn studied the lectures Richard gave him and also imbibed a great deal about forestry from the work he had to do in the woods. Perhaps he was not as studious as Richard might have liked. However it was, after two and a half years StJohn felt himself more labourer than student. He decided to emigrate to Canada, like his Uncle Reggie, organised his visa, and in due course was off. He went with a friend from London, and they somehow got themselves to the backwoods, where they were employed in such work as stripping the bark off tree trunks, and digging ditches. He joked that mosquitoes took chunks out of your ears and sat up in the trees to eat them. They shared a log cabin, and in wintertime one or other of them would ski several miles, over the tops of fences, to get their week's supplies. The miles of open land he found invigorating to the mind.

But they were young and basically sociable, and later moved into Montreal and found jobs and flats in different areas. StJohn worked first on the counter of a big store, and moved his way up to the edge of management. He made many friends, led the busy social life of a young man about town, acquired a car, and then, his dearest dream, a motorbike, on which he took himself, in a glorious and often talked-about holiday, to the coast of Maine. And there was another holiday to New York – to visit his father.

The fact that it is not possible to obtain Hugh's record for the Second World War suggests that he might have been in the secret service, as the story ran, although one statement obtained from Stockholm states that he was there on his way to Finland to volunteer for the Finnish Winter War, but was forced to stay in Sweden as the war closed the borders.

Whatever the facts, it was encouragement received in Stockholm that persuaded him to start to write about his life, and in 1942 *Som chef för Arabiska spyarkaren* (*Chief of the Arab Scouts*) was published in Sweden. He must have written it in English. As I was unable to find a copy, a friend painstakingly translated it for me. He was writing of events of nearly thirty years before – and was inclined to embellish – but I have included some of the stories as much for the picture of people and times in Egypt, as for his own story.

He said (in his own slightly random style),

> Destiny wanted me to end up in Sweden, where I was forced to refrain from the open-air life I was used to. In this situation, it was with the encouragement and friendly advice from three Swedish newspaper men that I sat down for the first time and wrote.[1]

---

[1]   *Among the Gauchos* was first published in English in 1944.

I can't enough point out my gratitude towards them and some other persons who have shown me friendliness. I don't claim to be a writer. I have only step by step taken down my memories.

This having been said makes it all the more sad that a letter was sent to him two years after he had left Stockholm for America in 1950, asking very politely for settlement of a bill for 439 krona.

He had left a letter saying.

In case of my early departure to the USA… I do hereby put all my effects of my apartment {as} guarantee of the above payment."

But nothing of any value was found in the apartment. Shades of his 1921 letter to the British War Office.

As well as the writing, he began painting in Stockholm and worked at it for seven years alongside a day job. He had been encouraged by Sweden's art critic Redaktor Hard. An exhibition was arranged for him in 1949 (in honour of the Argentine minister Don Hector F. Russo), and this was a success.

I am not sure how StJohn found out that his father was in New York. Canada is not a polo country, like America, and it appears that *Among the Gauchos* had not come to Canada. However it was, StJohn acquired his visa from Canada and found his way to the Studio, where he saw his father's book for the first time.

It was a big club – space over a garage – and contained a grand piano. He knew his father would be out when he arrived, and went on up the stairs. He was amazed by the spectacular pictures round the walls. Memories of his childhood flooded back to him, for they were portrayals of horses in motion – single animals, or dozens in rapid movement on the open plains, horses rearing and gauchos remaining seated, figures on the skyline, ostriches and cattle. He walked round in a strange dream, for a long while.

He noticed a certain amount of mess in the kitchen – bones left out for the cat, around the pot-bellied stove. He gathered up seven grubby shirts, washed them, found hangers and put them up to dry where it was possible. And he cleaned the greasy stove as best he could.

He said that when his father came back it was as if there had been no years between. His father had never shown much emotion – it had always been hero-worship on StJohn's side. Perhaps that lay uneasily now with his successful adulthood.

Hugh (Hugo to everyone) held a party on Friday evenings – part dance, part social occasion – trying to gather people who might buy his paintings. There was also still talk of writing, for magazines. Clearing up after these evenings was a fairly major job that StJohn experienced at least once – glasses, ashtrays, general disorder.

Next to the parking space under the studio was an area full of offcuts of wood left over by a furniture-making company, and this is what fed Hugh's stove. He asked his son to go down and fill his wood box, and StJohn went down the stairs with a torch.

As he gathered the wood in the dim light, something reared up startlingly beside him. It was a large man, swathed in overcoats, who had been stretched out to one side of the pile. He didn't speak. His eyes remained closed and he lay down again. StJohn filled the box and took it upstairs.

When he rejoined his father Hugh was amused at his shock: "Oh, he's just a tramp. He lives down there," he said.

At the end of his holiday StJohn returned to his little house and his job, which he enjoyed, with Marshalls' Silks. But there had been much conversation about whether he might come and work in New York. He kept three of his father's letters, sent in 1951, 1952 and perhaps early 1953 – and when one thinks of the length of three years out of a lifetime it is strange, and rather sad, that in all three he is expecting his son (whom he always called Johnnie) to come to New York. By 'the family' he means Dorothy, and her parents, now in England.

> September 26th 1951
>
> Johnnie my Dear Boy,
>
> Thanks for the letter, and I'm glad you had a good trip, found the family well. – I've been writing and must fight to get in the papers here, which is a very tough fight (he still wrote about horses and polo for magazines) I'm awfully happy with my studio and couldn't have found a better place in N.Y. but I have a hard time to keep things going – however I'm not depressed nor too worried and I think the break will come if I keep on plodding and don't give in. I'm glad the family liked the book (*Among the Gauchos*) so that they can understand that I'm no 'lazy guy'…

The next page is a rambling explanation of how StJohn might get a job in NY through links in Canada, or through the vice president of one of the biggest aluminium companies who was an old friend and might offer StJohn a job.

> Anyway Johnnie my boy I should love to see you again – write when you can as I like to hear all that goes with you.
>
> Best love
> Your loving Dad

The next letter, November 15th 1952

I was made to start writing again, so up I get at 4am to write (last week). Well I finished it, kept my promise, it turned out quite a story and tomorrow I submit it to the publishers and I hope 'True Mag'.

I got fed up with people and the Saturday before last was the finish because there were over a hundred people drifted in when I had only asked 30! You know the mess they can make and I had also asked a wonderful piano player and some singers but the mass of people blocked everything out. I had had the piano tuned also – so anyway that was that.

This letter must have been sent to England, as he ends with a long list of things, mostly underlined, that he would like StJohn to do for him in London, including visiting Jarrolds (publishers) for this, that and the other.

Also to buy 2 bottles of Dr Collier's 'CHLORODIN' can get at Boots, very cheap 2/- I think, good for stomach trouble. Please let me know when you intend to come as soon as poss. Because there is a room available a block away that you can have, bath complete and must tell the German woman to reserve it…

The last letter, a little more untidy, and undated, he is still hoping.

A friend of Ed Shindler who had that radio business on Broadway and who is a successful man spoke to me about you, he is an Executor in the Arabian American Oil Co. And he seemed interested to get you a position in his Co. I told him that as long as it was N. York you could be interested, so he wants to see you when you come back.

How are you getting along? Do you think it will take much more time before you can get away? To wait for the clearance of your papers will maybe take months, but don't you think you could get back and wait time as we discussed?

I held my last party last Friday which was successful but I want to finish with the big ones for a time and get the roof garden going and have summer gatherings of more selected people.
Write and tell me how long you are still going to be away, as I should not want interested people for your future to get cold…

Going into big business was never going to be a choice for StJohn – perhaps he should have told his father.
Or was he punishing his father – for being his father?

StJohn's father Hugo aka Hugh.

Hugh painting (one of five).

Hugh painting (two of five).

Hugh painting (three of five).

Hugh painting (four of five).

Hugh painting (five of five).

7: Part II of Alex and Nellie

The Second World War and After

Christine had married an English businessman, William Rose; and Irene had married a member of the Greek Bernachi family. Both were still in Alexandria.

In 1938, representatives from Mussolini's Italy were pouring in money for hospitals and schools and were offering young Italians in Alexandria holidays in Italy, where they could be exposed to right-wing politics. They issued them with black shirts, which set them apart from the blue shirts issued by the elected Wafd government. This though frequently dissonant and interrupted by the right-wing King Farouk, tended, initially at least, towards ideas of dialogues and progressive Egyptianisation of the country, towards independence.

In 1939, when Britain declared war, 1,200 Germans were interned. There were already half a million Italians in Libya, and in 1940 Italians in Alexandria and Cairo were also interned as enemy aliens. Even before the Italian legation left, Italy began bombing Alexandria – including the harbour, which was full of British boats.

Grafftey-Smith had returned from a stint in Jeddah, and was in charge of 'Information'. He began to recruit agents to move around among people. Most of them belonged to the Civil Defence Units, and could speak the language. He quickly learnt that German propaganda had preceded him – many villagers already believed that Hitler was a Moslem who had been born in Egypt (Grafftey-Smith was shown his house) and that when the war ended he would give the rich man's lands to the poor men. So Mohammed Haidar was prayed for every day.

Grafftey-Smith was genuinely fond of Egyptians, and aware of their general turn of mind. If information given looked like good news, it tended to be believed; but often when supplied with a fact, they would assume the opposite must be true.

When France surrendered, the French faction in the city was divided and there were occasional fights between Gaullist and pro-Vichy citizens. The French fleet in the harbour was disarmed, but fed by Britain, until it was persuaded to sail away and join the Free French in Algiers.

There was a huge build-up of troops in and around the city; Grafftey-Smith suggested the establishment of a centre outside with canteens, etc., but this was not taken up. There was some bad behaviour which upset citizens of all races. There was an increase in brothels. The harvests of 1941 had not been good; demands on the food supply were enormous and increased resentment. There was again the so called voluntary recruitment – the pay was reasonable. Food, vehicles and livestock were also requisitioned.

The Battle of Alexandria was similar in some ways to the Battle of Britain – the only city outside Europe to experience such a battle. Houses were shuttered, car lights dimmed blue; and when the siren sounded, some went to public shelters, others to shelters they had built in their gardens. A difference was that when it was hot they tended to sit on their roof terraces, waving to each other and watching the light show of searchlights, tracer bullets and explosions over sea and land amid a thunderstorm of noise. There were barrage balloons over the harbour.

There was also the Harbour Watch. Many people owned small boats, and there were routine patrols of the harbours in case of invasive craft – this was regarded as a sport. During the day the beaches were still crowded with people bathing. Alexandria, with its freshness and blue sea and skies was considered a holiday city from Cairo, and free of politics. Churchill visited troops in Cairo and Alexandria, and bathed in Stanley Bay, raising his legs in a V sign to the cheers of the crowds on the beach.

The Italian army was advancing into Egypt. Hundreds of Greek citizens volunteered to join the army alongside the British, and eventually the Italian lines were halted and surrounded. Many prisoners were brought into Alexandria – 'They looked miserable, awful, like beasts, like lambs' – and enclosed in a stockade before being trucked off to camps in the desert. And then it was refugees from Greece. Many came across in small boats – school teachers, professors, families – and camped on the beaches and in parks. Royalist and communist Greeks were fighting each other even as they were being liberated from the Germans.

Lawrence Durrell, the novelist, had arrived as a refugee from his home in Crete, and when recovered enough he signed up to work with the Red Cross. He also helped organise concerts for the troops and published a magazine with poems which Grafftey-Smith said, 'provided essentials in a world of flux and menace'. He remarked later, of the books the Alexandria Quartet, 'I recognise the city, but not the people'.

As in the previous war, people opened as much of their houses as they could for respite or nursing care, and Alex and Nellie in The Cloisters were among them – in 1940 Mrs Nellie Alderson was presented with a certificate of thanks from the Red Cross for help and co-operation – as probably others were as well. There were breakfast and supper clubs, tea parties and dances, concerts of all sorts run by those who could, and thousands of cups of tea. There was the British Benevolent Fund, the Greek and American fund – lectures, and tours organised by the archaeological society of Alexandria's ancient ruins. The wealthy – Greeks and others, (who owned three-quarters of the money in the Misr (Bank of Egypt) – gave with great generosity.

Out in the western desert, slowly advancing and threatening the fall of Egypt, was Rommel, with a huge army. Once they withdrew, with losses on both sides, then regrouped.

At this point there was panic in Alexandria, and a run on the banks, with people trying to take out money in order to escape – many Jews and Greeks and others left. People burnt documents of identity and company records, in the streets, which became full of blowing ash. Barclays had to organise and control queues.

British Intelligence had managed to crack the German codes. Also, there was a plot designed by an illusionist called Maskelyne. This involved the faked massing of tanks in one area, giving the impression of attack from that quarter.

So when Montgomery arrived and the American forces, with massive armament, joined the British and the bombardments began, they had an advantage. The battle lasted twelve days, and was the Second Battle of El Alamein, in 1942, and the bells of Westminster rang out to signal victory in the Desert War. Rommel finally retreated and escaped, but he shot himself two years later – on Hitler's orders.

The vital American help came at a high price. Britain's gold reserves were much diminished and not permitted to be used for trade out of Egypt. Many traders were bankrupted. A Bernachi sister poisoned herself from despair at the destruction of the city's prosperity.

Alexandria, at more than bursting point with shattered and wounded men, battled on. But the threat of war had receded – War from outside, that is. Many long-established families had already left, though some (like the Bernachis) stayed. The structures of government were being shaken from inside more strongly than over the last eighty years since Allen Alderson's had been established. George had had The Cloisters built for himself, and then Alex. Businesses were at risk of being taken over by the government, and it is likely that when Dorothy visited her parents, perhaps at the time of the Armistice, she had already decided to take them to England. With their wide business links, The Cloisters was sold (and perhaps it would have been attractive to an Egyptian businessman), supplying enough (but leaving a great deal) for Dorothy to pack up to furnish a flat for them in England. For their care had become her job.

It was probably through Church links that the flat was found. Alex and Nellie had given Alexandria all they could, and England must become their home.

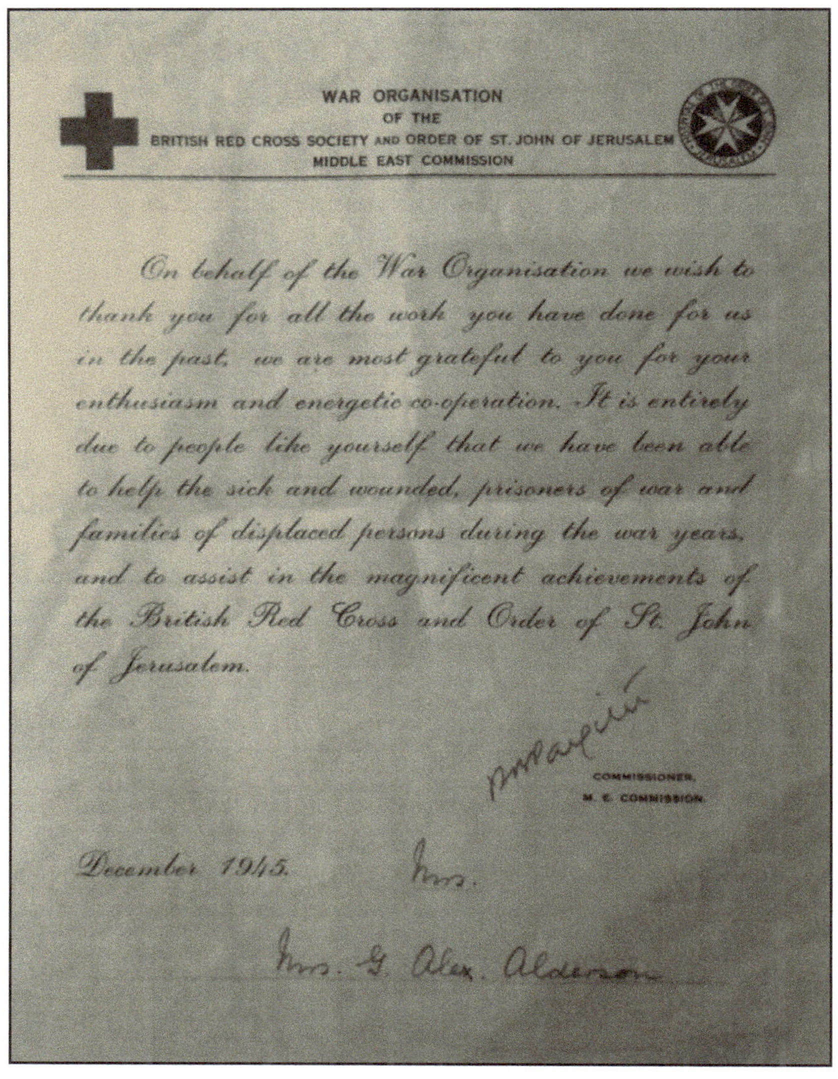

On behalf of the War Organisation we wish to thank you for all the work you have done for us in the past, we are most grateful to you for your enthusiasm and energetic co-operation. It is entirely due to people like yourself that we have been able to help the sick and wounded, prisoners of war and families of displaced persons during the war years, and to assist in the magnificent achievements of the British Red Cross and Order of St. John of Jerusalem.

COMMISSIONER,
M. E. COMMISSION.

December 1945.

Mrs. G. Alex. Alderson

Red Cross certificate for Mrs Alderson.

8: Yet Another Tale

There was a new face at one of the occasional dance parties held around the town among friends and acquaintances. In those days, you might get to meet someone by means of a Paul Jones. This consisted of a circle of boys holding hands, moving in the opposite direction to a circle of girls. When the music stopped you danced with whoever happened to be opposite to you. Sometimes neither could think of anything to say – they just danced until the music stopped again for another change of partners.

Thus I met StJohn, dark-haired, soft-spoken, extremely nice-looking. Conversation was not scintillating on either side, but he had a slightly appealing accent that he said was Canadian, and he told me he was in Tunbridge Wells temporarily.

My mother, who liked organising things, wanted to give me a dinner party for my eighteenth birthday, and booked a table at a familiar restaurant in the town. I tracked StJohn down through the host of the previous party, but learnt he was somewhere up north making sandwiches for flood victims; so the party happened, not very excitingly, among people I knew pretty well.

A few weeks later, riding along the road towards my bookshop on my bike – which I'd painted bright yellow (he christened it the Yellow Peril), I saw him coming along a driveway towards the pillar box, and almost fell off as I stopped. He dropped his letter.

So – corny story – he took me to a film, and another dance, and I liked the way he danced. It had a gentle swing to it. He came to dinner, and as he was courteous with impeccable manners he passed muster. He was already integrated into the town although he had not been there long – but he had joined the 'Cadena Crowd', who met at a particular coffee house on Saturday mornings (not my brothers' scene) and I saw his playful side – something very different from the more demure gatherings I was used to.

Looking back to that time over sixty-five years, it all seems extraordinary. He was just there – in Tunbridge Wells, of all places – and I haven't been able to find out why there? It was like "Why Brighton?" Probably Dorothy persuaded her parents to leave, in view of the growing hostility of the Egyptian Government, before all the assets of the company had been stripped away, so that this flat could be afforded.

He wanted me to meet his mother and grandparents, in a big block of flats tucked away up a long leafy drive five minutes from our house. I had never known it was there.

"Stairs or lift?" he said.

We walked up the stairs.

The room was light and sunny, his mother welcoming. And there were Alex and Nellie, though I never called them that. I don't think I called them anything. Alex was tall and imposing, a little foreign-looking, with a kindly face and tidy white beard. Nellie was very serious, with large blue eyes that seemed to assess me in a glance. I understood they had had to leave Egypt on account of Nasser – I had read of this in the newspapers, but knew nothing.

We met a few more times, and then my mother had the bright idea that I with StJohn, and John with my college friend, who was staying with us and whom John rather fancied, should all go for a weekend to the caravan – boys on camp beds outside, girls in the caravan. John, of course, would chaperone.

But shortly before sundown, John appeared on the platform of the caravan with his arm around Anita, and announced that they were going to sleep in the caravan if we didn't mind the camp beds. Anita seemed quite happy about it. Where was my self-respect, my fury, my family loyalty? They drifted into the balmy summer among the apple trees.

There was a brief equivocal moonlit interlude on one of the camp beds, but the next day when we went for a walk, John and Anita in another direction, StJohn said, "Would you like to be engaged?" which was an odd way to put it – perhaps a shy way.

I couldn't begin to explain that to my unenlightened 1950s way of thinking I would like it if we were engaged simply to salve my conscience. (But if I had backed off, we would never have shared those two best things – children and The Project).

It turned out that the shiny gourds I'd bought to decorate the caravan were called maté pots, from which you drank something called maté through a silver straw, if you were in the Argentine. I'd 'done' South America for my School Certificate geography, so of course knew all about it, and the pampas, and the wild horses of Argentina, where he had been born and spent his first precious years.

Dorothy and Nellie.

Wedding day – with my father.

Dorothy, StJohn, Alex and Nellie.

He sailed away (one of two).

He sailed away (two of two).

Nicholas at Grange Cote.

His mother came round to dinner, and to talk. My mother visited their flat and was delighted with his grandparents. My father interviewed StJohn (very seriously, he said), but he came though as acceptable. He proposed (again) and gave me a beautiful diamond ring. My parents knew that his parents had been divorced.

We had an engagement party. I stupidly left the ring on and I woke in pain and panic-stricken with my ring finger twice its size. My father tried to wiggle it off with oil, but it was no good – he had to cut it, and send it to be re-made.

StJohn's plan was for us to go to Canada, and on account of the wedding-plans' delay he resigned his remunerative job in Montreal, confident of being able to replace it when we arrived. So I would be emigrating! He already had Canadian citizenship.

I think my mother dispersed any regrets about my leaving among the interests of the wedding preparations. She gathered for me a wonderful trousseau, including a massively warm coat for the Canadian winters. She had taught me precious and unforgettable things.

The first I remembered for always was one winter evening as we came back from a friend's party when I was about three. At the top of the steps, she said, "Look up – look up at all the stars," and showed me stars this way, that way, in all the enormous sky for several ever-and-ever moments.

She had taught me the names of wild and garden flowers, taken me to matinées of plays in London and meals in Chinese restaurants.

We had sat together at the edge of a familiar field in sunshine, watching a great shire horse ploughing, and she said, "You may never see this again. You must always remember it."

And I do. All through my early life she had read to me.

She had always wanted a daughter, having been, by her own admission, "naughty about Guy", but added how much she valued his company when he grew up.

I disappointed her on occasions. She sometimes looked at me hopelessly and said, "Plain Jane today, dear." (As if I didn't know it!)

But then, it was not as if we had been at home all the time. We were all three packed off to boarding school at seven or nine – something I couldn't have done with my children, however exasperated I used to become.

She had a lovely wedding dress made for me. The four bridesmaids' dresses were of layered green-and-bronze tulle. This was flattering to my college friend, who had dark-brown hair and eyes; and to my childhood friend, who was green-eyed and auburn. Not so good for my pale and blue-eyed school friend (who had gone on to Edinburgh University to read literature) or my beautiful violet-eyed and graceful older cousin (who taught dancing). She was my matron of honour, patiently helping and cajoling me on The Day.

We were married in the local church, and the reception was in a friend's garden, full of July flowers. There were all the dear and well-known friends and relations; but there was one young man who stood out as alone and different, and I learnt he was Don, an old friend of StJohn's who had sailed his small boat from South Africa to come to the wedding.

When it was time for us to be driven away, I was ushered into the car, but StJohn wasn't there. He was not beside me – he was not outside. The car was moving. There were thumps – the Cadena Crowd had merrily dumped him on the car roof, where he clung for several yards before slithering off and getting in.

We had wanted a camping honeymoon – not approved of by my mother, who insisted on one night in a hotel. We complied, leaving the room awash with rice that kind friends had placed in our suitcases. StJohn had bought complete camping equipment, and my mother lent us her Morris Minor, which was very generous.

We hadn't tried out the tent. Having found a lovely field and arranged to camp in a corner of it, we took everything out, but when it came to putting up the tent StJohn had problems. I stood holding poles in various positions while he crawled about and fiddled and uttered words I'd never heard used. It was obvious to me as a bystander that it would work if you put the groundsheet out first and fitted the tent around it. A moment of factual conversation in opposition can be a watershed moment – especially when you are eighteen. It is different from the violent emotional opposition to something that can take place from the age of two, or the deliberate rule-breaking practised by those with that turn of mind. It was some time before my suggestion was put into practice. We then laid out our belongings and prepared for supper.

On this, as on all subsequent camping holidays, StJohn took charge of meals and cooking. This was excellent. I think he did it because he doubted my capability with the stove. The sun shone for almost the entire two weeks, during which we found two other enjoyable sites on farmland (we would never have gone to a camping site) costing just pence and enjoyed ourselves. He would plug his shaver into the light sockets of phone boxes, and sometimes we had fish and chips.

Dorothy and her parents moved out of the flat into a residential hotel nearby, where she could get a little help. It was the first of many such sacrifices she made for us over the years. We lived there while our array of wedding presents was crated up ready to be transported when we had an address in

Montreal. Bookings were made, forms signed and contacts in Montreal made by StJohn. By this time it was November.

A farewell party was held, and my father sang and played 'Shenandoah' to my almost breaking heart:

> Oh Shenandoah,
> I love your daughter,
> Away you rolling river.
> To take her o'er
> The stormy water.
> Away, I'm bound to go…

We went by ship, complete with party dresses for cocktails and dancing on board – one was a three-quarter-length dress in deepest scarlet, which I was longing to swirl about in and never ever wore. The ship ran into the tail end of a typhoon with a shuddering impact that cracked the bridge, and for most of the journey I lay in the cabin feeling more ill and miserable than ever before in my life while StJohn, distinctly green although an ex-navy man, mopped me up and emptied basins. His devotion, which I was not conscious enough to appreciate at the time, was remarkable. For the last few days we walked palely on deck or sat in chairs immersed in rugs, cautiously drinking bouillon.

The St Lawrence River ('Away you rolling river') was surrounded by the brilliance of autumn leaves. On both sides of the huge stretch of water was mile upon mile of rich colour as the ship swished gently thrumming on its way, and everyone stood silently looking at the loveliness after the fury and misery of the sea. We left the ship at Quebec – grey stone houses piling up steep hills. We went to a restaurant and I was overcome at how smartly everyone was dressed. Charles Trenet was there and sang '*La Mer*', but that this was something special I scarcely appreciated. Then we took the train to Montreal.

The enormity of the city appalled me.

"This is it, this is Montreal," StJohn said, and I began to gather my things to get out of the train.

But it went on and on, a built-up desert, flat and vast, spreading on both sides and extending behind like a huge prison between ourselves and green land.

The speed of the traffic was terrifying, and as this was 1953 (before London was fully furnished with high-rise buildings) I had never seen such tall walls. The outskirts were more friendly, two- and three-storey grey stone houses in tree-lined avenues, or rows of cheerful two-storey buildings called duplexes, which were separate flats upstairs and down. We stayed temporarily as lodgers in a room that StJohn had lived in for a while previously, while we tramped the streets looking for an apartment.

The cold of those streets was to me like a continuous assault, even when wearing the huge coat with quilted lining that my mother had provided. (Do people have trousseaux any more?) I would walk along feeling completely full of hatred for that cold – a kind of desperate fury at the cut of the wind on my face and the hard chaotic turmoil of concrete, vehicles, and crowded bewildering movement. The interiors of shops and other buildings were so extremely hot and stuffy with the unfamiliar air conditioning that I frequently felt faint after a few minutes indoors and would have to go out again to get air – the beastly bitter wind. It was not the crisp cold of white frost, or even the slate-cold damp rawness of an English January, but to me it was as savage as a wolf, violent and hostile.

Textiles were apparently in a state of regression and none of the places to which StJohn confidently applied for a job were interested. He had lost the one he had by meeting me and staying in England to get married. At any rate we were so taken up with the drama of our lives together that I doubt if he would ever have managed a regular daily exit from wherever we were going to live. There was something else too: despite our naïve hope that "Once we get settled down things will return to normal", there was no doubt that my waist was disappearing and I couldn't do up any of my skirts.

Traipsing round the endless streets made me long to go beyond the reach of the buildings, out of the city, and one day we saw in the newspaper an advertisement for a flat in a duplex on the other side of the river. It took us some time to reach it, but there was a feeling of escape and relief in being able to see the sky at ground level. The house we went to see was being built by a man who meant to finance it partly by letting the top half until his family could no longer squeeze in downstairs. The view of the sky, and a gate like a farm gate at the end of the road (which was also the end of the city), persuaded us, quite wrongly as it turned out, that this was home. We arranged to send round two trunks as a guarantee, and wrote off for our other belongings to be shipped out.

StJohn's third journey to see the place took three hours, and suddenly he realised that it was all absurd, that when he had a job he would be spending five or six hours a day travelling, and also that the housing estate was going to become a noisy French slum. So we backed out, and had to pay a month's rent to the understandably sour owner who was so unpleasant we were glad we were not going to live over him.

At last we found a semi-basement flat, in a road nostalgically called Kent Avenue. Outside was a square of green open space. The flat consisted of a large L-shaped room with a cupboard-sized kitchen next to a shower, a tiny loo, and an enormous fridge. The walls were of knotty pine. It was clean and warm and we could open the windows. Our belongings, which had somehow en route got tossed to Amsterdam in the wake of another cyclone, arrived on Christmas Eve. We unpacked a few things and ate stew at three o'clock on Christmas morning, using two 'Famille Rose' dishes which had happened to emerge instead of dinner plates. Then we slept till lunchtime. We talked for the next four months.

The talking, of course, should have taken place earlier, but there seemed to have been too many people about and too much going on.

Lesson 1 – Discuss aims and purposes with your partner before making moves.

We found that neither of us wanted to live in a city, but somehow we must seek space and creativity. If we had known it would take us twenty-five years to achieve the first and a form of the second we might have lost heart, particularly if we had been unable to see the cheerful and contented moments of the years between even through their problems.

My bulge grew larger with an inexorability that I found perfectly terrifying.

"We're not ready for this," StJohn kept saying, and paced the floor at night unable to sleep.

Lesson 2 – Before you act, think through the obvious consequences so that you will not be surprised by them.

All this time we were using up money that StJohn had saved, and another slice of it was used to pay an obstetrician, and for a private room in a hospital. And while I was in there, StJohn moved all our belongings to another flat, a little larger (but not nicer) with room to dry nappies. It was a decent ten months since the wedding.

If he had got a job, if we had not had the baby so soon, if we had not developed those ideas about its being possible to decide on one's life, aim for it and carry it out…

'What might have been is an abstraction, remaining a perpetual possibility, only in the world of speculation.'

Nicholas was born into the sunshine of a spring evening – though I didn't notice the sunshine until they unstrapped my arms and legs from the contraption they provided for the ordeal of parturition. To produce a baby without anaesthetics or drugs, which we considered the proper course and had followed through, was at that time and in that place unorthodox and worthy of several witnesses (though the father was excluded); and the idea that a mother might wish to hold her new child in her arms was not current. Instead, in the silence of the audience having departed, I heard minute breathings and suckings and stirrings from a cot on the other side of the room, which I spoke to. So there actually was a living, breathing baby. The stillness, the brightness and the sounds were strange – a sudden peculiar peace. At last had ceased a wailing that had continued from my entering the hospital that morning until now – a woman (Greek, I had been told) intoning rhythmically and apparently without stopping to breathe, "Mama mia, Mama mia, Mama mia…" until now, this golden moment, this first and private hearing.

We thought of pottery, and yet we felt it would be impossible to do it where we were. The enormity of the city, which gave way to an enormity of not county as I knew it, but wilderness, seemed totally inhospitable to the kind of project we visualised.

Lesson 3 – Equip yourself for the kind of life you feel you can fit into.

But StJohn, in the wartime navy and prior to that taking for granted his position on his father's ranch, had had little time to think it out, and I had never thought myself through. The vastness of Canada felt home to him, but I felt lost in it, wanting valleys, hills and slopes on a scale I could fathom. Before Nicholas was born we had twice gone with friends to the mountain slopes 100 miles from Montreal, and they skied while we walked about. But the utterly frozen state of the trees, the depth of cold! I tried, but I could find no joy there although I could appreciate the beauty.

We stood at the top by the huge trees and watched the coloured dots of the skiers fanning out, down and down; and if I had been a proper sensible person and not a spoilt child, I would have taken StJohn's arm and said, "Won't it be fun when you have a job and we have a proper flat and a car, and we shall come and teach our child to ski." Instead I stood dumb and miserable, hating the hugeness despite my admiration of it, hating the long stuffy car drive, and the turmoil and insecurity and lostness of our lives.

And having a child altered perspectives for StJohn as much as for me. As a merry, prosperous and popular bachelor he had had no cause to notice, but now, looking round, Canadian children seemed to us to have a shallow sophistication that was somehow un-childlike. And, brought up to believe that babies should have fresh air every day, I was appalled at the fact that they could not be put outside in winter unless the object was murder. Instead they lived in the deadness of air conditioning, kept out of the excessive heat of summer as well as the winter's cold.

So after all the performance of having emigrated we wanted to be back in England and start life on different terms. It was an expensive way of coming to a conclusion. We looked down at our small, fair Nicholas and desired for him something other than a house in a street and a daily-absent father. The idea was in contrast to that of our parents, and to most of their generation, who believed as firmly that a father's place was out of the house by day as that a mother's was in it. At about this time my father offered to buy us a cottage in England, as he had done in turn for each of the boys.

So – when Nicholas was five months old I took him back to England, leaving StJohn to settle things in Montreal while I was to gather information and look for a cottage. (I wondered later if in those weeks he went and saw his father one last time.) At that time you could buy a cottage for between £1,000 and £2,000. We flew in a BOAC strato-cruiser – the first time, apart from ten minutes in a two-seater plane in Italy, that I had been in an aeroplane. Nicholas behaved perfectly normally. I breastfed him in the powder room, where an effusive Canadian lady gushed her delight at seeing someone actually breastfeed a baby. In her country, as we had found, it was generally considered archaic and rather rude, while bottle-feeding and a ridiculously early stuffing with cereals was the norm. The results were the solid pappy babies who graced (or disgraced) the advertisements for baby food – babies that I found unattractive.

The powder room was pink and comfortable, and apart from that one interruption I was alone and felt luxuriously independent and adventurous. Something was beginning, and Nicholas's contented feeding, unaffected by the fact that we were in the sky, gave me confidence in two ways. Firstly, I was able to be his provider: this new person needed hands to lift and care for him, and he needed milk of a certain temperature, and I had these things – and though I never had much in the way of breasts, they proved, then and subsequently, quite adequate for their job. Secondly, in the consciousness of being myself a channel, the tenderness, as it were, passing through me, there was hope that such tenderness was a universal reality even if not universally expressed, a hope that perhaps, after all the coldness and problems and pain, we were experiencing a forgiving, a fulfilment. These thoughts were vague and unformed in my mind, yet at the same time strong and encouraging.

I went back to the house of my long-suffering parents, who gave up their spare bedroom and a little upstairs sitting room to us, and Nicholas had what had been my playroom. In due course the crates, repacked by StJohn, came back and filled up their basement. We should have been ashamed of ourselves – but I was too pleased to be back within the cycle of English seasons.

There were plenty of country trains and buses running then, and I went about calling on potters to glean advice, carrying Nicholas and a bag of his necessities. Potters I found to be friendly, helpful and tolerant, generous with information as to how much space was needed and what sort of running costs there were, and my affection grew for the smell of wet clay and the spin of the wheel. I had done some pottery at school – enough to feel I could at least assist. I took it for granted that StJohn would be brilliant at it. The arrogance of the idea that we should learn pottery, set up in it and make our living at it, did not strike me. It was all possible and joyous. What others were doing, we could do.

I saw a tiny pottery in a Wealden village using Wealden clay, with a brick floor and sun shining in through the lupins. I saw a neat prosperous little town pottery with the smiling wife selling in the shop. And a pottery with a vast wood-fired kiln and a great chimney that was built on the end of a small house buried among fields. Another was a huge London studio, light filtering through high windows, where I was shown small wooden boxes of cigar and cigarette ash used in marvellously effective glazes on models of animals. Potters of the exotic and of the everyday, makers of bowls and mugs by the dozen, or of unique creations that stood solitary and precious on a plinth or in a niche.

Sometimes my mother ferried me about, and we began looking at cottages. We visited dozens. So began the second round of house-hunting.

StJohn came back from Montreal and started commuting daily to the Camberwell School of Arts and Crafts. Soon he began bringing home things he had made – bowls, a teapot, some delicate globe-shaped pots with beautifully turned lids. He was involved – we were on our way. For several months we continued hopefully, but somehow, strangely, we ran out of steam. A kind of normality unnatural to us overlaid us. Scarves of convention wound about us from all sides.

It was in some ways all too easy – our tough times were to come later. We were living in a civilised environment lapped in the security of hot water to wash the baby clothes, and a nice kitchen that it was not my job or my mother's to clean. I cooked for us and generally we ate on our own in our sitting room. There were outings, dinner parties and, as all our contemporaries seemed to be getting married, many weddings. So many that StJohn one day (to my mother's great irritation) dug in his heels, declared he could not stand another one and took Nicholas out into the fields for the afternoon instead.

My father suggested that StJohn should take a correspondence course on business methods. This was a good idea, and he was later glad that he had done it.

Even as the meshes closed on us we thought wildly of selling everything and going off in a boat. Joshua Slocum, of sailing fame, had been StJohn's long-time hero. He had kept in touch with Don, who was on another visit to England in his boat on some business or other. In a holiday period from

Camberwell, to gain some experience, they planned that StJohn would accompany him back across the Channel.

They were caught in fierce storms. I listened to radio reports of ships in dire trouble in the Channel, cuddled Nicholas and wondered if StJohn had gone forever. But he came back with ecstatic and hair-raising tales of the adventure – which had encouraged him. He started going off at weekends to look at boats, and I wrote to several addresses asking the price of carved-built gaff-rigged cutters. I stood holding Nicholas, who was enveloped in a huge white and beautiful shawl knitted for him by his great-grandmother Nellie, on a very windy bare beach, while StJohn looked over a particularly attractive boat aptly named *Idle Hour* – which turned out to be completely unsound. Always they were either not quite right or too expensive.

Our sense of what was essential changed: all we needed was a cottage and a job – something to keep us independent. Pottery would have to wait until we could branch out into it. Finding a cottage suitable for pottery was taking too long.

And finally: "As soon as I went inside," StJohn said, "I told him this was it."

So just before Christmas, with Nicholas nearly two, we moved into the terraced cottage in a village near Sevenoaks, with its red-brick floor (the oldest kind of quarry tile), its Courtier stove standing outside the bricked-up fireplace warming the room efficiently except in exceptionally cold weather, its new kitchen built out at the back, and its new bathroom and two bedrooms. We felt that it was a refuge, a jumping-off place, and would have been appalled if we had known it was to house our frustrations and delights – and an additional three children – for the next twenty years.

StJohn bought a second-hand bike and found a job with Marley Tiles four miles away. I kept house and took Nicholas for walks in the fields. I did this with great zeal, having been brought up to believe it was what you do with children, and I still tend to think that children who are not taken for simple walks – rather than to places of entertainment – are deprived because a walk can be the most perfect form of education into the realities of things. Through daily walks you discover the changing seasons, the differing atmospheres of the unrolling months. You note the gold of willows and birches, the first to show their green, crocuses and daffodils, the russet of oak leaves that unfold last of all.

"What are all those little knobbles?" asks the child, trotting along in his tiny boots.

"Those are the buds, the leaves are all curled up inside, waiting to open when it's spring."

"Will it be hot? Will I have my pool again and swim?"

Camden Terrace with the holly.

And there is a lovely certainty he will have his little pool on the lawn and will run up and down with the freedom to be happy, to enjoy himself.

One child and a very small cottage, yet I considered myself extremely busy and fighting hard to find myself a little time to do things I wanted – studying this or that or writing or dressmaking for myself and the child (rather badly, but with great enthusiasm). At one moment adoring his presence, his speech, his sense of fun, the enchanting dearness of his limbs and movements and expressions, but sometimes resenting the continuity of his demands, his power to exasperate me, the physical work his presence brought me. And at one moment enjoying friends and conversations, and daily greetings in the village, and the next longing for total seclusion, a complete absence of meaningless 'good-mornings' and swapping of baby stories, desiring instead miles of greenness only, and hills and trees.

After two years StJohn left his job at Marley Tiles and joined a small new commercial art agency in London, less hierarchical, a little more remunerative and a great deal more interesting, but initiating us into the routine of commuter life. We lived in the commuter belt – our village was sprinkled with families of which the husband commuted and no one seemed to think of it as a ludicrous and extraordinary way to live, as we did, although we were doing it, and although it was the very way of life we had planned not to adopt. But we felt confident it was only temporary, until we could save enough to start the pottery – a few years. We never really rooted.

At weekends we explored. StJohn preferred woods, and led us through them with an unerring sense of direction, so that when we found ourselves back where we started after a long and interesting trail we were always surprised. We tramped through woods in the autumn, looking for chestnuts, admiring colours, smelling the deliciousness of leaf mould. We set out through woods in spring when beech leaves were soft as baby skin. In the snow all was changed. The once-familiar was all afresh, and we moved with stealth and wonder over wide places that had become scenarios, and into small clearings that had turned into secret pictures.

We explored every wooded place within walking distance as Nicholas grew from two to five. Sometimes StJohn would go out on the Saturday alone and discover the route of a new trek. He needed some solitude after London. Then on a Sunday we would go all three together, and perhaps make a small fire and cook maté and toast over it. When he was older Nicholas once remarked that this was the best time, when he was the only one.

But after five years we had Joanna. She was born in the cottage during one long night. Her brother heard her first cry early in the morning and called out, "There's my baby!" He was very curious and solicitous about her.

She was round and creamy and blue-eyed. Her hair was so long in coming that I lay awake at night fearing that she was never going to have any, and when it came it was a white bloom that turned, incredibly, into blond curls. Through her early childhood the honey-gold waves hung down her back and amazed me. But the anomaly was that only when they were cut off did the real quality of her face emerge. Beautiful in themselves, those fair tresses did not flatter her.

So here was another stage of life. We acquired an enormous black pram, a comfortable well-sprung 'nanny-pram' with a cream-coloured canopy under which I could set her angelic head on an embroidered pillowcase and admire her as I pushed. We paraded the lanes and avenues, in incessant conversation with each other, sometimes with Nicholas sitting on the end of the pram 'for a rest'. I felt important and proud, and the pride made me set a standard for myself that was probably healthy for the children. The many creative and money-saving things you can do at home – (making curtains, covers, clothes, cooking, playing games with the children) were usual then. I was impatient, probably inefficient, and definitely unsure, but I remember with gratitude and joy the small satisfaction of the days: sitting on chairs I had covered, looking at flowers grown from seeds I had sown, and sampling the intense interest offered by a short walk. Or a time at the recreation ground, where I could admire Nicholas's daring on the slide or climbing frame while the baby slept or later sat up and watched. And why was it – what had gone wrong? That a few years later the swings would be repeatedly damaged, the little roundabout heaved off its pivot, the steel plates of the slide, which had given pleasure and first 'speed-confidence' to so many children, would be bent up into lethal shards? The 'rec' that we knew, where we and our children could meet and talk, became a wreck.

Between the bricks in the middle of the sitting-room floor we pushed a long skewer and cemented it in. We used it as a tethering post for the baby so that Nicholas could play out of her reach and not always get his castles knocked down or his cars disarranged. Sometimes it all worked well, sometimes it didn't. But at least it meant that Joanna was not Nicholas's permanent pest.

StJohn was not a pram-pusher and carry-slings for small babies had not come into their own, so for the whole of Joanna's first winter, sometimes quite happily and sometimes resentfully, I stayed in at weekends while he and Nicholas went out on their own. But soon she was being carried, then humped in the pushchair, and then she was walking – and also requiring the monopoly of the conversation and quarrelling with Nicholas, forcing us to learn some measure of diplomacy, and the least-nice aspects of sibling behaviour.

By watching them, knowing them so much more fully than can parents (my own included) who hand their small children to others to care for, I was subject to great interest and delight – and frustration at times – and deep realisation of the tiny steps of their increasing knowledge and abilities.

The fruit-farm project had not been successful. My father blamed it on their constant cutting-down and grubbing-up. The supply of apples had been a joy to my mother. They had grown strawberries (we had all spent days picking), but the pickers of strawberries and fruit complained about the presence of bees, and tall walls of hessian were put round the hives (supposed to make the bees fly higher). My father hated it, and in the end, sadly, the farm was sold. A little later he was asked to remove the caravan, and my father offered it to us, which was generous – he probably could have sold it. But what to do? Where could it live? Of course we wanted it. I don't know what made me think of the vicar – who owned the Vicar's Field, down which the residents of the village tobogganed in season. With much trepidation we asked him if we could rent a corner at the top, and he graciously said we could. We also (later) rented one of his garages.

It arrived on a low-loader to the great interest of the locals, and StJohn managed to coerce a group of them to help us manoeuvre it into position after unloading it, which was a mightier work than the helpers had probably expected – StJohn took them all to the Pub afterwards.

It became another pleasant place to go at weekends, its near surroundings needing to be kept in order and enhanced with other plants. StJohn kept it well maintained.

9: Expansion and a Sketchbook

We were at number 2 of the terrace and at number 1 lived an old man with his housekeeper, his wife having died. He was an old sailor, rather gentle, with a kind smile. He grew roses and madonna lilies in a little wilderness of grass and rubbish on the other side of our 'rustic fence'. At the cottage end of this fence the polygonum or Russian vine we planted to hide the coal bunker swarmed along it for about three metres, a froth of white flowers. In the garden I grew sunflowers and candytuft, godetia and rosemary, and the scent of the lilies drifted over. We had made a brick path that ran neatly down the garden below the washing line beside our perpetually threadbare lawn.

The next-door housekeeper was a tall large-boned woman with a permanent gash of lipstick for a mouth. She was said to be a leftover from a batch of wartime London evacuees, and was looked on as an outsider. She was brash and noisy – pans clattered, water splashed, the kettle screamed and doors banged about her. Her summons to the old sailor to come for his tea, when he was at the bottom of his ten-metre garden, could have fetched him from across the village.

"Hallo, ducks," she said to Nicholas through the fence.

"I'm not a duck," he answered in a polite and informative way.

To get the pram into our garden we had to go round and past the back door of number 1, and the tall strange woman would sometimes emerge through the door and peer into the pram.

"Oh, yes?" she would say. "Oh, yes?"

I could never think of an answer.

Alex had died while we were in Canada, though Dorothy and Nellie were still living in the guest house. Dorothy was looking for a little house for them, so when the old man died and we knew that the landlord was going to sell it – as he had sold ours to our predecessors – it seemed like the answer to a prayer (though initially the price seemed above what could be afforded). The back of number 1, and its piece of ground the same size as our own, with the big barn belonging to the neighbouring builders next to it, were as familiar to us as our own. To combine them seemed the obvious thing to do.

So a rather strange period followed, in which with jealous eyes we watched through the front windows and the garden fence the people who came to see it. If anyone seemed too interested or came more than once I made a point of pushing a cargo of noisy children in the pram past the back door, even letting the gate bang loudly behind us. We were sure the price would fall to 'our' level if we demonstrated the disadvantages. We listened with interest to the comments.

"If it was mine I'd be glad to get rid of it."

"Where's the sanitary inspector been all this time?"

An elderly wife said tremulously to her husband, "You could build the kitchen out like that one," indicating ours.

"By the time you done that," he said firmly, "the rest of the place would have fallen down."

We longed to take down the fence and make a wider lawn, to have a square garden instead of a strip, and to make the two cottages into a little square house.

One day a keen young man walked up and down the garden talking to his companion with an earnestness that alarmed me. On the Sunday morning, when he came for the third time, StJohn went and talked to him with all the civility of a prospective neighbour.

"Do you think I could manage with just cold water?" he asked StJohn confidentially. In casual conversation he divulged what his offer was going to be.

Perhaps it was our wickedness on this occasion that merited our suffering from gazumping and other malpractices in subsequent house-hunting, for as it struck nine the next morning we phoned to submit a slightly higher offer, which was subsequently accepted.

Once we knew it had been accepted, with our fingers itching to start work, we were rather unmindful of the time that is taken in due process of law, and immediately took down the fence. I began clearing the garden (and how the old man had treated his lilies I wished I knew, for they never bloomed again), and the agent, coming one morning to check on something, almost fell into a ditch that StJohn had dug all around the walls to dry them out; and another time he was surprised to find StJohn's mother standing on a table and scraping away the flaking paint and plaster of the kitchen ceiling.

And here I must explain something that in all the excitement (the sense of possibility in uniting the gardens and doing up the cottage) I tended to overlook – that Dorothy was buying the cottage for Dorothy and Nellie to live in. The implications for personal good or ill passed me by – it just seemed the next thing for us all to be doing.

I think Nellie was being shared between sisters, who assumed that because Dorothy was the only one that was 'free' (they all had husbands) she should take the responsibility. Dorothy would come and 'camp' in the cottage as rooms were made habitable. Meanwhile, StJohn at weekends, and a member of next door's building team much of the time, would be at work.

We had japonica outside our front door, which gave us useful fruit for jelly, where number 1 had a large and beautiful variegated holly. But we found that not only were its roots bullying the front wall, but a thick and sprouting root had grown right through the house under the tiles to the back of the cottage. It was sad to have to destroy it all, because it was so much a part of the character of the front, but it was the only thing to do – a mighty and disruptive job.

Where our fireplace had been bricked up and fronted by the Courtier stove, number 1 had still an open fireplace, which StJohn set about repairing, and the room began to look 'real'.

StJohn with Joanna.

The earth outside was black and sandy, full of tiny bright pieces of glass and china.

We had been told that the stone barn which stood at the bottom of our garden and now belonged to number 3, had been the earth closet for numbers 1 and 2 (before number 3 onwards had been built), the product being thrown back up on to their gardens.

The children, following us about, were perpetually black, and somehow the blackness seeped into our cottage – towels were black and the walls were smudged, and all the floors scrunched for weeks. They were both excited with the new dimension, and Nicholas was delighted to help us peel off layers of wallpaper: little mauve violets, smart pink regency stripes, flamboyant roses, bunches of cherries – generations of changing tastes.

In due course, the cottage was renovated, and decorated, and they moved in. Nellie (Great-Granny) was settled in her wheelchair either in front of the fire or, in summer, in the morning sunshine just outside the front door, where she could watch the world go by. Joanna would sometimes help to give her her porridge. She did not talk much, and I still had very little idea about her.

As the level of the garden of number 1 was rather higher than that of number 2 we decided to take some earth away so that we could make a level lawn across the two. We found someone who could lend us a lorry in exchange for the earth, and we spent several Saturday mornings loading it. From that small square we took six loads. We set a plank against the open back of the lorry and, taking a good run, pushed the loaded barrow up the plank to tip it out inside. Not always, of course – sometimes we lost steam halfway up and had to teeter back again for a second try, straining not to go crooked and tip over. It was probably good weekend entertainment for the people behind the windows of the cottages around us.

On looking back, I am rather ashamed that I never tried to talk to Nellie about her life in Egypt and what it had been like to move to England; and now I greatly wish I had. At that time, Nellie was Dorothy's sphere; mine was the children, the garden, StJohn (now shared to some degree) and writing down reams of mostly tedious descriptions of it all.

Amid all this activity, StJohn learnt that his father in New York had been called back from work (which was interior decorating) because his studio was on fire, and he watched the destruction of all he had, including his paintings all around the walls. StJohn was concerned it would have been on account of his habit of overloading his electrical plugs with a string of extra fittings – all these years afterwards he was blaming himself for not having sorted them out. If this news came by way of a perhaps wild letter from his father, StJohn had not kept it. Hugh was living in a hotel.

A letter from one of the friends he had around him suggested Hugh might come to England to be with his son. The cottage being chock-a-block, and with his divorced wife living next door, the chance was as remote as finding somewhere else for him to live, as StJohn explained. The next suggestion was for StJohn to visit his father – friends were collecting money to fund this idea – but before it could happen he heard that Hugh had died in hospital. This was 1961.

He was given due honours. A kindly letter headed 'British Empire Veterans Fund' told of his funeral, attended by several British war veterans from New York, who paid their respects at Rose Hill Cemetery, Linden, New Jersey, where Hugh's name (as Hugo) would appear on the monument. There was nothing to send his son.

A copy of the death certificate was also included, which referred to him as 'widowed' and included his usual incorrect birthdate. Whether Hugh shared StJohn's address before he died, or whether it was found with his papers, I cannot tell.

We bought a car. It was an ancient Standard, and before long it belched smoke to such a degree that cars behind us kept their distance when going uphill. StJohn made a complicated arrangement of plastic containers that was supposed to siphon off the fumes inside the car. The word 'pollution' was not common currency then. But after a trip to the seaside, during which the fumes had overcome the bottles and nearly overcome us, and we had to push it up hills while Nicholas steered, we stopped at a garage where we saw the loveliest car any of us had ever seen. It was a green Citroen, a 1955 Light Fifteen, long and smooth with beautiful great wings and big chrome headlights. Inappropriately to it, wearing his seaside shorts and cotton sun hat, StJohn tried it out with Nicholas and bought it there and then. It had belonged, we were told, to the cricketer Denis Compton.

StJohn and Nicholas kept it clean and polished. I took driving lessons and, to my great surprise, passed my driving test. That car – that leather-seated comfortable purring spacious gracious car, took us backwards and forward across England many times during the next twelve years. It took me and the children and their friends on countless holiday outings, to Brighton and Canterbury, to swimming pools and rivers, to visit grandparents and friends. When once, early on, I grazed one cherished wing on a wall, it hurt me like grazes on my knees.

Outside the cottage on the other side of the road was a triangle of grass planted with shrubs by a village benefactress. It was called The Green, and it was the last remnant of the old village green, the outline of which could be seen on old maps, the church at its head, the smithy to one side, and our two cottages at its end. Gradually it had been whittled away by dispensations from successive lords of the manor to individuals wanting to build houses on it, through the eighteenth and nineteenth centuries, even to the early twentieth, when smart gabled red-brick houses were built for the last retiring groom, carpenter and butler of the local big house. This triangle, though now no more than a space between roads, I felt was precious – though it had taken eleven years of living opposite what was becoming a rubbish repository and dogs' lavatory before it dawned on me that unless something was done it would be gradually eroded away by parking cars.

Looking at it one day I thought "But this is my environment, my business."

We canvassed opinions around it. Some people would prefer a car park, but someone who worked for the council managed to obtain kerbstones and the neighbouring builder lent a cement mixer, and enough people turned out to do the work so that its edges were defined.

In the centre was a lilac, with a variety of smaller shrubs surrounding it. I felt foolish when I first went out and began to gather up bottles, tins and paper, and even more foolish when I took a pair of shears to it, meaning to tidy the side we looked on to. But there never seemed a sensible place

Citroen L15 outside Camden Terrace.

to stop, so I found myself shearing through to the other side. After that I took our sturdy little mower over it, fighting the tufts and bumps, and after a few months of doing it once a fortnight it had become a *green*. When I began planting crocuses a neighbour told me it was a waste of time because the children would spoil them, but that never happened, and people stopped taking their dogs there. Once it was under control, an hour or so a fortnight, and trimming the shrubs and raking the leaves in autumn, was all that was required. The view of the cottage was as much improved as the view from it.

Through an organisation, I heard of an elderly couple needing someone to do their garden, and presented myself on their doorstep armed with tools. This couple taught me a great deal about gardening. Their front garden was high with weeds, but garden plants struggled alongside, and gradually it all took shape again. It was the end house in a council estate, and when you have a proper garden you are entitled to angrily fling back a ball to a misfiring child, or even to confiscate the ball into your hall drawer in retaliation for its trespass. A child who treads a tangle of weeds cannot be yelled at with as much justification as one stepping on a freshly hoed flower bed.

Sometimes I would struggle to listen sympathetically to intimate explanations of my lady's bodily ills and the various medicines she had for them, while champing inwardly to get to work. Sometimes it would be gossip of the endless feuds that went on next door – saucepan-beating and door-banging – sometimes tales of rows, scandals and walkouts elsewhere on the estate, until I was nauseated with the whole gamut of human beings and their messy pointless affairs, in the middle of which were always children, who were always the losers.

The back garden was a small square suntrap facing on to the fields. It was also overgrown, but, taught by my host and hostess, I learnt to produce from it potatoes and peas, beans and lettuces, which excited me as much as them because I had never done it before. My host would sometimes sit watching me from an upright chair. He was a First World War casualty, with only half of most vital organs remaining, fragile and tragic, and yet with a gentle air of nobility. He told me with deep and loving pride about the pair of farm horses that he worked with and cared for before being conscripted into the army.

On account of his disabilities his wife had become sharp-witted. Her man was spoilt, and her bitterness for that shrivelled her mercy towards anyone she felt to be falling down on their job. Life had become a long fight for retribution.

Later on I applied for an allotment – the allotments, later built over, were two minutes down the hill from the cottage. The weed-filled rectangle I was given looked enormous – what scope for the relays of roots and shoots and rosettes and stems! I was filled with excitement at the possibilities. The earth was light and sandy – an easy soil for a beginner – and there was a wide view across the valley to the North Downs, though with rows of council houses in between. It took me some time even to learn to make straight rows.

In StJohn's evening paper we saw advertised a cottage in Somerset, with one acre. At that time we thought of an acre as a huge expanse. I prepared the weekend's meals for the family (labelled, for example, 'Friday supper, 20 minutes at 400 degrees') and leaving the children in Granny's long-suffering care, we set off to see it with relays of picnics in baskets.

It was early spring, and it was raining over almost the whole of the south of England. We reached the place and saw the name painted on a board stuck in the hedge: 'Potato Cottage'. We sat in the car and ate our lunch, finishing as usual with maté out of a Thermos. I doubt if StJohn would have taken to me if I had not taken to maté. We were struck by gales of laughter – it was as much the peculiar freedom of having no children to chivvy as by the absurdity of the situation: the fact that the little household next door was just established, the children at school, my parents in convenient range, and here we were in green and rolling Somerset looking at a cottage at the bottom of a valley with no road leading to it.

We had to leave the car by the sign and walk down a steep little path that in places ceased to be a path and was no more than a series of rocky outcrops for stepping stones. There were primroses in flower and ferns among the stones. As we reached the bottom the rain stopped and sun came out. We walked across a little wooden bridge spanning a stream to where the cottage stood, stone, sturdy and in good repair.

Suddenly there was light and warmth and stillness, like a welcome. Inside was dry and snug. Along the back was a huge storeroom, which I began planning into a playroom. 'Spring water supply', the details said. We found, above the stream bank, in a tiny orchard made fairylike by an abundance of lichen, a hollow in the ground filled with clear water. We splashed it away; magically it filled again. We drank from our hands, sacramentally.

There was no electricity – could we fire a kiln any other way? And anyhow, what about humping clay and finished products up and down that slope? But the feeling of welcome – that vision of the children paddling their way through the summer in that curly stream! We left the place, conquered by it, and on the way home our minds were for the first time unhinged from pottery. We thought about some form of craft using wood, anything was possible.

We should have been ordered back into line – stay in the norm, forget your selfish romantic nonsense, think of your parents, give your children the same as everyone else does – FORGET IT! And the next morning, on waking, those relentless waves of a cold and sensible sea broke over me one after the other. But finally, stretching into daybreak, I basked in the sunlight over that little footbridge, watched the children barefoot and free on the grass, packed up beautiful small creations StJohn had made to take into town.

All fancies!

Still sweating in his office, StJohn attended the auction by phone, to find that others, far richer, had been captivated too. Sometimes in the ensuing months, when awakened for the commuter slog, StJohn would sigh, "Oh, Potato, Potato!"

Earnestly hoping to do the proper thing, we looked at town houses, picturing ourselves joining groups or organisations, being sociable, giving parties, but it felt like dressing up for charades (children's birthday parties excepted – they were special). We had no clear idea of what we aimed for, only a shared feeling – a longing for something green and spacious and productive – and blamed each other for restlessness. Scattered through the years were cottages that we saw, became excited about, then, for all kinds of reasons, dropped. All the time our ideas were changing, a sort of purpose developing.

Dorothy could not have been more kind to us. Sometimes she invited us all to lunch, yet in retrospect I was mean about inviting her.

We never argued, but sometimes I seethed with fury into my diary, with disagreeing words that I could not express. I knew I was disapproved of and never quite up to scratch – which probably I was not. I think we were both conscious of StJohn in the middle, and neither of us wanted to load him with *stuff* when he came home. And I knew I was fortunate in being able to offload a child or two every now and then.

Knowing that she might have been alone all day, StJohn would often go round after supper – children as they grew older were sometimes on their way to bed, and there was peace, quiet, or the televisions. It was perfectly understandable, and sometimes I welcomed the time alone. But if it got late I would bang furiously on the bathroom wall, and I vowed that never would I live next to a married child of my own.

Her caring for Nellie was an amazing achievement which I never properly appreciated. She had a nurse's training, but Nellie was quite a dumpy lady, needing to be moved from chair to sofa bed and back again. Dorothy looked after her till Nellie died, there in the cottage. She arranged the cremation and car, and she and I went together and left the urn in its little alcove.

Our third child, Daniel, was born in the cottage, like his sister. Why, when a good deal of the time I longed for more time to myself, I was so desirous of a third child, heaven knows, but there it was. There was bliss each time I picked him up and held him. He was endowed with caramel eyes and vitality and joy.

At weekends StJohn had been working on the conversion of the loft into a room for Nicholas. At first he had worked both Saturday and Sunday, but we found that one free day to go out all together was essential for all of us. The only thing we had professionally done was the putting-in of a skylight, and the rest of the work took two years. The room was A-shaped, and StJohn built cupboards all along one side and made the bed, low and on castors to pull out at night from the other side. The skylight made it the brightest room in the cottage. He constructed a ladder that stood hooked to the wall at the top of the ten twisty wooden stairs. Nicholas was eight and needed a refuge from his siblings. A fortnight before the baby was due, Nicholas climbed the ladder into his own new room.

StJohn was still working with the same advertising agency; but as a projected partnership seemed not to be forthcoming, he became sporadically sleepless, and would be downstairs into the small hours, standing motionless in thought or covering scraps of paper with figures, preparing himself to start out on his own. This was not popular with his boss, who denied him some holiday pay that was due to him. On an impulse StJohn filled in a Pools coupon – something he had not done before – and won almost the exact sum.

He found himself a little office in Great Newport Street. He scrubbed it all out, and decorated it with the help of one of the artists, who left and came with him. It was white and pale yellow, which was restful to the eye and encouragingly light. Its particular smell, a combination of all kinds of paper and cardboard, became known to the children, for he took each one up with him for the day as a special occasion, to sample London, the office, and even visits to clients.

For a while, near the beginning, Dorothy commuted to London with StJohn to help him in the office by taking calls and messages when he was out, before the answerphone became standard practice. This was a great help to him and I think she enjoyed it. The steadiness of their relationship and her calm approach were always helpful. She came back a little later than he did, when it was less crowded. I have no record of how long this continued.

Briefings of his little team of artists often took place at home, and the children would be interested when they saw book illustrations or newspaper advertisements that they had seen as drawings spread out on our table.

Gradually, by means of conscientious hard work, the business was built up until StJohn no longer had to go out and get work, but to keep up as best he could with work that came to him.

He was more successful than I was. Snatching time at odd moments, chiefly early in the morning, I wrote stories and articles and plays, a novel and a children's book. I sent them here and there, but they always came back, again and again and again. I tried not to go on trying, because the continual rejections were so depressing, but couldn't rid myself of the habit, which stung and buzzed at me like a fly. Paper and stamps were a constant outgoing expense which it seemed I was never even going to recoup. Anger at continual failure made me more angry with my absurd instinct to keep at it. I almost longed for StJohn to seem so fulfilled that I would be forced to find other outlets, other routes, but always when I asked him about 'getting out' he would say, "If we found the right place…"

The cottage was overfull of children. Hugo was born when Daniel was two, in the maternity hospital nearby, and I did not relish the return to nappy days. In order to avoid his waking everyone in the night, I slept for several weeks downstairs in the living room with his cot beside me, and during this time his thoughtful dark eyes and his watchful presence of mind won me over. Even at a few days old he had an aura of intense concentration and wonder. It was so calm, so free in the night, the small low light at the head of my mattress on the floor, and the quiet responsive infant. I had been told that I had not enough milk to feed him, and for the first time in my life mixed bottles, but after three or four days I was able to discard them and manage without. Hugo as a toddler was chubbier than any of the others had been, and all the family fell in love with his cherubic curves, particularly in evidence when he stood at the top of Nicholas's ladder, ("Please, Ikkus?"), requesting admittance.

Dorothy made us the generous offer of her front bedroom, so that the two small boys could have our room. Gingerly StJohn knocked through the wall upstairs between the two cottages, and we passed through what had been her clothes cupboard out into the other room. It was odd to look at the cottages from outside knowing they overlapped.

***

Thick snow, and all six of us walk deep into the woods. We find a clearing where Hugo and I tend a small fire. We admire snowflakes, twigs, tree bark, lichen, while the other three children and their father, in two teams, at opposite ends of the clearing, pelt each other with snowballs, gather piles of ammunition, or dive for cover. Then Hugo and I hand out toast, which tastes as indoor toast can never taste, and we all drink maté round the fire.

There is a place on the North Downs where the beeches grow very tall, and the ruins of their forerunners lie on the chalk. There are also sinewy old yew trees, the flaky roseate trunks patched with areas of exquisite rich smoothness, and the darkness and density of their fronded branches suggest mystery. There is a hollow in the side of the hill, floored with the rich green of dog's mercury. On the slope above, under the long yew branches, lie heaps of flints of all sizes, leached out of the chalk by rain or pushed up by roots. This hollow being surrounded by trees, is protected and sheltered.

There is an aura of ancientness here – the yews, the flints, the ruined beeches beneath their younger offspring – and even when the wind rushes overhead, between the treetops and the flying clouds, it is very still.

We came there one February, in gumboots and thick coats, squelching through the clayey mud of the path, carrying picnic baskets, rug and cushions (we always took cushions – comfort could prolong the enjoyment). We had been there before, and we found the ring of big white stones that had been our fireplace. We took out the leaves that had accumulated in the middle, and went our separate ways to collect firewood, the children knowing what was needed: a pile of little pieces, a pile of larger pieces, and a pile of big ones. As we collected, the atmosphere of the place drew us within it. The white-grey of the sky, the warm grey of the beeches and the hospitality of the clearing included us in the enormous past.

As the fire burnt and the food cooked, the children collected flints and experimented, knocking them rhythmically or randomly against each other, producing sometimes a large flake, sometimes a small point, or a spark. We wondered – had others done just this, just here, thousands of years before?

StJohn artist's agent.

The grey light deepened as we ate, and the fire was a friend. We moved closer to it, using the larger bits of wood to burn, while we set in the embers chestnuts that we had stored in sand the previous autumn. They tasted delicious, in tune with the out-of-doors. We stayed there round the ring of stones and the companionable warmth, talking more quietly as we became an island – a family and a fire.

So many times I walked with small children through the village, through the churchyard and out into the field behind. It was a wide field sloping down to a hedge and some great elms. A stile led to another field, then we would walk across the railway line to the stream, and opposite were the chalk hills with the white scratch of a path, up which again I walked with relays of children. I wondered about the hill and the stream, about the thousands of other feet that had walked these ways through thousands of years.

When Hugo started school, there was all of a sudden a new dimension – it was the first time for seventeen years that there was no child in the house. I began to find out all I could of local history, starting with the happenings back in the enormity of time, when the great sea that covered that area laid down over aeons the white bed that was later upthrust into the long roll of the North Downs, and that now bears (or did when we were there) thyme and scabious, harebells and tormentil, yew, birch and beech, and the black and scarlet berries of the wayfaring tree.

Then there were the cave dwellers of Oldbury Hill, where our children clambered up and down the little rock faces, and where all those centuries ago people probably made better use of wood than we shall ever know. One day a week for two happy terms I caught a train to Maidstone, the county town, and worked away in the archive department of the town hall, leaving my bike at the little country station of Kemsing and getting back in time to cycle from there up the narrow lanes to meet Hugo at the small primary school of Seal St Lawrence.

The more I searched the archive, the more there was to find, and avenues were endless. To me as precious as the contents of an Aladdin's cave were the maps and documents, little tattered lists of names and solemn declarations. I taught myself, with the help of a book from the library, to read earlier documents, and brushed up my Latin. It was like a private treasure hunt, endless, bottomless, absorbing. To find familiar places bought and sold hundreds of years ago, to see the shapes of streets and fields changing – there was a fascination about it, deliciously dry, detached, out of oneself.

Then there were the parish registers and the vestry records, those meetings of village elders that preceded the parish councils. I spent happy solitary hours in the vestry making notes, finding the same names recurring in different lists, the same people on parish relief, bearing children, dying. I followed people taken to the county court for trial, registered in other parishes, walking from one parish to the next and sent back again. Given some pennies to keep themselves alive, and sometimes 'Woman [or man or child] found dead on road.' Finally the parish council meetings, accounts of the first tarrings of roads at the advent of cars with the subsequent nuisance of dust, the first arrangements for rubbish collection and the laying-on of water, and all the efforts by people through the two wars.

But peering over my shoulder in all this delectable work I felt the 'real' historians, the people who really knew that they were doing – for something in me scorned my own amateur enthusiasm.

Sketchbook of Children

When we were digging out some buried sheets of corrugated iron in the garden, we discovered pure-white sand about four feet down. We excavated a wide hole and took out several sackfuls, which later we used in a sandpit for the children. Despite the disadvantages of sand in clothes and shoes, a sandpit is the most scope-full spot for small children, and we blessed that haul of clean silver sand. Through the following years I would sometimes take out a cup of coffee and perch with it in the sunshine on the edge, to watch a child. Each manipulated the sand in their own individual way. For Nicholas it was a world to be sculpted at will into hills and valleys and bridges with routes for his Matchbox cars and lorries. For Joanna it was a medium with which to fashion shapes, some with the hands, some turned out of containers in rows and patterns. For Daniel, the entire bulk of sand must be energetically shifted – to one end, or up into a corner, or into the middle – a mighty and laborious task for a small body, undertaken with great earnestness. For Hugo, it was something to mix with water and pour about, to experiment with consistencies, textures and comparative pour- and build-ability, in concentration so deep as to be tiptoed to and from by a spectator.

***

The last week of the summer holidays. All morning in the garden Nicholas has been working on a tracker-bike, busy with bits of metal. Sometimes barking out a reprimand to an over-inquisitive sibling, or calling for my aid in bringing them to order; otherwise he is absorbed. Hugo sits in the sandpit happily pouring rainwater from one coloured pot to another. Rarely, for that holiday, the sun is shining, and seeing them all through the kitchen window I realise that this is the last holiday of Hugo being a baby, of Nicholas, ten years his senior, being a child. I plan a picnic, for once with them alone and not their friends as well, up on the edge of the North Downs.

We drive along the narrow ribbon of the Pilgrim's Way.

"This road is *good*," says Nicholas – high praise.

We park by a lane and set off with the pushchair and picnic basket.

"Stop – listen how quiet," Joanna says, and we stand for a moment in the delicious stillness. "Our place will be like this," she says – the place that we seek, and that she will never, as resident, experience.

***

One of our holidays included a visit to the farm in Dorset where StJohn had worked for Richard St Barbe Baker. He slowly and thoughtfully worked his way to re-finding it, and we waited while he called at the farm.

The wife (now ex-wife) was living there with a farmer, and recognised him, though not with enthusiasm. He was, after all, from a former phase in her life. But it was agreed that we could camp. Where and on what terms? It seemed a long time before he came back and showed us where we would be, on the very field he had ploughed with the awkward horse, planted and harvested, all those years ago, after the war.

We set up the tent – Nicholas by then had a little one of his own. Being at the top of the hill, we seemed always shrouded in thick mist for breakfast, but would then go down into sunshine, to The Swannery, at Abbotsbury, and to the Chesil Beach.

Here we collected a huge pile of driftwood beside that spinning sea, at the edge of which Hugo perched himself on a lilo and pushed out for a voyage. Fortunately Joanna noticed him before he was out of her wading distance, and brought him back as we cooked lunch (thanks to Joanna, still complete) in our own wild and sunbaked world.

StJohn fixed everything. All broken toys were left for him on the mantelpiece. In the evening he would delve into his cupboard under the stairs, which substituted for a workshop. It had tools hung in rows on the back of each stair, and every sort of item arranged in dense layers back into its deep recess. He would seek out whatever was required and make ingenious repairs, drilling holes in metal cars and inserting wire, sticking plastic and shaping replacement pieces of wood. On coming down in the morning, the children would happily reclaims their belongings.

Sweet Tuesday house, shining clean from all directions.

Granny kindly offers to have the boys while Joanna and I go shopping, but first Nicholas has to be seen off to technical-drawing coaching. He is dismantling a scooter engine to draw its parts for his A-level exam. He comes back firing blithely round on his machine but says something is not quite right. I fret. He goes to the village mechanic to get a little bit of copper. He fiddles. I tell him there is a bus in two minutes that might be more reliable. He fiddles long enough to miss it, and finally putters off.

Sticking to a resolution, I give Daniel one sentence of dictation.

He writes, 'A big lorey is pacd outsid. It is full of barrels of oil.'

His spelling is being ruined for ever by the ITA (Initial Teaching Alphabet) system of learning to read, which is being tried out (with unfortunate results) at his primary school. I set him the corrections to learn, and Joanna and I go to get the bus, because the car has blown a gasket.

She is very pleased to be going, just the two of us. She is totally wrapped in her present moment. She suggests Millets for her jeans. The boy serving selects two pairs.

"They're not Westcotts. I don't like them. They're not very strong. They won't fit. We'll have to try Youngs."

Then silently she puts a pair on. She pulls out the front crease. Looks in the mirror. Turns, pulls out the back crease, looks in the mirror. She stands and looks, legs apart. Turns, twists round sideways, at one with her reflection. That innate dress sense – from StJohn – not from me!

"Can you wash and dry them before tomorrow?" she says.

Next, shoes – the fashionable so-called granny shoes. We have already tried every shop in the town on another day, but as we pass a rather cheap one we decide to try again. And there we find a pair of black lace-up broad-toecapped fairly low-heeled granny shoes. Her bliss knows no bounds. She squeezes my arm with painful strength and kisses the shoebox and clasps her hands in delight at the look of her clumpy little black feet in the mirror.

We run to catch the bus, with our successes.

And the scooter had made it all right. It went better, he found, without the little bit of copper, which he took back to the patient mechanic.

All afternoon I cook and unpack groceries delivered by our Co-Op and wonder if I can squeeze fourteen meals out of what is there. The garden is full of hyacinths. Hugo is full of joy. And it is not everyone who has food to cook for days in advance.

Then there are days when I go on and on doing and on and on doing, and always when I get round the corner of one lot there is another lot of doing, and I think, 'Why do it? Why not buy hot cross buns – they'd probably be nicer? Why bother to make French bread for Easter when it goes even faster than the other? Come to that, why make bread at all? Why not be normal – buy it? And I get scratchy, arguing with children who always want to do the opposite of anything I suggest.'

Only when going to bed do I realise it's not the doing, it's the *being*, and now there's waste ground to make up.

***

I overheard this one-sided conversation after tiptoeing up the ten twisty wooden stairs to check the boys for peace. Somehow I found it reassuring.

Hugo: "Daniel, our Mum and Dad match, don't they?"

Daniel: "Yeah."

Hugo: "Because they're the same, aren't they?"

Daniel: "Yeah."

Hugo: "I like Marga. She's nice, isn't she?" (Aunt.)

Daniel: "Yeah."

Hugo: "Like you and me – we match, don't we? We're the same because we're brothers."

Daniel: "Yeah."

Hugo: "Nicholas and Joanna – do they match?"

Daniel: "Yes, we all do. Goodnight. Let's go to sleep now."

Hugo: "Goodnight."

Nicholas is going to a disco. He wears the latest craze – a tummy-button-length T-shirt with lacing at the top of the front. When he stretches, an expanse of skin is exposed. The girls, he says, tie their shirts up at the back and dance – he demonstrates with an undulation of his middle. He goes off across The Green, thumbs in the pockets of his flares. Twice he turns and waves, for which I am gratified and touched.

***

There is to be an exhibition at Goldsmith's College, New Cross, which Nicholas and the two other metalwork sixth-formers wish to go to. They are going on the motorbike of one of them. Nicholas plans to go on his scooter. I picture him pushing it back from New Cross. It so happens that there is a lecture near here that evening, for which he has consented to usher, so he must be back by five thirty.

Two days ago he and StJohn spent a long evening taking the whole thing apart and putting it back together – almost. The next evening, just as StJohn was coming in, Nicholas appeared black, dripping with sweat and close to tears. He had knocked off some vital corner of the engine with a mallet.

159

On the vital day he works on it from 7 a.m. till school time and sets off with his packed lunch and my prayers. Would that 'chuffeting' green-and-yellow machine really get him there and back?

It does. He triumphantly returns just before five, having been to the exhibition and then ridden up the King's Road over Vauxhall Bridge, round Piccadilly – and back to the school where the lecture is, to directi traffic in the car park.

He has won the school metalwork prize, most of his races in sport and the swimming gala. He retains unsightly fluff down the sides of his face, as the fashion is. But as yet he has made no start on his thesis for Shoreditch – he thinks he will sail in on the wings of his optimism.

He can be gentle and humerous, can be ratty and rude, and frantically explosive when things are awkward – which I annoyingly tend to find funny. He goes quite often in a group to a mental hospital to do voluntary service – once, I know, he had a fit of the horrors at the helplessness, the confinement.

He had literally fought his way to acceptance at the secondary modern after the transition from his prep school. He was teased and mocked as a 'posho', and he found his status by challenging individuals to fist fights – and winning them.

Joanna objects to wearing skirts longer than twelve and a half inches and looks totally tarty. She is maddening, yet enchanting, tries everyone's patience to the last degree and watches their reactions with clinical interest. Why?

She longs for fun, for clothes.

"I want that blouse tight, tight into the waist with long collar and wide, wide cuffs. I can't wear those trousers any more because I like them tight to my legs, then out. If you could alter them I'd wear them."

Sometimes I can still manage to supply her with a blouse or skirt she finds acceptable.

Streaks of sunshine in Daniel. He comes bouncing back from Cubs and cannot be hurried to bed because he keeps thinking of things that he finds irresistible to say and has to stop what he is doing in order to say them.

Eventually he dances his way upstairs, taking my hand and swinging it as he goes and singing, "We'll both – fly – away. We'll both sing – anyway." Then, head upside down on his pillow, he composes, "With a splutter, he fell in the gutter and didn't come out any more." And collapses with laughter.

The younger boys are doing a charade. At least it was going to be a charade but dressing-up took over. They appear with black creases drawn down their faces. Daniel also has black spectacles drawn round his eyes. He wears a tweed sports jacket that would fit Nicholas, knee-length red cotton shorts and a pair of my gardening shoes. A stick is a cigar; the poker is a walking

Joanna with a pet mouse on her hat.

stick. Hugo, in enormous grey corduroy shorts and a fur hat that comes down over his eyes, is Bertie, the pupil at the lecture.

The lecturer points to an invisible map of the world: "As you know, the world is filled by England. Africa is a small place down here."

"No, no," says Bertie from the sofa, "England is this big and Africa is huge."

"Quite wrong. As you know, America is a small spot down here. People in America speak Welsh. Tell me if I put my cigar in my pocket?"

"You put your cigar in your pocket," says Bertie.

"Quite wrong. I would never do anything so foolish."

Noisy and dramatic slapstick as they beat out imaginary flames.

Nicholas's eighteenth birthday. He has been working hard to finish work for his A levels. I've been typing his thesis till midnight, and it is very interesting.

He seldom grumbles, and at last, sometimes, he's able to treat Joanna with a kind of joviality that begins to override the sparring that has frazzled us since she learnt to talk. And he has a place at Shoreditch College not conditional on A levels. He decided on teaching years ago.

***

Joanna went to her first 'real' disco in the village hall, and came back in throes of delight. She went with two friends, both girls, and wore black corduroy bell-bottoms and a mauve blouse. She said they danced and danced – the non-significance of partners certainly lessens tensions. When there was a waltz she and Elizabeth danced round together (so it had been worth teaching her the steps).

September 1972

We took Nicholas to college, and on the way we stopped in the last field before Egham and had a picnic. Aeroplanes growled in a half-circle round us and dropped down to land at Gatwick – a sideshow for the boys. Nicholas was in an amiable mood. After several false trails we found his lodgings – the bungalow of an elderly man in felt slippers with a smelly dog and a parrot that might bite.

We left his belongings, and then went to see round the college, which Nicholas had of course seen before. After that we took him back again to the bungalow and left him walking back over the grass with the kindly-faced old man, a bag of sandwiches in his hand, and his hair wispy on his collar.

***

A week goes by, I enjoy the one-less-area-of-friction, find less of certain things is consumed, and find there is more peaceful time in the evening. I think of holidays that never happened, of gifts I would like to have given, of possessions I would like him to have had by now, of opportunities I wish had been available. And suddenly, strangely and unexpectedly, I am crying and saying, "God bless my son Nicholas, and keep him safe."

It was becoming difficult to get spare parts for the Citroën, which was needing more of them, more often. Things went wrong with it. On one occasion it failed us on a steep curved hill on a main road – after some time a passing police car stopped, and drove us home. StJohn and Nicholas pushed the Citroën home that evening. Another time we phoned for the mechanic who knew and cared for it to come and rescue us. In between times it was out of commission for weeks while we waited for this bit or that, and it was all becoming too expensive. So, sadly, we sold it by the time Hugo started school, and bought a mauve Mini Moke instead, which I never grew to love: but we were actively saving for the move and so used it as little as possible. Petrol at seventy pence a gallon seemed hugely expensive. The allotment was providing many meals and saving more pounds. I would go down to work there early in the morning and be back by six forty-eight, which was when Daniel liked to be woken.

He is absorbedly asleep. It seems cruel to wake him, but he is emphatic about the timing of his routine. A touch rouses him, and he slides out of his bunk. In a few minutes he is doing his exercises, and counting energetically as he stretches his bars. Next he polishes his shoes with equal verve as I lay the table, and he checks his watch to make sure he is on schedule.

***

This discipline was his personal fight-back against bullying that he experienced in the village – a statement of his own ability and strength. (Nowadays parents witnessing that kind of self-imposition are more likely to reach out for 'counselling'.) He did suffer, and from psoriasis, and when I look searchingly at all four of them, across the packed density of those years, I find culpable omissions in our care and concern – the idea that the good times would somehow heal over the bad ones, and that overarching family love and activities of life would carry them through the problems. They carried themselves.

Thinking to benefit Daniel, we moved him (to his initial excitement) from the small country primary school up the hill in the woods to a prep school, but after a week he remarked, "I'd rather work on a manure heap than go to that dump," which was not encouraging. We had to catch up on his tables, and on spelling, – neither was well covered at the primary school. Gradually he held his own, won his races, and began to express himself in art.

We moved Joanna to that primary school from another school, where she was not happy. She stayed there until she moved to the secondary modern. The teaching may not have been brilliant, but it was peaceful and on the whole cheerful. When Hugo started she had already moved on, but I was one of four parents in the rotas transporting five children to and from the village to that school for several terms.

Hugo, on waking, would moan, "Ooh – I don't want to go to school," which I took as a fairly normal state of mind for a child who was perfectly happy occupying himself. He was actually bullied at that little school, and his vindictive, even violent, punching of cushions around the room before breakfast was his repudiation of it.

Joanna meanwhile lies like a honey-and-cream dormouse just capable of opening an eye, and only after a series of taps on the ceiling above my chair (which is below her head) as I give StJohn and the boys their breakfast does she emerge, pink, soft and gentle, sometime after I have waved Daniel off to school, breasting the wet gale on his bike. StJohn, complete with large parcels of artwork has set off for the station before Joanna has managed to decide the details of her clothing for this wet day. She goes off at last with scant time to spare, curls bouncing on her back under the red umbrella.

Finally Hugo and I get ready, Hugo topped rather charmingly by a hat of his father's to keep the rain off. He rides on the back of my bike – another method of saving money until he will be old enough to ride his own. It has taken a little while to adjust to this – during the second week I several times woke in the night with a dreadful feeling of aching limbs, but since the third week it has been under control, and has entered the circle of activities as normal as gardening. In fact it has led to many delights, as the way is through woods not properly appreciated in the years of driving the previous contingent.

Water is over the road, and we enjoy the satisfying whoosh as we go through. Pigeons flap through the rain across the bright- green golf course. The rain enhances all colour: lichens glow sage green; brown beech leaves shine, and Hugo points out the beads of rain decorating the hedges.

It rains all day, and when I go to fetch him the air is clear, empty, liquid as birdsong, and the sky is thronged with clouds of exciting colours. Above the sun, which sends gold rays diagonally down to the tree line, are brown-edged puffs, above us slate grey, ash grey, purple grey, all billowing like a magnificent crowd above the trees. Hugo hums loudly in sheer joy, and homewards is downhill almost all the way.

***

On the way home in the morning I would sometimes push the bike a little way into the woods to collect a bundle of firewood to tie on the carrier, and fill the basket with fir cones. In summer there were lovely opportunities, for I could take some small treat and a Thermos of tea when I went to collect him, and sometimes whatever book I was reading him at the time, so we could sit under a tree and enjoy it, riding back in time for the others who came in a little later. Those were beautiful times.

***

Christmas, and it all went all right. Now it's another 'last Christmas' – a little dazzling melée of rustling paper, fairy lights, cracking nuts, hugs, and the occasional drama. The tree still stands in its box on the lawn, faintly sprinkled with crumbs of silver. My parents came for lunch on Christmas Eve, the ivy along the beam shaking in the warmth of the open fire, candles alight and the cottage looking like a proper cottage, almost persuading my mother, who always said she didn't like the cottage, that it was not such a bad place to live in.

After lunch on Christmas Day, we went for a walk to the golf-course woods. We found embers of a fire still hot and built it up again with twigs. Then we played Rescue – all but StJohn captured, and then as I turned I saw them all released by Joanna and running off silently in different directions – too charming a sight to interrupt.

That evening after the little ones were in bed, Nicholas (on holiday) and Joanna, began to show us how they dance at discos. It seems an odd kind of dancing to us, but there is a rhythm and grace about it. And Nicholas was showing her something, and that was heart-warming – one of the best half-hours. (Sixty years on, Nicholas is still dancing).

***

After a few days back from college Nicholas slowly softens and links up. He goes to a tough job at Marley Tiles, getting up at six fifteen – I get his breakfast, and sandwiches to take. Today he voted in the local elections for the first time.

It has not seemed strange that StJohn suggested their working in the holidays, because my brothers had done so.

***

"Why is it Chooseday?" said Hugo one day.

I said it wasn't Chooseday – it was Tuesday. Monday is Moon Day, Sunday is Sun Day, Wednesday, Woden-god-of-war's Day – but I couldn't remember the origin of Tuesday.

Hugo said it;s Chooseday because they couldn't remember and said they could choose.

***

Pouring rain. Lessons, (sums, dictation and spelling for Daniel; sums (which he loves) reading and writing for Hugo, who is exasperatingly slow at getting to the reading. He comments on the picture, the page number, on how many more pages to do, on how a word would be spelt if it were not spelt as it is – and eventually he reads the sentence. Sometimes I give him a large sheet of paper covered with little sums to keep him amused – and it does.

June – after long and lovely heat, the earth is so parched that it amazes me to find savoy, cabbages and broccoli seedlings surviving at all. The ground is so hard that for the first time ever in this sandy soil I can scarcely get a fork in – and now, at nine in the evening, there is a thunder storm.

The boys, out of bed to relish the storm, lean from the window, revelling in the enveloping pinky-white flashes that switch the roofs into shining slopes, the trees into tossing round waves. They exclaim at the water that rushes along the road with a white frill on its back. They delight in the rumbling thunder.

"I would like to be out in it in just swimming trunks, rolling on the grass," says Hugo, but we doubt if he really would.

The lovely rain falls on the leaves, delicious on the warm earth, feeding my plants, feeding the minds of my children. Joanna finds excuses to run into the garden to see that everything is put away – she loves to feel the rain. Never before having children did it occurr to me that someone might really get struck by lightning.

"Come in, darling – silly to get wet," I say as the flashes show her sharply in a darting run over the lawn.

We are all doing different things and playing records. We put on Los Paraguayos, and immediately they were all movement – heads, hands, shoulders – Hugo and Daniel all energy, Joanna all grace. Then Daniel becomes very busy. He collects together a small cushion which he puts in the middle of the carpet, and some red paper, which he crumples up and lays on top of it. He balances a bit of plastic pipe on a chair, and hangs a small jug on the end of it over the paper. Then he sits cross-legged beside it. He is a gaucho before his fire, brewing his maté. Lovingly planted family lore.

I came back from the allotment to find Joanna feeding boyfriend Pussy with mushroom soup and coffee. The impression is of a young lion, honey-coloured, wild but amiable shagginess, mildly proffering a paw. I was told that his parents had moved house and told him they didn't want him any more. He sleeps in Knole Park or the bus shelter, has been beaten up, robbed of £15, and works on the industrial estate during the day (has a badly cut lip, cannot speak very clearly). What should one do? I don't particularly want to encourage the friendship at Joanna's age, and also don't quite know what to believe. However, we did what we had planned to do, which was to go fruit picking and have a picnic, and we included him. During the day we heard of a childhood in Cornwall as well as Wrotham – both possible I suppose.

StJohn took Daniel camping for the weekend, leaving on the Friday evening when he returned from London. Daniel was like a little silver spring with excitement.

Joanna's Fifteenth Birthday

On the last night of Nicholas's Easter holidays they had a mini-disco, carpet rolled back, records and all dancing. Nicholas has not been home much – he was driving a lorry in Oxford. The entire Oxford traffic was held up for a while as he negotiated a lorry round a corner between two brick walls. He and Joanna worked out a complicated series of steps danced opposite each other like a curious minuet. Meanwhile Hugo performed his own invented dance, quite absorbed, walking forwards and backwards with small steps and nods, in perfect rhythm. His highlight came when Nicholas, picking up what he was doing, did the same, then Joanna, then Daniel, and they were all doing Hugo's dance.

When Joanna came back from school I was playing my new Yehudi Menuhin/Stèphane Grappelli record. She took off her galumphing platform shoes and danced away (fast and enchanting) in her socks.

Re-Cap

5 November. Air sharp and clear, stars pricking through a dark sky. In our strip of garden, a small hooded figure waves a sparkler, his hand at first guided by a parent's hand until he discovers for himself the lines he can

weave, golden curves and circles surrounding sizzling falling stars. He runs about and laughs with delight.

His father, a magician of light, brings forth showers of green, blue and silver, or sends a rocket whizzing on its path until it melts into a sprinkling of stars.

Five years on, and a smaller figure joins the first. Joanna, vying always with her brother, runs beneath the starlight scattering gold dust.

Five more years, and now the garden is opened up to twice the size, and our strip has become a square with a little hill up to the sumac tree. Granny holds the baby, Daniel, up to the window of next door. He traces the path of the rockets with wide butterscotch eyes, wriggles and laughs in her arms.

Two more years and the three children run past the window waving their sparklers for Hugo – intent and solemn he follows the movements of light and figures.

Ten years on – a wet November, starless, and the garden is once again the narrow strip of twenty years before, and the dividing fence partly hides the sumac tree. The big downstairs window of next door is dark. The cottage is for sale. Granny has moved away. Hugo plays apathetically with his sparkler. The two oldest children have moved on, and a larger more exciting party has taken Daniel. Not to attempt the magic would have seemed a betrayal, but in attempting it the magic is betrayed already, for "It used to be all six of us, and it was fun then."

New Year's Eve, 1974–5 – Nicholas is now twenty-two and he and his college girlfriend have decided to get married. It seems to us all an unlikely and ridiculous thing to do. We met her once at the college, and last night he brought her to see us here. She seems intelligent and mature, and they are obviously fond of each other. But we feel we must persuade them to wait. They want to marry in July – but their lives have hardly started – why take it all on? They will have missed out the stage of being both young and independent (as I did).

(And if it had been the nineties instead of the seventies – if they'd hung around instead of doing all the proper things, without the drama of a big family wedding, and moving into and setting up a home – would the relationship have ended sooner with less heartache, an unhappy child, and the dreadful overhanging involvement of sparring lawyers?)

My precious father is in hospital after a slight coronary and last night I dreamed of the front door handle being violently shaken from the outside against the locked door – threat, intrusion.

Moment of Decision

Before he came, our hands were joined.

The morning, though full of normal activities, carried some awareness already, so that when he came in, soon after midday instead of early evening, he was already part of the hour.

He said, "Shall we go up the hill? I've got a bottle of wine."

We didn't keep any drink in the house or go out for it, yet the sense of an occasion was palpable, as if we had spoken of it.

"Get a quick picnic," he said, and went to change out of his city clothes.

We took the car up to a particular spot on the North Downs (a few minutes' drive) that we knew was for that moment. Our previous years, and the ones to come, swung on either side of us – we had reached a balance point between them.

Quiet in the gentle sunlight, with the scent of thyme and our simple meal, how did we know what we knew – that the arduous yet rewarding years of his business life – commuting, navigating relationships and transactions, earning enough to keep us, (the children all at school that day) – and the friendly, busy, committed village life (normality) were to end? That our lives in their parallels of village and city life would rejoin? It was a sacrament of farewell, a christening, and a moment of deep weariness.

We stretched out in the sun and slept, hand in hand, knowing that the journey on the other side of the transition would be hard, maybe long and to the hilt of our endurance. But that day wedded us firmly to the further side, over months, almost years, of seeking – to the fraught, agonised, blissful, enrolment in the new.

***

Hugo's bike is gradually coming together. We found the perfectly sound sturdy frame under bracken in the woods, and now various new additions, newly painted, are hanging to dry. They add to the clutter of the chaotic little room (roughly five metres square): records, record player and sewing machine about, StJohn's tool cupboard open, boots drying by the fire, large folders of artwork ready to take to London, my in-the-making rag rug with bits of material waiting to be torn into strips. Will I ever feel nostalgic for all this? Will I ever live differently?

***

Saturday – we all went into the deep woods to the oldest dump. I was at first disdainful, but became interested on finding a pile of old but solid seven-foot poles ideal for runner beans. And at the back, the oldest side, under leaves, I found a grey-and-white marble washstand top, with a low back, all undamaged. StJohn made a set of straps out of some plastic tubing and somehow took it on his back. The cold wind howled, the black twigs shook, the dark rooks called, as thus laden we fought our way back along the path and loaded the Mini Moke. And more of the marble washstand top much, much later on.

***

Hugo decides he is not going to ride his bike. I have taken him out several times and sat him on the saddle. He marvels at the scenery from that height, but every other sentence is "Don't let go."

StJohn took him out and, when he sat on, gave him a push and let go. Hugo rode – and went on riding.

Daniel and I do spelling, which leads to derivations. I say "'Undulating' – unda is a wave in Latin. Spell 'philosophy' – love of wisdom in Greek. 'Philippa' means lover of horses. Think of hippo-potamus – river-horse. What is the Thames?"

"A hippo?"

Failed again.

Another try: "Spell 'bicycle'."

"B-Y..."

"No, you see, 'bi' means two. So it's a Bi-cycle. So what is a biped?"

"A bicycle with two pedals."

Very logical.

"Actually *pedes* is a foot, hence pedestrian. And we are bipeds. What have you learnt?"

"An undulating hippopotamus is a biped, and a philosopher is a lover of horses."

How to muddle your child.

As I peel potatoes I listen to a terrible story from Joanna about someone who has strangled his girlfriend.

"And he's a very nice boy. I knew him – he helped at the youth club to break up fights. Should we have 'crime of passion' here, do you think? That boy's going to prison and he's not like that. I don't think it's fair," says Joanna.

"I don't think we should. You can't justify things."

(What can we know? What is justice?)

Enter StJohn in the shiny black coat Joanna loves. Enter Daniel at the back door, chilled and balaclava'ed, bursting with affection, hugging us all with joy.

Joanna did well with her O levels, but had no idea what she wanted to do, except leave home. (She does not always get on well with her father.) She was sensible, capable, kind. A course in childcare perhaps?

But meanwhile our lives were not straightforward. Our house- hunting was centred on the West Country, and during many weeks when decisions for her had to be made we were involved with the possible purchase of a cottage in Devon, while also involved with on-and-off arrangements for the sale of the two cottages. She was unenthusiastic about the two possible colleges in Kent.

I sent for details of several Devon colleges and we went through them together. She was not inspired until it came to Tiverton.

"That's the one I like."

(Tiverton is where several of her forbears had lived and were buried – which she had not known.)

Gradually it was arranged. Accommodation was found (the first unsatisfactory, then the next with her best friend and her kindly family).

So she was cast off into Devon. We took her there, and left her there. The Devon cottage had finally to be rejected.

Vision of a Child

I have seen you soaring through time and space.

Golden, fearless and free you have hovered on the
    horizon of the universe,

Alone, glorious and entire you have stormed the
    barracks of darkness and returned in peace.

And in your shell of quiet, curled close, wings
    furled, moon-calm.

10: And Then – Out

In all the years before the move, we thought it would be beneficial to the two younger children, who would accompany us – not only 'getting away from the rat race', but to give them a different challenge and purpose. Doubt about its being beneficial only started in the long months when the search became intense, and Daniel joined with it, experiencing some strange travelling weekends with his father – looking at gone-down cottages on Exmoor for example, and sometimes staying gratefully in the holiday place of some friends. He shared the let-downs, and also failed exams that everyone thought he would pass. Definitely our fault. Equally heart-and-mind wrenching was the process of closing down the business, deliberately over many weeks, maintaining enough activity to keep us going while agonising about how long it would all take, yet without the spur and anchor of continuity. StJohn gradually brought materials back from the office ('keeping everything in case' was his hallmark, which I was often to regret). When I look back, I find sweeps and wells of desperation, rolling black masses that might envelop us, both in the months of uncertainty before the place was found, and again after that, before the move could take place. For Granny had moved away, so we had two cottages to sell.

StJohn saw it first – and said, "I think this is it."

We went together during the drought of 1976, the grass pale and parched as we never saw it again in the next thirty-five years.

We walked down the steep track between the tall trees, and he said, "Come and look at this," and we branched down over a little field on the lower side into a copse of oak, ash and hazel, with a stream flowing along its edge. This convinced me before seeing the cottage – a conviction that remained. The cottage, with five acres, was on the edge of Cornwall.

Before winter set in, Daniel sawed up the sandpit to burn on the Courtier stove as we waited. It had been made from a crate that had carried our goods to and from Canada, twenty years before. I thought of the succession of small brown backs of children who had played in it – our own and their friends

– in all their different ways. Little fragments from all those years were now warming us over this last weekend, as the snow piled gently into the little garden.

It was January and still snowing. We were booked to move on the Monday and there had been some resentments at packing up at Christmas time. It had not been feasible to wait until spring. We moved away from the village where they had all lived all their lives.

It was StJohn who wept, standing on the brick floor of the cottage at the last moment, in the empty room – after its years of capacity fullness. But I was glad to leave. I could not wait for the longed-for experience of our own five-acre space in which to create a whole new world.

We ran into a blizzard over Dartmoor, and the car broke down. Hugo and I, with the cat in a basket, waited inside the totally stacked-up Mini Moke while StJohn stood in the snow and battled with whatever had gone wrong, and solved the problem, and we reached the entrance in the dark.

As we turned in, on to the thick mud of the entry yard of the farm, in flowing sleet, we were handed a five-gallon drum.

"Your drinking water. I'm afraid the water system isn't quite working."

As we bumped along towards the slope of our track StJohn said, "It's all a mistake. We should never have bought it."

This remained his conviction for many months.

We had become friendly with our removal men and Daniel had travelled beside the driver in one of the two vans (something that seems improbable now), which were already outside the cottage. He was tear-stained. The delay had made us late and he thought we weren't coming. He was helping to lift out plants, planks and tin baths into the yard when we arrived.

The main room of the cottage was bleakly lit by a very yellow strip light, and in the smaller sitting room a pile of wet roots smoked in the fireplace. ("I'll have a nice fire ready for you.") The whole place felt extremely damp, which it had not on either occasion we had seen it. Chaos was piled on chaos as both rooms filled up with furniture and boxes. Later the empty vans had to be pulled up the slope by the farm tractor. We slept on lilos on the floor upstairs. The children wept copiously and the cat, shut in the small middle bedroom, clawed the door the whole night.

The water tank, which was in the boys' bedroom, had overflowed the previous morning, the pipes being both blocked and leaking. It was extremely rusty, and had been painted inside with bitumen, which had not worked, as black water had flowed through the boards and down the wall of the main room below. When we had last visited, hot and cold water was running from all taps and the toilet had worked. We kept our coats on inside, and lit our oil heater, which gave out warmth, but added to the moisture.

Fortunately we had brought a plastic and a china potty and toilet paper. I selected a suitable place for a compost heap among dry leaves at the side of the field beyond the cottage, where we planned to have the vegetable garden. We christened it from the potties.

We were able to plug in our electric kettle and so have maté. We had brought plenty of stores and I made sure where they all were through the packing and unpacking. We had loaves of home-made bread, eggs and cheese, butter and jam, cake and vegetable-and- cheese pies, fruit and plenty of our own vegetables and chestnuts for soup and casseroles. There were also such things as sardines and baked beans. We positioned our little fridge and filled it. We did not have to shop for three weeks.

Our electric cooker was in place in the long room outside the main room, but it lacked a particular piece of cable to make it usable, and until the right piece was found we cooked on a fondue set that adequately served the purpose for several days.

We were still having breakfast the next morning when we saw someone coming down the track. It was the driver who had brought the caravan from Kent on a low-loader. He said it would be impossible to bring it down as it would skid all the way. A honey sandwich in his hand (still my blessed father's honey), StJohn went up with him and watched the caravan, spick and span in green with scarlet decoration and yellow wheels, being gently lowered on to the side of the track above the slope, outside the bungalow where lived the farmer from whom we had bought the property, with his wife and three children.

After his breakfast Daniel went and paced out the square on which we planned to keep it, above the vegetable garden field, by a sheltering hedge, and found it large and flat enough.

A builder friend of the farmer's, called Graham, came down to help us. Water came through the hot tap complete with globules of bitumen, but not through the cold taps. Graham made a hole in the plaster and discovered a stopcock. He jammed a wire into the pipe.

Upstairs StJohn tracked where the wire had reached and jammed, and hit the pipe with a hammer. The wire inched forward. StJohn pushed another wire into his end and continued to hit the blockage. A slooosh and rush of sand, cement, bitumen and water came out into the bath on the other side of the sitting-room wall.

StJohn and Graham went round the whole cottage discussing plans. It all seemed possible, even probable, and he thought we could do it inside a year. StJohn became more cheerful. Graham stayed for some soup.

While they were talking we heard a rumble on the drive and went to look. Round the corner came the farm tractor, very slowly, and behind it the caravan. I ran up beside it and there it was, superb on its own gently creaking wheels. The sun shone on its gleaming sides, and it seemed the most beautiful and perfectly proportioned shape that had ever existed.

As StJohn came out it began its last few yards up a gentle slope to its destination. It had to be turned to face diagonally – a fairly sharp turn – and we had never seen the turntable so far round. I thought it would tilt too far, and fall over – that its journey would end in splinters.

The tractor inched forward, paused – and cut out. It had stalled – the battery was finished, and another tractor had to be brought down to finish the job. Gently, gently this one moved into position. Whatever his other faults, the farmer was a skilled tractor driver. He began, gently, gently to pull the caravan round. The huge ridged tractor wheels skidded, throwing up mud. The engine roared, and beneath was the gentle creaking of the caravan, like a wise old voice. Some branches had to be trimmed back. Six feet more, four, two and the wheels were straight again, still whole, despite their look of slenderness. So there it stood in the appointed place, amid deeply churned mud, but level, whole and splendid.

Later we battled to get some kind of order into the clutter indoors. When the children grieved, I chivvied, while StJohn told them he was also miserable, and that it was more difficult than we had realised, but that it would be all right. We heated necessary water in the kettle from drums brought down for us, then we brought out more clothes and blankets and talked of how it would be.

And the next day the sun shone, and we walked about together looking at what was now ours. The snow had melted and there was a great deal of mud and water, but for me it was enchanted mud and water. The cottage stood end on to the bottom of the track, its front and front door facing the morning sun and a square space of about forty feet to the stream and outer field hedge, with a tiny orchard to the right and a laurel hedge (which made a marvellous shelter from the wind that swept along the valley) fronting the leat to the left. Beyond the hedge and the leat was a low meadow bordered by the stream which flowed to the river about 100 yards away. Our boundary, not yet fenced, was to enclose a portion of that field, in the top half of which we planned to make the vegetable garden. Once the mill had existed on the leat end of the cottage – a leat that had been dug from further up the river, turning at a right angle past the back of the house.

***

The upper storey of the mill house had long ago gone, leaving only a large asbestos-roofed lean-to which extended from the lower storey of the wall. Behind the cottage the ground sloped up past the well into a steep field, halfway up which our boundary was to run, joining the lower field boundary beside some corrugated-iron barns and several large oaks.

We walked along the top boundary, looking across at the hills that overlapped each other as literally as in a child's picture book, with wooded combes leading down to the central river valley. As we climbed down a wooded bank, across the track and into the other little field bordered by copse and stream, the boys were stirred from their solemnity (perhaps it would now be called trauma) and began to be excited about seeking climbable trees, and about paddling through and jumping over the stream – to be free within their own acres – and we left them to explore.

We used the fondue set until the third day, when a suitable piece of cable was found to connect up our cooker, and I could give them proper meals.

We positioned two compost heaps, later increased to three, beside the vegetable garden, divided by corrugated-iron sheets, because these, though not beautiful, served the purpose and were about. It was in those first few days, when there was no running water, that we constructed, behind the

The Mill in winter.

laurel hedge, a comfortable 'throne' on which to place the potty and became used to the completely non-unpleasant method of lining it with newspaper which we could then fold over after use and drop on to the compost heap, layered in with other compostable material. It was a method that, in our creed of utilisation, we continued for the following thirty-eight years. Though we had a respectable toilet for visitors, we found we preferred the open air, and it seemed strange that such a simple system, involving no accumulation or the need for disgusting cleanings-out, was not in more general use elsewhere. The resulting compost, which I never needed to turn over, was crumbly, completely odourless, black and full of worms. Now our successors have a compost loo.

After a while we could even use the bath, as there was an immersion heater, though the water was still speckled with bitumen drops as with some exotic oil. But when the boys were in the bath they would talk to us in the next room continuously for reassurance, because StJohn had pulled two dead rats from among the pipes, and might not a live one climb down and out through a hole on to a boy's defenceless body? On one occasion Hugo sat weeping as he washed remembering the clean white walls of the other bathroom.

"I don't care what it's going to be. I'm not talking about that – it's *now*," he wailed.

At such moments my enthusiasm turned to aching guilt.

We set the little Courtier stove we had brought with us against the utterly hideous brick-built and red-painted fireplace of the main living room, and when Daniel discovered an area of yellow clay we dug up chunks of it and stuffed it round the sides. The boys searched about the barns for scraps of dry wood and we tried to have something of a fire in the evenings – the clay helped to stop the smoke coming from the edges. The smaller sitting room to the side was solidly filled with furniture and boxes.

Rubbish was littered all around the cottage and in the copses. Bits of bicycle, bedsprings, jars, tins, china, old clothes, bottles, wire netting, breeze blocks, planks, cutlery, and even tools – some of them useful ones. In the copses were old cars, half burnt, which eventually were removed for us. StJohn made a stretcher from iron sheets with pole handles, and in sessions over many days he and the boys gathered up unusable junk (carefully retaining the usable) and carried it beyond our boundary to a truck belonging to the farmer, whose rubbish it was.

The boys started school, Daniel walking to the main road to get the secondary-school bus, Hugo riding his bike the other way to the primary school. When I visited the schools, and later at parents' evenings, I found them warm-hearted and friendly. The much touted theory of choice in education is not a factor in a rural area unless you are prepared to chauffeur children for many miles, in which case they would meet no one in their own area.

For Daniel, the contrast of his commuter-belt prep school with a rural secondary was a challenge to his personality, and his natural ebullience was not always appreciated. It was tough for him to integrate. The position for Hugo was more familiar, but it was even tougher for him when he joined his brother later. His nature was the opposite of that of his brother, but he fought to emulate his brother's means of self-defence.

When the boys were at school, there were days when we would look at some area of the cottage, start a job and become baffled by some problem, and when the boys returned we would seem to have achieved nothing.

The month 'anniversary' of our arrival was the worst day of weather we had had. There were some phone calls to make (we had had the telephone removed because we had calculated that paying for it would take us outside our budget) and this was the pre-mobile age. As I rode down the hill to the phone box the rain fell in solid rods. It roared and poured and stung my face like needles. It beat into my mac and saturated my trousers so that standing in the phone box I could feel the water seeping up to my waist and had to control the chattering of my teeth. Yet there had been something exhilarating about the ride down – the strength of the wind, the swaying trees, the hill-scapes grim under layers of slate-grey, flannel-grey and silver-grey clouds.

But the cottage was not a cheerful place to come back to. It was dim, battered, cluttered with goods – books in boxes, saucepans in a tea chest, carpets in rolls against walls, windows curtainless, and all the objects seemed to absorb the light and breathe it back in a pall of melancholy. And Hugo with a bad cold lay in bed, his face hectic with crying.

"At my old school – we used to have good games. There were the woods – there was Simon. We used to have fun. I was happy then."

The joy and freedom we had envisaged for them – how had it turned into this cruelty?

The deep cupboard under the stairs was inches thick in coal dust. Under the coal dust was what looked like chicken droppings, and under them the old slate flagstones, very pitted and damaged. The smell of dusty ancient dampness seeped into the room as StJohn, a handkerchief around his nose, scraped and scrabbled the rubbish away.

I counted what the month had achieved: one twelfth of the vegetable garden dug, with Daniel's help; compost bins and cold frame built; a great deal of earth moved from against the back wall of the house in preparation for a retaining wall and herb garden there; many yards of ditches dug; eight square feet of lawn laid; many trees relieved of banged-in nails and barbed wire;

the first few feet of fencing up, with hawthorn and hazel and oak seedlings planted alongside; and there were lettuce and cabbage seedlings appearing in the improvised cold frame.

Fencing was essential as we were continually ousting sheep, about which we complained fairly often. On one occasion StJohn went up ready to fume and found the farmer bottle-feeding a lamb. How can you fume at someone bottle-feeding a lamb? Our exact boundaries were not properly defined, and over the months, totally ignorant of the Land Registry protocol, and interested only in perfecting (as we saw it) what we wanted, StJohn haggled with the farmer (who was either ignorant as we were or simply more interested in any extra payment he could receive from us for small areas and corners here and there). This made enormous complications many years later. Each time we had an arrangement we marked the line, and gradually planted along the line with infant trees to make a hedge. It ran from the bottom of the outside field by the stream, up the side past the barns, and along the Top Field – the planting taking place over the next few years. Ash, and hazel, oak and beech, apple and blackthorn – which is lovely in flower, but constantly suckers outwards.

We had several other people to advise us about the cottage and give us estimates, but they all said different things and had different ideas about priority work, and we realised we had to decide and act for ourselves. StJohn painstakingly considered problems from every angle (until I was in a state of exasperation) and then tended to come to sensible conclusions for reasons I would not have thought of. The resolution of the problem of the relationships between stove, pipes, tanks and rooms was arrived at gradually over several months.

As the cottage sat at the bottom of a hill not much above stream level, the water needed to be directed around it to flow away behind. StJohn broke up the concrete that had been laid close up against the front wall (which was damp) and dug a ditch instead. He channelled the water that flowed down the track away into the leat, and he dug ditches across the track to divert the water down to the stream. We blocked up what had been the back door, facing the track, because water had flowed straight under it into the side room. Each ditch, each decision, each spade-thrust even, was chipping away at the block of the entire project – a shaping-up of the whole. The boys were extremely helpful. Daniel worked valiantly at anything.

To produce food before the money ran out was my priority. The four allotment-sized vegetable plots and smaller seed plots, and the paths, were marked out with posts and lines. There were a great many stones, and we piled the larger ones on to the paths, to be laid gradually as stones accumulated. Much of the turf was chopped into the trenches as I dug, but wherever there was a good smooth square I cut it out and took it over the leat bridge to the 'lawn' outside the house, laying them tightly on the area prepared little by little in advance. This instant lawn gave us hope – it was a great day when there was just room for the four of us to sit on it.

In addition to the chopped turf, there was crumbly black loam of old manure that we found under corrugated-iron sheets opposite the shippen, where there had been a milking parlour. This was a treasure trove.

We were all awestruck by the rainbows. Several times during the first few weeks the curves of the hills and the great slate-blue clouds were overarched by a stupendous sweep of colour, more glorious than we had ever seen before. Rainbows became for us a symbol of hope and beauty compared to our present squalor – a kind of proof of the vast imaginative and creative Power active in the universe, freeing our joy. We would all stop to watch them. Pausing with my spade, mentally on my knees, the rush of happiness would be like the paean of an organ. That we should be here – in this hollow of grass and trees, slopes, stream, barns – even the little house, for all its problems! In such moments I felt that the yearning we had felt for just such a place was not a discontented desire merely for another thing, but a valid travelling towards something we had always been part of. I knew that in spite of their pain and sense of disruption there were deeper, lovelier things that the boys were going through and gaining. And although we did not really know what we would do here or how we were to survive, we had challenged ourselves, our faith in things we believed to be natural and purposeful, and in the ultimate source of all we felt was good. Every now and then (despite StJohn's doubts), in the rainbows, the boys' laughter and their rising to tasks and occasions, in the growth of seedlings and in a host of expectations, there were gleams of something *real*.

In those far-off days of the seventies a butcher used to call at the farm along the road, and I would go and purchase from him there. I walked up the track with the boys on their way to school on a May morning sweet as honey.

Daniel said, "This is the kind of morning that reminds me of camping. I can remember looking out of my window in the other cottage at the roads and the roofs and thinking, 'There's something I want. I don't know what it is.' And now I look round at all this lovely country and think, 'This is it.'"

But Hugo said wistfully, "I don't. I like lorries that go by with such a roar that you can't hear yourself speak, and main roads with lots of cars. I'd like to be able to see a train. When I grow up I shall live in a city with lots of noise."

(And so he did for a few years, and then settled for rural peace.)

I waved goodbye to them and Hugo rode off. The fields were pastel green and brown and there was a warm haze under a light- blue sky. A procession of black-and-white cows filed down the side of a field and ran joyously into the next, while first two then three more figures came from entrances along the lane and joined Daniel, all walking to the busstop.

Overhead a rook wheeled, calling caressingly, "Come and try the sky this morning. The air is a gentle pillow. Come and ride the breeze with me."

And another rose to meet it. A lark began its musical ascent a few yards from me. The wait was not a waste of time.

The well had not only been abandoned when it proved inadequate for mucking out the milking parlour as well as household use, but it had been used as a giant rubbish bin. When StJohn talked of restoring it, I begrudged the idea of spending time on it when the cottage needed so much work, and I did not at the time appreciate how useful if would be, or that a well is as much a feature and part of a place as plots and paths and trees.

At first they hooked out the rubbish – a mixture of metal and wood, stone and cloth, including piles of black-stained towels and curtains that we suspected had been used in desperation to mop up the cottage on the day we arrived. Then StJohn stood on the rubbish and handed it up to Daniel in or on a bucket. As the level went down, he tied a rope to a birch tree that stood a few feet from the opening, climbed down it, and eventually sat on a piece of wood in a loop at the end of it. Daniel lowered a bucket down to him on another rope from a second convenient tree at the top, pulled it up and emptied it. StJohn would pull himself up, with the help of his feet against the wall of the well.

After the first effort he and Daniel were more or less prostrate for a day or two, and he was fighting to keep desperation away, while my guilt was directed also for Daniel. They decided to do it just once a fortnight.

The lower he got, the nastier and smellier did the rubbish become. His hips would be sore from the rope, and his throat from the foul air, but they bravely persevered. At last, thirty feet down, he found himself on a stone base. He stood in his boots on solid rock and could see clear water seeping slowly in. And how many bucketfuls Daniel had heaved up over the weeks, how many stretcher-fuls the three of them had piled and carried away, I hate to think. StJohn scraped the sides of the well where he could, and they emptied several more buckets of dirty water. Then the top was covered with a large slate and it was left alone for two years.

At the end of this time the water was clear, and we found that even in the height of summer it would be over half full. StJohn tied a not-too-large bucket to a rope and we learnt to drop it in such a way to fill it for pulling up. We used it for our drinking and watering for all livestock later.

A May evening, champagne light over the hills. Daniels sits on the ground modelling a head from some of the yellow clay. We are also using it mixed with stones to fill some of the holes in the track. Challenging and strong, the sounds of Britten's violin concerto come through the open window. There is a feel of summer. The growing lawn threatens to become a meadow, and all around is billowing greenness that might grow altogether over us, a flood out of control.

It was a blessing that we met Pat and Hilary. He helped us with the track, and both floor and roof tiles, and she knows about wildlife and remains a valued friend. It was with the help of another neighbour's low-loader, and Pat's know-how, that a load of suitable old slates was brought down for us, and he and StJohn, with his application of ladders and planks, were able to strip off, insulate and retile. Later the precious bats re-emerged as usual.

The haystack.

Roof rebuilt by StJohn and neighbour Pat.

11: Towards Completion, With Subtractions

Apple blossom was a feast to the eyes in the tatty little orchard, many of the trunks damaged by the horns of cows that had been allowed to wander in. By June, we had some vegetables. On wet evenings we all went out and collected bags of enormous black or brown slugs and later loosed them into the stream from below the vegetable garden.

Around us hay balers clackety-clacked in other people's fields and our own grass was thick and tall. It seemed a right idea to cut it even though we had no animal to eat it. A neighbour kindly lent us an Allen scythe – a heavy and noisy contraption that spent more time being taken apart in efforts to make it work, than it did in cutting. Its vibration and the efforts to manoeuvre it were exhausting. The three of them pushed it all the way back up the hill to where it had come from and the farmer at the top of the track cut all three little fields in about an hour and a half.

Adorned with rows of bright hay the whole place looked cherished and in proper order. But we had to learn how to turn, gather and stack it. On a blazing day we worked in the Top Field. There was a breeze up there and the scent of grass was delicious. Like so many other tools, there were excellent hay forks and rakes in the barn. StJohn shuffled the rows over very fast with a wire rake. We tried the forks as well and the boys worked nobly – but Hugo found it tough.

In the bottom field there was no breeze, and we thought, 'This is intolerable,' but there was no escaping it. The weather held, and over several days, turning and re-turning, all of them bronzing by the hour, it was done – or almost done. Another small section was left when the rain came, and we went indoors soaked and shivering. When we uncovered the last load we had piled we found it dusty and musty. We spread it again, shook it out and then stacked separately that which had lost its sweetness – but none was wasted.

August. After a stay with friends in Kent, Daniel was homesick for both, and StJohn decided on something new to undertake: we would take down the red-brick fireplace in the living room. We cleared the room as best we could, took out the Courtier stove, and covered everything else with dust sheets. Then StJohn attacked the bricks and the extremely hard cement that bound them together, with a cold chisel and various iron bars. There were twenty-two rows of bricks in fancy steps up to the ceiling, and in the middle was a fireplace sixteen inches deep and a foot wide. We carried out the bricks and cement in buckets while he levered and bashed, and the red screen gradually disappeared to reveal a mass of large-size breeze blocks, heaped together rather than built up. We gradually lugged them out as well – as a great stone chimney space was gradually revealed. After removing more rubble we could all stand in the square space and see daylight at the top of the stone tower above our heads. An iron bar was fixed across at about seven feet up. We hoped it had been for smoking flitches of bacon, but it may have been put there as a support at a later date.

On one side was a slightly frayed small metal door. After some work on the hinges it opened to reveal a dome-shaped clome oven, cracked, but not smashed. The whole dimensions of the cottage expanded for us that day.

Above, in front of the fireplace, was a hefty seven-foot-long beam. The fireplace was not central to the room, but in one corner – the clome oven was inside the wall next to what had been made into the bathroom. We wondered whether the reason the chimney space had been stuffed with blocks was that it was liable to collapse, and StJohn put a prop under either end of the beam in case. It had many splits in it, which he was convinced grew wider every day.

We built a fire on the hearth that evening, even though it was summer, and waited ceremoniously for the moment of glowing warmth. The flames gathered and shimmered and the cottage seemed full of magic. Who had last made a fire on that hearth? What had been cooked there? Had a great iron pot hung from the bar? Were there children and was there storytelling, the flames flickering on the stones and on the slate floor? The black chasm of the chimney was lit by the flames as they reached back into it and upwards through that beautifully shaped funnel. For a short while the magic held – but then our eyes began to smart and we realised the whole room was full of smoke. We tried opening the door or the window – this door or that door – and on subsequent days we tried with different wind directions, and with a cowl, and with variously inverted slates on top of the chimney but it was no good. To light an open fire was to be smoked out.

Shopping days stretched from two weeks to a month now that we had vegetables. We still had no freezer. We were able to buy milk from the farm at the top. I'd always made bread. StJohn, going out shopping with Daniel, roared the Mini Moke up the track without pause, to the top. To pause meant backing down to start again.

Daniel and Hugo in the woodyard.

A school visit to The Mill.

Hugo with a dragonfly.

The wall of weeks building.

StJohn and brother-in-law at sitting room fireside.

(My father, driven up on one occasion, arrived at the top pale and shaken and remarked, "You have to have courage to drive up there.")

Meanwhile Hugo and I took sandwiches to a special little corner, and he showed me the village he was making under the big oak trees, with roads, fences of tiny sticks, and little houses. Every time StJohn did any cementing Hugo would gather up the crumbs to make his roads. He was sweet and peaceful like the day. He told me that he had seen two lovely things as he rode back from school the day before – a double rainbow, and a white owl on a post.

"It looked at me, and it was so beautiful."

Later I stored the provisions, wanting them to last forever, and prepared supper to the music of Maxwell Davies, wild and glorious. The mist was creeping up from the river across the garden, making us an island of laughter and revelry.

We found another builder to help us along, and he came and took away the ugly square of red bricks that had been built on top of the small chimney at the other end of the cottage, over the room now a storeroom, one day to be a sitting room. He mixed a load of cement – and then it rained, and he went away and left it. So all day long StJohn cemented the inside of the big chimney we had opened, filling cracks, pushing small stones into holes – and lying flat inside it, he also repaired cracks in the bread oven.

So the next day was special because the great chimney no longer looked as if it would collapse, and we decided that the splits in the beam were not getting larger. And because, after long dry days, the seedlings of sage and hyssop and lemon balm, which had stood making do with watering, had stretched their little leaves up to the rain and changed into baby plants. And because now, in the cheerful wind blowing clouds across the sky there was a new breath, a hint of something entirely different from what had been current, there was a suggestion of winter's closure, the silence of frost-grip.

On this day I worked under the oak trees above the vegetable garden, where there had been an old barn. We had pulled away layers of collapsed galvanised sheets, old planks and decaying beams, and beneath was a mass of ancient horse manure. After it was uncovered there had grown a host of the most delicious mushrooms. This was a magical happening – and I say magical not because it was unnatural that mushrooms should grow from old horse manure, but because it is one of an infinite number of things that no amount of recounting of cause and effect (which is all that scientific explanations are) can diminish the marvel of it. You can describe the physics of the rainbow, but that explanation does nothing to explain why the laws of physics should exist in such a way as to result in a rainbow, or why the loveliness of a rainbow should call forth such delight, or why mushrooms coming unbidden can be so utterly beautiful, and utterly delicious. At about this time Hugo, who himself had a streak of magic, became acquainted with a robin so tame it would perch on his hands, and on his head.

∗

One evening we took our maté into the garden and sat in a row facing the house on the new square of lawn. I was reading aloud – I think it was *The History of Mr Polly*. It was a soft, gentle evening and twilight began sliding down the hill towards us.

Someone said "There goes a bat."

I looked up as another swept out from under the porch roof and wheeled over our heads. Eleven emerged at intervals of a few moments, some from the porch, others from under the main roof – a battalion of tiny lives dwelling with us, flicking over the house, round the trees, across the darkening sky. They remained as companion-residents over the years, even after the roof slates were removed and renewed.

Part of our bedroom ceiling collapsed on us one night – we propped it up by a sheet of cardboard on a post until it could be done.

"I don't believe there are curtains that pull," Hugo said gloomily as we hung the rug on its nails over his window and said goodnight.

But his room was the first bedroom to be finished: gleaming white walls with a board for posters, blue floor and blue curtains on a bamboo runner.

It took an hour to dig one row across the garden in front of the cottage in preparation for a lawn, and each row produced a barrow-load of roots and half a one of stones, some quite usefully large. A perfect wild garden was already there – eight-foot-tall thistles, burdock full of bees, hogweed, dock, and a mass of nettles, all being wound and drawn together with long strands of bindweed that gradually enveloped the lot. There was a conflict between the part of me that wanted it wild and the part that craved structured order with space to put in what I wanted. But now the goldfinches that used to come to the thistles cluster on the teasels and the coal tits that ate the burdock seeds now pluck out the seeds of centaury. One morning, looking out at the weedy space that would be a herb garden, I saw a dozen yellowhammers, bright as celandines, finding something they liked, but I have never seen them here again.

When the whole space was dug over it was possible to draw out a plan and mark the spaces out with sticks – a big half-moon island bed with a path beside it. Because of the winter bogginess, which we had experienced, a path would be essential – but it would have to be made of what was at hand, as carefully as possible. Into the double-dug and composted space of the flower bed went minute plants grown from seed that made no immediate difference and had to be regularly cleared of weeds. The latest turf strippings could now be laid against the curved edge.

Blackberries were everywhere. We picked into a bucket those for bramble jelly and a small bowl for 'specials' to layer with a little sugar for supper. I also made blackberry and elderberry syrup, which was delicious with sponge puddings and, diluted, for drinks. When the hazel nuts ripened we gathered them as well. The ones we had brought with us, in sand, had stayed good till we finished them in June, and we began storing this new harvest. Sad to say, since that time the grey squirrels increased to such an extent that we could no longer gather more than a few hazel nuts – and we felt guilty at taking those few from the dormice, nuthatches and wood mice. We had dozens of hazels. Not only did the squirrels increase in number, but they became far more destructive – they stripped the trees, dropping broken shells long before they were ripe as if they had somehow become nature's idiots. The test of any fruit's ripeness is when a blackbird takes it. But the squirrels also stripped off hawthorn berries, splitting some of the seeds, which they rained down around them in a manic and infuriating fashion – something they did not do before.

They also destroyed our trees, particularly oaks. The Long and Short Copses running either side of the track became largely populated by broken-topped oaks, having been debarked. We planted three scarlet oaks – one in particular did well. But when it was fifteen feet high, the trunk about eight inches across, it was entirely debarked from the base up to three feet, and subsequently died.

Any so-called animal lover who defends the grey squirrel has no care for the countryside or its truly native wildlife, flora and fauna. We killed them when we could.

Our neighbour at the top had offered us wood from a copse he was planning to cut, and StJohn set Daniel to bring in ten trees a week. Now I am appalled and ashamed when offspring get paid, or otherwise rewarded. Then, it seemed a challenge for him to be proud of.

We tried to keep Sundays different and special, unless there was anything essential to do, such as haymaking. We had long chatty breakfasts and picnic lunches, the boys doing what they wanted. Daniel was constructing a cabin beside the stream, with a little stone chimney built up from the hearth. Sometimes we walked by the river – the boys trying to persuade StJohn not to load us all with wood to carry home. It was not always easy to cope with being physically tired, for we were still developing the strengths we needed – and life was not predictable.

October began as an Indian summer, but left us in a sea of mud. A vigorous wind hurled itself down the track like a coach and horses galloping through our trees. The three of them were gathering up apples in the orchard – I was longing to go out, but cooking. When they came in, glowing, with a great basket of Bramleys, I had finished, and went out to imbibe the wind and the night, to stand by the big oaks and watch them in movement so wild that the pliability of such large branches seemed incredible. Birds must crouch low in sheltered places on such a night.

In December we bought a second-hand Rayburn. It was brought down the track in a van, rolled into the cottage on metal pipes (luckily there were no steps) and placed under the chimney beam.

A plumber came, bringing us a new lavatory and yards of copper and plastic piping. We had finally decided to make the central room into a kitchen/living room complete with sink unit and cupboards, so that the pipes had only to go from the stove and sink through the wall beside the bread oven to the bathroom, where the hot and cold tank would be. Again the cottage resounded as holes were banged through the stones of the walls. At last the pipes were all in place – water ran away through them, and the Rayburn would heat the water. There was only one problem: the Rayburn was slightly in front of the chimney space so that I would not hit my head on the beam every time I looked into a saucepan, and this meant that the cast-iron flue pipe, which rose from the stove into the chimney through a metal sheet overhead, had to be set at an angle to the stove. The plumber had brought an elbow pipe, but the angle was too acute and it didn't fit into the flue pipe anyway. When he discovered this fact the plumber lost interest in the whole affair and began packing up to leave. We followed him about, trying to discuss the problem and holding up the catalogue with pictures of other pipes. But it was no use – for him the bell had rung and he was off, with such haste that a tin of glue on the back of the van tipped over and poured out as he roared with necessary speed up the track.

We came back inside. The new pipes round the stove gleamed efficiently in the cold room. Above the Rayburn the flue pipe disappeared up the chimney – with a half-moon gap between its base and the stove top – this half-moon was the difference between function and non-function, between warmth and cold. StJohn had put his back out the day before and could scarcely move. He thought of bits of metal he had in the shed – I went out and picked up the things he indicated, because he could not bend. When the boys came back from school, Daniel and I supported the pipe while StJohn, sitting on a chair behind the stove, sawed and snipped at bits of metal. He put them in place supporting the pipe and covering the gap, and smoothed it all off with fire-cement. The boys fetched in twigs and logs. At nine o'clock we lit the stove, and I set a saucepan of water on for maté. After a while we turned off the oil heater, never to be used again, and never used the electric cooker again either. Suddenly the cottage was alive – it had a heart once more. The children kept getting up from the table to touch its warmth, and its shiny front rail.

More waiting then. If StJohn came down and sat in a chair he got stuck. It took some weeks to master the Rayburn and understand how to get it hot, or rather (for someone used to electric cooking) I learnt to give it time. You could not come rushing in, put wood on and expect heat, and I seemed to spend long hours into the evenings reading aloud while supper was cooking. Daniel brought in his ten trees a week from the copse and he worked like a beaver at the sawing, taking turns with Hugo. This meant that much of what we were burning at the time was green wood, which did not give out so much heat. One day I was chopping up small pieces when a chip flew up to my mouth, splitting my lip. I sat in the woodyard holding up a bloody handkerchief. My tongue fitted into the split, and I thought I would be harelipped forever. When I finally went in StJohn wept at the sight of it, but he fitted across it a strip of plaster with such skill – instructing me not to smile for a week – that it healed almost invisibly.

Waiting. In the stillness of Sunday morning, waiting. And I was afraid of the time, of the Nothing, of the pain in the back, of my own purpose faltering, of the boys' discouragement, of Christmas that is not Christmas, and of next year.

One day, when the ground was frozen solid and the heaps of stones waiting to be laid as paths were as immovable as though cemented, I read to StJohn the whole of the book of Job. It voiced so much for us.

> I am made to possess months of vanity and wearisome nights are appointed to me – I am full of tossings to and fro into the dawning of the day. When I say my bed shall comfort me you scare me with dreams and terrify me with thy visions.

We became aware of Job, struggling, oscillating, exasperated both with his friends and with his own searching and longings and pain, one moment reaching out his heart and his hands for help, the next hiding his face in hopelessness. Then came Elihu, daring to speak after his elders, pointing out a more positive, more hopeful way, not the punishment of evil but the helpful love, the power and the beauty. And finally the voice from the whirlwind, commanding only that we stand still, look up and out, that we acknowledge, that we begin again, that we gird ourselves in whatever we can understand of that majesty and wholeness, accept it, presently.

Nicholas and Dorothy.

Standing beside the trusted Rayburn.

Dorothy at The Mill.

We unearthed the Christmas decorations and hung the row of gold and silver bells (made from the once current milk-bottle tops) along the beam. They swung and tinkled over the Rayburn as they had along the tidy white mantelpiece of the other cottage. Out came the red paper lanterns, paper chains, crackers and cut-outs that the children had made over the years. StJohn, gently mobile, caught a spark and began fixing sprays of berried holly across the walls, with silver stars and tinsel. He knelt stiffly down and wrote 'HAPPY CHRISTMAS SILKIE' on the cat's box.

We were waiting for Joanna to come – ("Why do you always flap? Coaches are always late!") – and she appeared. And that evening the three of them performed a crazy not always complimentary and impromptu charade, which held us in long minutes of laughter more nourishing than the turkey. Daniel, five years younger, had grown taller than his sister. I was glad we had the tree and the little bells cheerfully clicking over the fire. I ached for the circumstances that we had never intended, whereby she was so far from us – the irony that had put us in Devon just as her training in Devon ended and she began her first job, in Surrey. She was the one left most in limbo by the move, which had been planned so long to bless us all. The guilt for this would never leave me.

The very depth of winter came in February, the ground wooden-hard under days and nights of frost and then beneath successive falls of snow. The transformation of every copse and corner of the fields was magical. Hugo and I went down to the river, where sheets of ice bordered the banks, and here and there were ice-flowers and ice-bottles built around the ends of trailing twigs and brambles. We skidded stones over the ice, and listened to the crisp squeaks as he tested the edges with his foot.

"It was a lovely time by the river," he said as he got into bed.

The water pipe froze, which meant that as no water was coming into the system we couldn't use the hot taps – instead we had a six-gallon iron pot (hauled from a Kentish dump years before) on the stove, filled with stream water, and collected drinking water from the farm. No baths.

The cold of the rest of the cottage and of outside was like a pressure, reaching and touching. In the contrast of the one warm room with the rest, in the relentlessness of the cold and the earth's hardness, I could perceive what it could mean to be helplessly in its grip and unsheltered without respite. We have wood we can saw and chop each day to fill the baskets, but I can see how it would feel if the room was still the dead shell of walls, floor and ceiling, heartless. Each morning I rekindle the stove, listen to the crackle, and hear the steady hum of its draw through the pipe and into the big chimney; and when I go out to the woodyard, smoke streams comfortingly forth, scenting the air.

'All Devon roads closed.'

'Roads blocked half an hour after snow-ploughs.'

The pipe finally thawed, but then the power went off. In the mellow light of a little oil lamp I luxuriated in a lavish hot bath, listening to the roaring of the wind. Schools were closed, and the snow had drifted against the top gate so that we could walk right over it.

We tobogganed down the top field, on plastic bags slightly filled with hay, which ran faster than the narrow runners of our sledge. You could go either long and slanting or short and fast. StJohn usually ended upside down among the bracken of the copse at the bottom like a stranded beetle, needing to be pulled out by the boys.

It rained all through March and the ground was so sodden that nothing would germinate. I had enlarged the cold frame and filled it with pots of what I'd hoped would be early vegetables. But, on looking into it one morning, three pairs of bright mouse eyes looked up at me from among tumbled pots and a mound of neatly shredded newspaper that had covered them. We fetched the cat and opened the frame – the mice ran off; the cat, switching its tail, stalked off in the opposite direction. Not a seedling remained.

The boys went back to school, and suddenly Hugo was in top form, bright and keen, almost adoring his food. And while Daniel still thought of Kent, he was going out skate- boarding with his friends, went off in coaches to play in school football matches, and was cheerful about sawing wood.

We were offered a Devon Red cow that had lost her calf. StJohn went up to see her, and watched her large bulk being manoeuvred into the barn. He thought of that weight on our fields, which were either sloping or inclined to be wet, so we turned her down. But we set up the marble washstand top (from the Kentish dump) across the end of the side room, and StJohn partitioned off the room as a larder. We also partitioned part of the barn as a loose-box. I filled a rubber glove with water, pricked holes in the finger tips and we all practised milking it – StJohn, having milked before, had no trouble. On the morning when StJohn walked up the hill to decline the offer of the Devon Red, a frightening thing happened.

Ditcher

We often heard the rolling heavy sound that preceded the roar of the tractor's engine when it was being bump-started down the top of the field above us. It always alarmed us a little because the hill was steep and our cottage was at the foot of it. So we tended to look up when the rattling started and the engine would start before the machine appeared over the hill. The fence was stretched across the middle. This happened because our neighbour did not believe in having charged batteries in both the tractor and the ditcher.

One day we heard the usual noise and looked up.

Hugo said, "Look – it's the ditcher."

The rolling was turning into a roaring clamour and I came to where he stood at the corner of the house. The ditcher was rolling and rushing, banging and clanging down the field. It ripped the fence, reached the belt of young trees, forged on down amid smashing greenery and clanked down on the other side of the track, where we lost sight of it. It had taken four or five seconds to come down and had stopped at the side of the stream. The farmer and his father were running after it.

Hugo's face was white, and I was in a peculiar dream of fury and shock.

Daniel had come behind us and was yelling, "Bloody marvellous, isn't it – bloody marvellous!" at the top of his voice. There was a welter of smashed trees along its path and I was crying for the trees and the boys' terror.

I sent Daniel to fetch his father back from the other farm – he had heard it and suspected the event – as our neighbour stared at the smashed-up front of his ditcher. It had been parked, as always, facing the hill. Someone had come to overhaul it, and got his hand caught. In the process of extracting it and going to attend to it the brake had been left off. Both parties were terrified and chastened.

It was Hugo who first realised that a half-inch difference in the angle of the steering wheel would have brought it across the space by the well, over the herb garden and on to the kitchen and sitting room. It was this that froze us later, kept StJohn awake and re- upheavelled all his doubts and guilt. But the route the ditcher had taken was merciful to us.

After flattening the latest sections of my hedging line it had (vitally) veered a little to the right after crossing the trench ready-dug for our water pipe. The bucket being down, it held a straight course, riding over the tree trunks of the copse.

We all began the therapy of carrying the broken trees to the woodyard.

***

We replied to an advertisement in the local paper – for a two-year-old Jersey heifer, in calf.

The vehicle was opened at the top of the track and the little cow emerged. She promptly escaped between us all, careered across our neighbour's field and stood proud as a deer on the hill, her rich winter coat shining in shades of brown from black coffee to auburn. She had been running free in the field for the two years of her life, and it was some time before we managed to coax her into the barn, having been advised to keep her in for a week and get to know her. We left her with hay and water, but as we walked away there was a clacking of hooves as she jumped clean over the three- foot wooden barrier into the other half of the barn. We shooed her back and added another bar.

Each day we talked to her, cleaned up around her, and admired her. As our three fields were unfenced we planned to tether her, Jersey cows in Jersey being traditionally tethered. We had ready a fifteen-foot chain and a metal post about two feet long, and at the end of the week we drove the post into the ground in a sheltered corner of good grass by the woodyard. We put on her halter and drew/dragged/shoved her towards it. We spent most of the day sitting on logs in the woodyard watching her – how she ate, how she moved with the chain, how she responded when we talked to her, how she got up and lay down. We brought our lunch out and went on watching her almost till supper time. Then StJohn took her back to the barn, by main strength. She plunged and pulled in all directions, and I was very nervous of her tossing hooves. Hugo christened her Betsy. We had a pile of fodder beet proudly harvested the autumn before ready to be chopped into her manger each day. We had two-year-old hay for her bedding, and the previous year's stack for her food. She was due to calve in June, and this was April.

I had never seen a cow calve, and was amazed to see a pair of small white hooves dangling out like something that was there by mistake. But then, after it was born, and after a long moment of utter stillness, it was a marvel to see the first quiver of life in the seal-like wet body on the ground, and the agonisingly slow but insistent process of its repeated efforts to rise, approach and feed. Lovely also was the new soft call that Betsy made, even while it appeared that she moved away every time the calf got its mouth near enough to suck. But its hunger forced it to try again, and again, until the udder looked at bursting point, and there came the supremely satisfying sight of the still cow, with the suckling calf leaving little puffs of white froth on the grass below.

Milking was no simple matter at first. Betsy was young and restless, we (I in particular) were inexperienced, and we frequently felt like throwing the spilt bucket at her head. I would milk in the morning and StJohn in the afternoon. A cow on the place had the same significance as the stove inside: she made a warm hearth/heart – a centre and purpose to the fields. And the milk was so delicious – quite different from the farm milk, not only in its richness, but in the loveliness of its flavour. And we began to make cheese. First curd cheese, then 'Cheddar'.

StJohn built the chicken house on the end of the barn, using mainly wood that had comprised a chicken house up in the field, which we took apart. The idyll of chickens pecking about free is unrealistic here, for two reasons. The first is the destructive effect of chickens on a garden, on lawns and edges, plots and beds, and the second is foxes. They came and collected their lunch while we ate ours in the garden, and thus we lost our first precious trio of North Holland Blues – we arrived a few seconds after the last squawk. So we built a proper run with six-foot-high netting, which became a double run so that one can be resurfaced with weeds and grass while the other is in use. We started with Warrens (after the loss of the expensive North Holland Blues) and gradually built up a flock of Marans, which returned to their broodiness in their third generation. Then we had eggs, cheese and milk, fruit and vegetables.

One year I costed out the shop value of vegetables against the price we paid for seeds and sundries. We found that the bills were paid off by April.

Cheese production slowed down and we started to eat the first of the crop. They were very good – sweet, golden and firm. The making of cheeses is simple.

Dear cow.

Milking.

The cheese cabinet.

We put the enamel preserving pan on the cool end of the stove with two gallons of milk in it – I suspect that the logic of English measurement was that a gallon of milk made a pound of cheese. (If there is anything as logical about litres I have not found it out.) Whoever is inside when it is lukewarm, or just over, stirs in a teaspoon of cheese rennet in half a cup of cold water. Books recommend something called 'starter', but it does not seem to be necessary. The milk soon sets to a junket and is cut into columns, and then horizontally into squares, with the stirrer. For the next hour it needs to be stirred every now and then to keep it broken up, and the cubes shrink, until they squeak when you bite them. When they were all just rubbery I would fasten a muslin square across a bucket with an elastic band and strain the whey through. I then gathered the edges and tied it tightly with a string hooked under the marble shelf in the larder, and left it till the next day.

When unwrapped, it is a beautiful ivory-coloured bouncy substance with a completely wholesome and delicious flavour. It has then to be pulled apart and crumbled finely (a good finger exercise), and a scant tablespoon of salt was stirred in.

***

You could buy, at a price, stainless-steel cheese moulds, but we used sections of six-inch plastic pipe about eight inches long, lined with a pushed-in circle of old sheet into which the curd was packed layer by layer, and pressed down and around, down and around. At an even higher price you could buy cheese presses. But we sometimes had three or four cheeses being pressed at the same time. StJohn perfected a system of pressing by breeze blocks, at the side of the orchard. A slice of a tree exactly the size of the mould, called a follower, was set on the cheese, which was set on a block a half-block on top, and another was added each day for three days. By the fourth day the cheese was ready to be taken out, greased, wrapped in muslin and stored for at least six weeks, though it would keep till spring.

If the nourishment for your soil consists of compost, ash and leaf mould, all of your vegetables and most of your fruit will be free. It is surprising how little money you can live on if your tastes remain simple. As I read somewhere, 'A man is rich according to the simplicity of his needs.'

I watched the three of them in the courtyard below the window. Daniel was now a fraction taller than his father, as Hugo was to be in a few years, though now he was still, for a little longer, a child. I couldn't hear the conversation, but Hugo was looking wide-eyed from one to the other. In a typical gesture of goodwill, Daniel thrust his hand across on to his father's shoulder and said something, head thrown back, and they all laughed. He was everything golden-brown and caramel. I believe he was telling his father of his plans to leave home, and bowls of strawberries and cream made not one iota of difference. He had been working on a building site in the holidays, saving his money, and while I tried to arrange for him to do his A levels locally (at that time the school did not undertake A levels, so pupils moved into various other colleges) he hitch-hiked to Kent and arranged not only to do them there, but his own accommodation at his old prep school, in exchange for some work in and out of the house. I knew only too well the pressures that drove his action, and the strength he needed to carry it out, and afterwards to get into art school in Kent.

The day he walked away up the track, pack on back, was very grievous. It was more grievous in a way than leaving Nicholas at college, which, though heart-rending, was the delivery of an eighteen-year-old to the training he had long since chosen. It was grievous in a different way from the delivery of sixteen-year-old Joanna to college in Devon – which had been horrible – because after all the planning, the excitement, the sharing, he was choosing to go back. Over the next few weeks I repeatedly retired to the Dingle to shed tears. It felt like the beginning of an end. It was lonesome for Hugo, and could there be the same sense of purpose without his energy and enthusiasm and imaginative company? But I knew that our lack of transport and social contact had made life difficult for all the children.

It was after he had gone that Hugo built a raft of driftwood, on a part of the riverbank a little way downstream that formed a catchment point. It took him several weekends during the summer holidays. On its completion he ferried us each in turn up and down the river, quanting with a long pole in what was for me one of the most blissful hours ever – the bright sky and water, ripples and movement, and the pride of his achievement.

During the process of Hugo's moving on, and out, in gradual and often painful and difficult steps, we walked one day by the river during a visit of his, beneath the calling of a buzzard.

He said, "That sound reminds me of my raft. I was happy then."

So at the end of a mere seven years, that which had seemed the motivation for the whole project, at least for the two younger children – to provide a different and (we thought) deeper experience from the normal – was all over. For the first time months were no longer divided into terms and holidays. Seasons, work and day-lengths alone regulated activity. But the worrying, of course, went on.

One night I woke at three in the morning besieged with anxieties for each child in turn. I slipped gently out at four, in a turmoil of distress, seeking some kind of escape – no point in waking StJohn only to bombard him.

He's off.

Onward.

I did something I'd never believed in doing: I opened the Bible at random. I found my self at the book of Esther, for no comprehensible reason. I read it through from start to finish – a strange, exotic and savage tale of slaughter, or raging anxiety and guilt. Beyond, somewhere, was still, small, cool reflection.

I'd fallen far short, not always properly taking in their troubles – walking on the bright side can sometimes blind you. I knew that StJohn could be mean and unfeeling (he could switch off like a gas ring). I'd assumed he'd helped with certain problems, even though I knew he'd sometimes denied the children's legitimate needs. And I'd credited the way of life we'd chosen with more than its weight of healing power.

I had left facts of life for the boys entirely to him, and was no better with Joanna, feeling myself incompetent (She was helped by an older female cousin).

In this day and age, no one was likely to be in the position of my great-grandmother, Matilda, 'who was married, as was proper, knowing absolutely nothing'. She was so appalled when her new husband started to take liberties that she hit him, but perhaps he was kind and patient – the marriage was long and happy and she became a Suffragette.

After this cooling-off hour, at five I took the big pot of chicken food out of the oven and put it, as usual, into the porch to cool. Intelligible life had to go on.

> I will give you rain in due season, and the land shall yield her increase, and the trees of the field shall yield their fruit. And your threshing shall reach into the vintage, and the vintage shall reach into the sowing time, and you shall eat your bread to the full, and dwell in your land safely.
>
> *Leviticus.*

> These things, these things were here and but the beholder wanting, which two when they once meet. The heart rears wings bold, and bolder. And hurls for him, O half hurls earth for him off under his feet.
>
> *G. Manley Hopkins*

When our searches had begun to take us further and further west, my father had said "Don't go so far away." But somehow, it happened.

When they came to see us, my father sat in the woodyard, appreciating the peace, and the view, but my mother walked about restlessly, and afterwards said, "But I don't like the mill," as she had said, "But I don't like the cottage," of the Kentish one. She really would have like me in a Georgian house being a little bit rich, successful and socially useful, as she had been. And though she was a good and knowledgeable gardener, she did not really grasp our concept of the development of our life at the mill, and self-sufficiency. She once said to StJohn, "I didn't bring up my daughter to be a gardener."

Over the years I made little islands of journeys – sad ones, and joyful ones. The Kate Gathering was a joyful one. I cycled to town with my suitcase, left the bike in the store of a familiar helpful shop, and caught the coach to Victoria, where I stood with my case and bags of eggs and home-made cheeses, and flowers, among the sea of faces, wondering how we would ever meet. But Joanna found me, and steered me through the chaos to the Tube and to her little two-storey 'flat', and I watched full of admiration and surprise as she prepared a supper of trout and vegetables. I was with what she was with and where she was at. I slept on a futon under a skylight that kept me in touch with the night sky and unfolding of daylight, and the next day we travelled again to be met by Nicholas, and Daniel, Hugo and my brothers.

Kate had first come to the family when she was sixteen, as a lady's maid to a great-aunt. Then she was married, but sadly her husband was killed in the First World War, and she came back to the family. She came to my great-grandfather in Bath and was then with the family in Brighton. She retired to a flat back in Bath, from where she sent the three families (my father, aunt and uncle) a parcel of *real* Bath buns each Christmas. Everyone had been fond of her. My grandfather had left her an annual stipend, but she never spent it, living on her pension, and when she died it came back to the family.

Guy was hosting the gathering at his home in London, for all the descendants of the Brighton family. Kate had collected a great number of hats and everybody was to wear one. I think she would have approved.

Pushchairs and carrycots appeared, first meetings enjoyed. Little descendants played with balls, dogs and Lego inside and outside the house, while the older generation (I am *there*?) who had enjoyed holidays together in their youth rekindled relationships.

Coming home across the spacious landscapes of the south-west of England, I thought of all the diverse people, experiencing their own routes, separations and coming together through childbirths and setbacks, and individual visions of fulfilment. I walked down our steep track holding back my bike between the encompassing trees, to our own space, to hear details of StJohn's three days, back with my own person, in my own space, to tell my tale.

With years between, I travelled to see some of Daniel's paintings hanging in a gallery in London. Joanna was there and Daniel's wife as we walked through London streets, and Joanna pulled me into a shop to buy me a typewriter. And Hugo was there, and we all ate in a restaurant. And we were amazed at the paintings almost sculptured to depict great landscapes of boulders and waves and clouds. Those paintings served him well.

In the two days I was away had begun the alchemy that would turn the close clods of our clay-based soil into something that would crumble and host seeds. A row of cabbages from the cold frame braved the wind and cold, and beside them, as fine as fine grass, onions recently turned out of their seed pots. So it was started – the long haul to refurnish our provisions while still living on the labours of the previous year.

This challenge – the age-long desire to have and work a little land, a scrap of it or a few pots – bubbles on, erupting in allotments and city farms, New Age diggers, communes that begin in earnest and sometimes founder on acrimonies or idleness. And it may even be seen in parks of retirement bungalows with gravel and decking, but also raised beds and production and amazing shows of vibrant plants.

The satisfaction continued to flow for us, glinting among the new green rows, turning up with the autumn digging, hovering about us as we laid the vegetables away in sand. Only tremulous when some arrow of guilty comparison pricked contentment: other people are helping refugees, being assets to society, ferrying their children towards worthwhile attributes to learning, while there we were busily discovering old truths – that the earth can grow food for us, that the sun warms our skin, the wind exhilarates us – and digging gives us an appetite.

Renovation and decoration had continued slowly over the years – StJohn worked with extreme care and thoroughness. It was a good day when the outside of the cottage (white walls and sky-blue windows) was all completed.

When, to our delight, Hugo came to visit, he said "It looks like a real house."

I took him across the river and the sun-drenched fields to the opposite hill, where mushrooms grew in abundance. He stretched out on the grass and I moved on, picking about ten pounds. No one else seemed to pick them. The large ones I dried in strips on trays, the smaller I threaded on strings along the beam (special treats for winter) leaving ample to eat, now.

After a change of ownership of these fields, for days the horrendous whine of chainsaws and roar of ditchers appalled us as we watched from a distance the felling of hundreds of large and small trees grown up along the hedgerows. An area by the river that had become an oak-and-ash copse with primroses and bluebells, was bulldozed back into a field.

And after that the mushrooms ceased to grow and soon it was ploughed. They joined the ranks of the Dear Departed. Larks over our heads for twenty years until silage, then mowing took the place of hay, lapwings along the river field, and cuckoos. They ceased to come.

Song of the Seasons

A haven for birds and a Jersey cow,
A green field in the sun,
Rich earth that yields its harvest up
As days and season run:
These were some of the visions we saw
In embers' gleam and glow
Of a winter fire, with night shut out,
And, beyond us, storm and snow.

Winter Views

But now the oaks in clamour are tossed,
The rising stream sings loud.
The river beyond is over the field,
And the great winds hurl the cloud.

At times the joy of the wind is ours,
Laughing and strong and free.
At times the droop of the falling leaf,
Or cloud-spread solemnity.
For why are we here and whom do we serve,
And what did we seek to prove?
And where is the fire and deep desire
That brought about The Move?

Wave after wave of onslaughts tempt
The mind to close, and deny
The validity of the golden times
That come, and reign, and fly.
Heavy the great grey sky above,
Heavy the earth on the spade.
Many the roots of thistle and couch,
Many the rows to be laid.
But resting shoulder and back, we see
Mid swirl of the keen March air,
Arching the valley from hill to hill,
Transitory, mighty, the rainbow, still
A covenant, rich and fair.

Spring Views

In soft dawn glow, to a blackbird's song
The calf just slid to earth,
Sees light, and shape, lifts fawn-like head
From the strange warm mass of birth.

Early spring is sodden and sad,
Slug-ridden, stressful and slow.
But an alchemy changes the cold stiff clods
To a loam where seeds may grow.

But always subtle the change, and always
Sudden the tide of May.
Like children alongside a longer stride
We tackle the work each day.

Green against blue, green across brown,
Green surging up and through:
The rainbow's promise fulfilled in full,
Its daffodil, rose and blue.

And we but serve the urgency
Of the season's ripple and flow,
Preparing, caring, fretting and sweating,
Coaxing up row by row.

Summer Views

In these short months must all be grown
That time and effort can,
Of greens and grain, legume and root,
Of herb and tuber, flower and fruit,
For cow, and hen, and man.

And during sunny days, with always
Fear of sudden rain,
The shining grass falls to the blade,
And fragrant, rustling hay is made,
Which must before its essence fade,
Be turned, and turned again.

In openness of summer skies,
Our problems shrink and are small.
In flow of warmth, in sunlight's wealth,
We are one with the fullness of all.

The zestful busyness shines and runs,
But a robin's smallest song
Whispers of challenge, hints at the change,
But we are supple and strong.

Autumn Views

(With a respectful salute to Shakespeare's icicles hanging by the wall)

When beech is russet and oak old-gold,
And starlings wheel and sweep and scold;
When ripening cheeses line the board,
And fruit in cold or glass is stored;
When sturdy carrots, marigold-bright,
Turnips and beetroot, sweet and right,
Are laid in sand for a winter's night;
Then onions, plump as an Eastern dome
In clusters hang, and wood hauled home
O'er river and field, sawn, split and stacked
Defies cold, storm and cataract;
When last year's waste is this year's mould
To soften and darken, enrich and enfold—

Then do we know that life is good.
Labour and Earth a parenthood
That generates both health and food.
Then do we start to understand
That cycles of seasons and of land
Encompass man's essential moods,
And needs and aims and gratitudes,
Past literary platitudes,
To essence, soul, *reality.*

I hope there may be some who share my unfashionable delight in rhyme and rhythm, in words and phrases that skip and sing and embrace each other, that move as music.

Bounty.

The Mill front garden.

We've made it.

12: And So – On

On a frosty winter day as I went towards the vegetable garden a young fox walked quite slowly under the trees, behind the compost bins, turned to look back at me and continued on its way. It walked along the top path and stopped where a clump of creeping phlox spread over the edge into the plot. It had sensed a quarry and began to scrabble the edging stones out of the hard ground. Every now and then it stopped and looked at me – I had moved several paces nearer to see it more clearly – but it was too occupied, or too hungry, to worry. Front paws shoving and scraping with all its strength, it danced from side to side on its back legs and gradually a section of the edge clinked and collapsed, and its nose disappeared down a hole. I was still not close enough to see clearly the swift dives of its paws or whether it caught two or more animals, but its head and paws darted like a juggler. Something long swung from its mouth; something shot sideways and was impaled by a nimble foot. Sometimes it tucked its head upside down between its forelegs as if about to somersault – I suppose in pursuit. It was all a rapid series of deft movements and gyrations so beautiful I would have loved to see them in slow motion. And as mice had gnawed holes in the tops of half the beetroot crop I did not mourn them. They were eaten in quite slow chomps up their length and then the fox sat down like a weary dog. Two magpies flew low overhead, perhaps hoping for remains, and it raised its head and watched them. I walked towards it. It still sat, possibly nursing the pleasure of having something in its stomach on this harsh winter's day.

Seen from our cottage, the opposite hill was clothed with trees up to the level field at the top, but cut into the bank a little before the top was the railway line. The motivation for its building was to enable farmers and others to get their produce to London from a local station. The labour involved was huge, with cliff faces blasted out with dynamite, and endless levelling and shovelling. While horses were used as the work went forward, the steadying of the slope below, too steep for horses, must have involved the heaving and banging in of rocks. Hazels were planted along the lower edge as a retaining hedge.

In the year 1886, when this stretch of line opened, Alexandria was still recovering from the bombardment. Allen and Alderson's were back to business-as-usual, and ideas about democracy and socialism were beginning to circulate in England, to the alarm of some of the aristocracy. A party of local dignitaries travelled from the station 'built of local blue stone with white stone facings, of Gothic style presenting a very picturesque appearance [as the local paper recorded] and the scenery maintaining its romantic character all the way from village to village.'

We had been told that daffodils had been grown by the mill and taken by cart to the station to be delivered to London. This was borne out by the fact that every year a few daffodils appeared on the strip of land indicated. Whether or not those living at the mill minded the sight and noise of the trains puffing along just below their horizon we don't know, but the fact that it meant business for them may have compensated. But they would not have had to take the horse and cart up the steep track we had to use, for the old track lay along the lower edge of the field in the opposite direction, towards the ford. It would have been almost impossible for carts loaded with flour to use that steep track – a fact we didn't realise till long after we arrived. Our absorption with having found the place blinded us to its background at the time.

The leat below and parallel with the old track had been dug as one of the many initiatives undertaken to encourage employment and activity in the countryside, and it must have been a massive labour. It brought water from the river to just above the cottage, where it turned at a right angle to flow past the back of the mill house, where the wheel was placed.

The leat had been filled in from our boundary, across what became our woodyard, to the waterway behind the cottage that took water from around it down to the stream. But there was a section out in the field where you could still see its rectangular outline, still shoulder-deep.

Just as the railway, to the consternation of some, had superseded the old canals, so the roads superseded the railway, and the stretch was closed during the Beeching cuts as uneconomic. The lines were taken up, and farmers could take the sleepers from their lengths of it. It remained a strange often dank and wet space among the trees, and the drainage culverts so carefully dug and cared for were smashed by the tractors. All that pride and labour, appreciated and utilised for so little time. But there remained some magnificent trees on that slope – great ash, oak and sycamore trees – so many dear and familiar to me over the years as I walked with my saw and wood bag for the day's supply in dry weather, or string to tie a bundle at other times.

At the foot of the slope opposite to us, by the river, pines and spruce firs had been planted in a regular pattern, probably as a screen for the railway.

If they saw them at all, those conifers would have been insignificant to those dignitaries on the train.

Yet 130 years later they had grown to their full height and glory. There were ravens always nesting in the tallest fir.

All through the woods ash twigs clacked and leaves rustled. But there by the river was the swish and hush of wind through the needles.

The lower branches of the firs had fallen away, but with the help of a propped-up branch, our boys on separate occasions climbed one. As we watched from across the river in the vegetable garden opposite, each waved a handkerchief from very near the top.

During a storm years later, one of the pines crashed down into the river. Gradually over many days it was dragged from its base, and we could see why it had fallen. A second tree had been planted close to it, and rotted into the main stem behind, weakening it.

Foot by surging foot of water current, the tree was pulled across the river to a corner near the edge on our side.

Wood! A tree-ful of pine! We asked, and were given permission, to take it – though not the trunk.

For many days following, after chores, we assembled saws, shears, billhooks, ropes, and sacks, working at first amid the sage-green sea of needles, clinging to branches as we moved cautiously along the trunk. StJohn sawed off the larger branches, which we manoeuvred towards the bank (it would have been both impossible and unsafe to use a chainsaw). Each day we took back bundles, sacks and lengths. The scent made the atmosphere delicious.

Then when we had practically finished, it began to rain. The trunk rose as the river brimmed and swirled. The trunk shook and tugged and then sailed majestically downstream.

It jammed for a few years by the Big Ford, and then vanished – we never saw it harvested. A year later we began using the wood in the Rayburn. It was too inclined to spark for the open fire.

And the river flowed on, speaking out with its many voices across the valley, rushing through consciousness like a purifying force, washing away childhoods and regrets, harvests, guilt and anguish, away, and away.

Returning from the forestry, where I'd collected an old larch pole (many felled at the top of the slope were never collected as those lower down were), I thought, 'That is a strange place for a cow to be lying down., I put down the pole and walked across to her, and realised she was immersed in mud to within a few inches of the top of her back. She had evidently been struggling for some time. She mooed to me, but I could do nothing to help. I walked hastily home, and StJohn went up to the farm to fetch Michael, its owner, who had been down only the evening before. Sitting on a bale of hay, StJohn rode down with him on the back of the tractor.

We had never seen a cow mired before, and neither in his childhood or adult life here had Michael, so deep had the mud become with the winter's quantity of rain.

They walked around her, mud to the top of their boots, working out a strategy. Then they put a halter round her head and attached the rope's end to the tractor bucket. Lifting the bucket with great caution, the front of the animal was raised a few inches.

Then Michael took the rope, and lying along her back he pushed the end of the rope down into the mud on one side of her behind her forelegs. Leaning down, struggling, he worked it beneath her, his cheek and shoulder against her neck. At last he was able to pull it up on the other side. When the end was again fastened to the tractor arm, StJohn moved the lever to lift it. Gradually, amidst huge squelchings, the heifer rose. Grunting and shaking her head, she lurched forwards, a great pad of mud and turf falling from above her front leg. Slowly the back legs emerged as Michael heaved, and she staggered out on to dry land. A few days later he had that crossing bridged.

The sun came out now in a golden haze, and an exhilarating breeze ready to give the washing its freshness. When the children were small, before the move, I had a little washing machine which we brought with us, but it ceased to work after a short while, and for thirty years I did the washing partly inside and partly out, by the leat – sheets were better washed outside. Rainwater, from the big barrel, or the well water served for rinsing, and there were bars in the big chimney behind the Rayburn for drying. It all worked. And there were rubber gloves – how our predecessors would have appreciated those.

＊＊＊

Easter weekend. Last night a gale repeatedly slammed against the end wall of the house and tore through the trees. After I was in bed the reading light went off, on, and finally off. Thinking StJohn was still on his rounds outside, I went to light a candle for him, but found him, towel round his waist and beautiful in the candlelight, having found his own. This morning still no lights, but no matter – I don't need electricity for anything. I sit here with my pot of tea and can see birds and trees. Blue tits are working their way over the elder which has tiny leaves. Probably it was the transformer; probably they will come and fix it.

I think about that special morning. The fishermen, who had stopped being fishermen to be disciples, unsure what to do next, shattered by the way things had turned out, depressed after a fruitless night. Then sunlight. A whiff of smoke from the shore. And, suddenly, the admonition to reset the net – and its filling. The reunion – the meal. Surely that meal, that morning, more to be commemorated, to be moved towards, than the gloom, guilt, pain and sadness of the death that was past.

I remember a three-hour Good Friday service held in the village church when I was at school, to which we could go for as long or as short a time as we wished. I was surprised to find I stayed the whole time. I can't remember how the service went, but certain things those three hours taught me: that time, as an experience, is elastic and variable; that one's real existence happens in one's own thinking; and that the depth and actualities of that existence can only be experienced solo, and are not truly transferable to others.

One day StJohn came to the vegetable garden with his hand folded over a bird. Sapphire head, long beak – amazingly it was a young kingfisher. We see and hear them calling as they fly along the river, but never before had we seen them here. It was quiet in his hand, but every now and then turned and gripped his finger with its dark curved beak that was serrated along its edges. He had disentangled it from the loganberry net in the garden, gently freeing it limb by limb and strand by strand. He held it until he felt it was revived enough to fly, then set it with its feet astride a small branch. It crouched for a moment, then sped off like a little azure rocket. I took the net away.

When I open the door into the morning twilight pipistrelles arrow over my head. Wind through leaves, wind over the hills, trickle of the nearby stream, murmur of the river, a rush of water drops from a branch. Sounds of robin and wren, chaffinch and magpie, blackbird and rook. I marvel more, not less, at the turning world with every passing year, the deepening into night, or opening into morning. I want to say to everyone, "Do you see it?" The shifting accents of light, melting to a secret envelope of darkness or the wide triumph of day, and embrace of sunlight – to be here, within that perfection! Such heaven almost frightens me – is hell to come?

And here we have the heaven of a haven, yet of the earth earthy, labour and disappointment, the ideal, the vision always beyond itself.

Throughout the years, we completed the cutting of the hay, with our scythes, raked it into a big old bean net and dragged it down to the stack. I watched StJohn climb the ladder to the top, immersed in the loads he carried on the pitchfork, so that he could level the top with the last of it. Then we unfolded the canvas cover, and with difficulty, drew it over, and fastened it down. The older end we used for bedding; the rest provided sufficient feed, with fodder beet and some barley, for the winter.

Six pounds of redcurrant jelly – one of the most exquisite in colour and flavour.

One day as I reached the river with my bag and saw to collect wood from the other side, I saw, like a scattering beam, a line of bubbles through the water and stood still. A flat brown head and sleek shoulders arose facing me – my first sight of an otter. I was surprised at the size of it. Without haste it turned and curved downwards. I saw the long smooth tail, then it emerged, and swam to the opposite bank, disappearing in a tangle of weeds.

StJohn, carrying a long pole, saw the head of an otter swimming downstream. He stood stock-still, and it came out on to a little shingly stretch of shore and stood up, a few feet away.

He said, "Eyes met eyes."

Unhurriedly it returned to the water, and then turned on its back, paws angelically on its chest, stretching and rolling, like a little child in enjoyment.

We witnessed a bird ballet as we sat having lunch in the garden. It took us a few moments to realise what was happening, as there was more and then more movement. A pair of flycatchers swept out from the hedge, snapped their beaks and returned, and surprisingly a pair of chaffinches did the same. A robin was stalking and pecking up and down, and we saw that the path was crawling with ants getting ready to swarm. Then three swallows swiftly circled in, four more, and more still, whirling over our heads, lower then higher as the ants rose. This continued over many minutes, the flycatchers still busy in an unforgettable pageant of wings.

A hedgehog was tucking into the whey left in the bantam run after we put the bantams to bed. Its head was fastened against the rim of the bowl as endearingly as a babe on the nipple.

At last we have a satisfactory water supply for the vegetable garden. We managed to acquire two 300-gallon drums that had held orange juice, and set them on cement and rubble bases just outside the vegetable garden fence, having rolled them, on delivery, down the track. The gutter of the barn above the garden empties into a fifty-gallon drum, and we buried a pipe across the track and down the bank, long enough to rise to the top of a big drum. With a little persuasion and experimentation, water would flow with a melodious musical song, and through a pipe at the bottom I could fill cans or run a hose.

Jackdaws elected to nest in the small chimney on the other end of the house (a chimney StJohn had climbed to and perched beside over the years), and their huge bundle of sticks clattered down the chimney and scattered on the floor. We decided to make a framework to fit across the top, and StJohn, knowing the dimensions, shaped one. But he did not feel confident now to go up the ladder, and I said I would do it. I had not realised, til I reached the top, what a terrifying distance it was from the ground.

Somehow, having had the wire tied behind me, and with more concentration that I had ever had to summon, I managed to undo it and push it in. Then, thankfully, I managed to get down.

StJohn rebuilt that little fireplace in place of the existing tiled one, with stone we had gathered, and he built a mantelpiece. Sometimes we would light the fire there during supper, and afterwards go in and enjoy it. I would read aloud, which StJohn loved. We read *Kon-Tiki* and Arthur Grimble's *A Pattern of Islands*. And we read also Flora Thompson's, *Down the Bright Stream* and *Lark Rise to Candleford*. And Dana and Ginger Lamb's explorations of the jungle. Precious times to remember.

I had forded the river with my saw and bag, leaving the barrow on the field, and was busy gathering into lengths the wood I had sawn, when I carelessly tripped over a bramble, and crashed down on my arm. I filled the bag with one hand, dragged it to the river, and somehow manoeuvred the barrow back to the house, leaving StJohn to fetch it in. As the arm remained stupid and black the next morning, and having endeavoured to organise some meals for StJohn, the ambulance team I'd called for took me to the hospital, having ascertained that the elbow was smashed.

I was fitted with a metal elbow, my own being in pieces. I was the only person in my ward, and most of the second night I stood by the window, overlooking the multitudinous city lights, and gathering myself together on the strength of that brilliance and breadth of great and small illuminations.

I managed bread somehow, and didn't go back to the river for a while, and when I did it was touched by the fear of my own stupidity. The comfort was that I am left-handed, and it was my right arm that had been broken.

There was a last visit to my father, where he was in hospital, briefly. Perhaps it is only in retrospect that you really understand what you have experienced.

When they were engaged, he wrote to my mother,

'I went to Church this morning. It was terrifying. He never went by the book of words. I don't think I could face it again without you to hold my hand, sweet one. But I really get much more spiritual uplift (you know what I mean by the term, and I take it that's the idea of a service), from the supreme beauty and glory of natural scenery. Well, anyway, he read out our Banns, quite correctly, and nobody had "just cause or impediment.'

After a tear-ridden coach journey home, too conscious of times past and of what might come, I learnt that he had died. I was at least glad of words we had exchanged during that last visit.

There was his funeral, at which John read from Ecclesiastes which he had so often quoted to us.

To everything there is a season, a time to every purpose under heaven: A time to be born, and a time to die; a time to plant, and a time to pluck up that which is planted; A time to kill, and a time to heal; a time to break down, and a time to build up; A time to weep, and a time to laugh; a time to mourn, and a time to dance.

The last time I saw my mother, in the home where she lived after my father died, she said, after I'd been with her for a couple of hours, "You're not my daughter, are you?" I could only put my arms round her and realise how little I'd done for her, on account of our great faraway project. For it was John and his dear wife, Margaret, who coped – and our mother was not easy.

After she died, I had planned to go to her funeral – but again the project intervened, for the day before it our calf of the time became ill, and I could not bring myself to abandon the situation. We spent the whole of that night in the field (the cow, strangely and totally, unconcerned) with the dying calf. And on the horizon, the aurora borealis shimmered all night – something we had never seen before, making those hours even more strange and unforgettable.

When StJohn's sister Joy died, sometime after her husband John, her ashes were delivered to us by arrangement at the top of the track by a pale and punctilious man who handed me the urn with gentle respect. In affection and sadness we scattered them round the roots of our favourite apple tree. She died seven years before StJohn.

Joanna had always been close to her Aunty Joy. (My only regret in this was that she had introduced Joanna to cigarette smoking, which later gave her one of the hardest fights in her life to give up.)

But Joanna had always loved going to stay with Joy and John in their elegant house in Surrey, Moorponds, finding her own home rather unsatisfactory on return. But I was always glad she had that relationship. She was deeply grieved when Joy died.

There remained the indelible glories of earth and skies, supplies, affection. I crossed the field heavy-hearted, and the river with tears, for his weariness and pain, the projects lying fallow. In the woods I came to the great sycamore, its trunk crazed yet smooth against my forehead, soothing thought. On, up through the clustering trunks to the oak – and I reached out my hand.

But the oak said, "No. Do not reach out. You must stand your ground sole on the earth as I."

So I stood straight, and waited.

Below the steep treed bank the river flowed rippling, each stone a voice. The voices all said, "Gentleness. Gentleness."

Against the sky, close to the spread of the oak, was an ash with crooked, broken twigs, and stumps of fallen branches, yet a multitude of leaves showed its green vigour. And it spoke of the validity of what we had tried to do: our losses, failures, deaths and exhaustion; and harvests, triumphs and moments of serenity or exhilaration.

A holly branch was across the path, but I pushed past it on my way, on, through and out to an open space where once a grandson watched hornets in a stump. I took blackberries – a gift, cool and sweet.

The river still said, "Gentleness. Gentleness."

I walked back through, and said to the oak, "Yes, I will stand."

I gave thanks to the sycamore – spokesmen, to me. I had always taken his strength for granted, but he was ten years older than me.

StJohn's burial ground after thirty-eight years at The Mill.

Flowers at the burial ground.

13: And So – Forth

A Great Time

Sweet chance, that led my steps abroad,
Beyond the town, where wild flowers grow—
A rainbow and a cuckoo, lord!
How rich and great the times are now!
Know, all ye sheep
And cows that keep
On staring that I stand so long
In grass that's wet from heavy rain—
A rainbow and a cuckoo's song
May never come together again;
    May never come,
    This side the tomb.

W. H. Davies

All the earlier years at The Mill the cuckoo called for us, the rainbows came for us and for our children, but the larks were driven away from the top fields by the silage and then the lawn mowing, and the cuckoos ceased to come – but the rainbows and the cuckoos and the larks had been, had been for us, and no one can ever take that away.

It isn't just that he was the rainbow and I was the cuckoo (though I probably was), or even that he ended up totally cuckoo (though he did). It is that apart from all the absurdities and tragedies and tediums in the world there are also the amazing drifts and billows of beauty and magic, the laughter and love of children, the wonders of sunsets and moonshine, unfolding leaves, the unstoppable cycle of seasons and days. The enchantments and necessities carry you on, take you with them, and you do the spring cleaning because it is spring and make love because the moment is radiant with the same magic – the marvellous plant is there in front of you, of itself; the strong eyes of the unknown animal hold you in that moment of beautiful sunshine, long, long ago.

There was the time when he was feverishly ill in the night, getting worse, and I cycled up to the phone box to get the emergency doctor. He came down by the light of my torch, came in with his bag and saved his life – and after a while he was sawing again.

Another time he tripped over a step downstairs and put his shoulder out – it took two hours to get him up into a chair, and a neighbour brought their van down and took him up to the ambulance. All day I pushed him around the hospital as he was sorted out. I left him there and came back in a taxi late at night, down the track with a torch they had lent me. I relit the Rayburn, and wondered: the Rayburn – just for me?

Over weeks it was as if necessary work and the time needed for it somehow expanded beyond proper attention, and instead of leaving him to get up and get his breakfast it became dangerous not to be walking down in front of him, one step then the next, or not to be walking behind him going up, so that morning wooding was cancelled and other things took up the day. He didn't mow any more. I could not live there without the patterns and order and provisions of supplies we had established for all those years. I could not see it go back into the wilderness we had made into our self-sufficiency and order – the vegetable garden, herb garden, flower garden, mown paths, trimmed hedges.

We found – in, I think, *The Smallholder*, to which we had contributed articles – the perfect agent for our type of place, but when I was witnessing the viewers and prospective buyers it was as if I was acting for someone else. It did not seem a reality.

In order to do it I could not really be there, and was surprised at how freely StJohn chatted and explained. It sold well, but our years of it, our *doing*, was a sealed box, invulnerable.

There were big complications with Land Registry, the muddles we had made without realising it, and a long process of realignments. But like one shining stone in a sea of mud was the fact that it was already loved, for itself, as it was; and the caravan, regarding which we had been guilty of cruel neglect, was to be restored.

Nicholas searched for a house for us. No good another cottage on its own needing attention. No good a town house. He and his partner knew what he was wisely looking for. And because each foray, and getting in and out of the car, became more difficult for StJohn, from the same zone of unreality we acceded to what was practical: a bungalow in a park of bungalows, a minuscule bit of garden, all mod cons and a price within our means.

In the last few weeks at The Mill the reservoir of bitterness was resolved by bonfires. We had prided ourselves on the fact that we had contributed so little to general pollution, but the enormous volume of material I barrowed round and burnt in huge conflagrations was nothing to be proud of. I turned out, discarded, shut things out of my love. Why should I want pictures of Tunbridge Wells or Knole Park – or various others – in this different place? Slip them into a bag, smash the glass, and bag up; burn the remainder. I parted with my bags of pieces of material to a sewing group, burnt old clothes (most of my working and non-transferable wardrobe), my piles of previously useful rags, some of the books. There was no time to try and sell things. I kept what might be useful to the children – passed down some specials – but disposed of innumerable flammable barrow loads. Also, our neighbour at the top of the track ferried up for us trailer loads of rubbish, and hospice-shop material, all of which I could not have barrowed up. They were so kind.

Not having my outlet, StJohn suffered horribly. All garments and objects he possessed were precious to him. He had always collected and prized things, including gadgets and tools, acquired and never used, curious things. He packed up his quantities of tools into many boxes and Nicholas took them to our new garage, where they were never to be used again apart from the few the children selected or I came to need. I packed things up against his grief, his constant questioning about this or that – many things I didn't know the use for. The tool shed was left almost as complete with tools as when we came – hay forks, pitchforks, the great scythe he had used, others we had acquired, wedges, sledges, many spades.

So one day in December (how had it always been in winter?), the ground outside the house a sea of mud, the removers left their big van at the top and managed to bring their trailer down many times. They waded through the mud carrying our furniture, and they were amazingly kind.

With a driver who had ferried StJohn several times, we arrived at the park after the removal van, which was there, as was Hugo, helping us, helping them. I'd selected only the furniture we would need for the space – there was to be no clutter, and there had not been time to properly distribute. In the garage were put the three wooden boxes for food – a boon to this day. The kitchen cupboards were excellent, and no ash, no smoke, virtually no dust, finger- adjustable warmth and hot water.

StJohn was slipping away in his mind. Sometimes he wore a boy's face, and sometimes it held a strangeness I came to recognise, knowing that then he was not seeing what I was seeing, but was out on a road, or by a river, maybe with people I couldn't see, or he was about some urgent purpose I was too stupid or too selfish to share. When you are in the mental vacuum you come to inhabit after being repeatedly pulled out of sleep, you can find no way of obliterating his knowledge of a dog making a mess by the wall, or a baby precariously on the chest of drawers.

With his face all crazed, and wriggling to the edge of his chair, he would hold out his hand and say, "Just pull me up and we'll go – we'll get out" – to that place of rainbows, where we had belonged.

After the Move

The glory of it,
The sounds of its waters.
The song of a single stone
In the shallow stream.
The roar of the river, gathering,
The stream rising,
River and stream, two voices blending.

The sounds of its waters.

How many thousands, millions,
Have wept for the sounds of Home—
Afterwards.

It was not long before we had to acquire a wheelchair for transport from room to room, because I could not help enough in any other way, and I was grateful for it. Nicholas had found for us a large adjustable raiser-chair, and that helped as well. Yet somehow StJohn was growing more remote – if I tried to put my arms round him it seemed everything hurt. I failed him in so many ways.

Trying to transfer from wheelchair to raiser-chair became harder, the space, the half-turn between the two, more dangerous, and after twice spending several hours in agonisingly attenuated struggles to get him back up again, I was offered twice-daily carers to transfer him with the help of a stand that turned. This meant twice each day being ready for them, having him fed and dressed by the stated time and being ready myself. And not being a natural nurse myself, I had to bend tough stems within me to 'toilet', dress and wash him. Just being willing to doesn't make you good at it. The carers were faultlessly patient, kind and efficient.

***

With a conspiratorial sideways glance, he says, "Who's over there in that corner?"

"I can't see anyone."

"Can't you tell him to go?"

"You tell him. He'll take more notice of you."

He makes a formal speech, very politely: "Can you please all go now – we want the place to ourselves. Please pack up your belongings and leave." And later: "Have they taken the little children?"

"I'm sure they have. You told them."

"Can't you help a bit? Can't you co-operate?"

At 4 a.m. he shouts, "There are five cows there by the wall. They're dunging everywhere."

As it's the third or fourth call of the night my resistance is low.

"Darling, no cow can get in here. There are no cows."

"There are five cows," he shouts. "Please come and get your cows." He calls out many times, then calls, "Don't forget I love you" – and goes to sleep.

As disturbed nights accumulate I get up feeling as if immersed in cotton wool, with no moorings or exit or meaning. Sometimes when he asks for it at night I bring him a thin slice of toast with marmalade, or pieces of cut-up apple, and witness the few moments of conscious activity.

This is winter – the terrain of our lives is frozen hard and unforgiving. For sixty-two years we've rattled on, occupied with a hundred things, quarrelling sometimes, hating sometimes. (I threw my wedding ring at him not long after we married and never worried about it, though my mother did. I found it later, safe in its box, and could get it nowhere near passing my knuckle onto my finger.) We were always busy – harvesting, cutting wood, quite often hugging each other, doing things with the children, mourning over their leaving us.

He is convinced there is water all around the bed; "Don't let the covers get wet."

"I can't keep this up," I shout at him, and he says, "If you wanted to you would keep on. Strength is there for the asking."

And I'm not completely asking. The exasperation and exhaustion – the excuse to not deeply trust, or deeply ask. We are going to look round nursing homes, and for him this is treachery and abandonment.

He shouts into the night, "Why can't you love me?"

'Love is not love which alters when it alteration finds., Any alteration? Total alteration? Was it not love, then?

'The rivers shall not overflow you' – but they have, and they are.

***

Leaving him with a carer, Joanna, Carole and I visit several homes and, over lunch, evaluate each, and select one. We ring up the chosen one and arrange for Madam to come and evaluate this old man, with a view to placing him in her care. He will be better looked after, have more about to interest him. No one angry. And I am forever culpable.

That night he calls me, and when I go in he says, "Can you take away this pig?" His eyes are shut.

I say, "Yes, of course. I'll get it out."

"Thank you," he say, and remains asleep.

The lady comes and talks to him in a way to which he responds, and she makes him smile in a way I seem to have become incapable of evoking – that dear smile. Yet he was even more desperate now to get away.

"Just take my hand. We'll walk to the corner and get back to our place."

I get him wriggled back again into the chair.

"Look – there are people out there. Go and ask for their help."

In a quick flip, I say, "All right," and put my coat on. I go and stand outside, look at the trees and sky, go in again and say, "They're too busy, I'm afraid. They say we'll have to manage."

I have never before found myself in a situation where I have two courses of action and both are impossible. How can you peel off the living skin of a shared life and put it aside as if it were Velcro? How do you cast off the person you've cooked for, cuddled and cut up wood with, brought up children and argued with.

How do you say, "We shall be separate now."

Yet to go on is also impossible – because I am no longer doing it well enough to be fair to him. Will his life be better when professionally managed – the only minus the absence of me? Exchanged for people who can manage better, who are not distraught?

And I have to admit another serpentine thought: perhaps there are things I can do. Can I be rightly free, mentally explore, not merely a failure – and he in a right place?

So amazingly it is all to happen – am I being carried along, or did I choose? – and this is our last day here.

I get up at six, wash and dress him and give him his breakfast so we're ready for when the carers come for the last time. Later, with the wheelchair fixed to the floor of the wheelchair-taxi, he almost dozes. I thought I had spoken enough, prepared him enough, but instead I hopelessly try to heal his pain and confusion when he thinks he is coming back with me.

"You didn't care enough to stick it out."

And I walk away, and come back to this, my unlikely home.

I often asked him if he'd like some records – "What about Los Paraguayos?" – but it would be too painful, and nothing else had appeal for him. Now I play Stravinsky's 'Rite of Spring' and it crashes it all out for me. The Khatchaturian piano concerto that bled out the harshness and crashed the airwaves for my fist. Didn't you know, when I was angry and shouted and protested at your obtuseness in believing you'd just walked back from Plymouth – didn't you know it was not at you – at the man I used to know – but at the imposition of the cuckoo that had entered your head and taken you over? But what have I done? What have I done?

I went and saw him with one and then another of the children. He talked to them, but he wasn't really there. After two weeks they phoned to say they had sent him to hospital, and I went there by taxi. And the nurses were so kind. They put a bed for me beside him, and they looked after him so beautifully. He did not speak except to complain if a movement hurt. Late into the third night, his eyes tight closed, he began to breathe with a rasping sound – a tortured engine that insisted on grinding on, and on. I was holding his hand, stroking him. How long can he – can I – endure these ever-and-ever moments? (My mother had said, "He just stopped.") And at last the engine paused, slowed, three slow, smooth breaths, and silence. Silence. Stillness like a huge fullness of peace, an infinite space unfurling into a sky of quiet darkness. I sat in the silence, the allness of nothingness, perhaps for an hour before I pressed the bell, and got dressed. I didn't look at him or touch him again. He was gone.

They called a taxi for me, and I came back to my home at two in the morning – my home, no longer *our* home. Light, warmth, food if I wanted it – all there, just for me; and I was so grateful that we had planned ahead, for three days later, with the help of Nicholas's arranging and Nicholas and Hugo dressing him in the morgue, three sons and three grandsons carried him under the shroud down the great open field of the natural-burial site to the plot we had bought a couple of years before, and all seventeen of the family were assembled. We needed no one else. Nicholas brewed maté and we all drank it, some from those little maté pots I had bought in ignorance all those years ago. Nicholas and a grandchild said lovely loving words, and when the shroud was lowered we all threw our bluebells and other wild flowers, and handfuls of earth and some resentments. A great-grandson threw a picture he had drawn, while his little sister sat on the grass among the buttercups.

And then we all went to an organic-farm-restaurant – again arranged for me by Nicholas – and had a meal and walked about and talked in blessed sunshine. The little 'greats' were loved and talked to; and some who met seldom, enjoyed meeting. StJohn would perhaps have congratulated us all.

There is the luxury of knowing there will be no calls in the night (though sleep can come tardily), of being able to enjoy a phone conversation with an offspring without being challenged by a need, or impatience for the time involved. Small feathers along the wings of my mind began to lift and shake themselves. I can listen to music while darkness deepens, read long and peacefully enough to understand.

But then grief strikes randomly and unexpectedly, like a great dark cloud thrust across the whole vision, edged with guilt, saturated with tears, "Why can't you love me?" meant "Why can't you love me out of this suffering – out of here?" And under that shadow anything beyond seems meaningless and unobtainable.

I remembered visiting a very beautiful villa in Italy – a delicious meal on a verandah overlooking the sea in a bower of flowers. But the aura that overhung it, completely oppressive, was of sadness. The hostess had lost her husband some time previously, and now herself dwelt in this solemnity of grief, in which joy would be disloyalty. Any sense of beauty or enjoyment was shut out of that marble shrine of loss, which had become impregnable, though many had tried to penetrate it.

I was only young then, but leaving that outwardly idyllic place was a relief we all felt, we knew, and my father pointed out that this emotional shrine was an insult to everything lovely in the world, even to love itself. (And I know that much, much later, each agreed there must be no all-stifling mourning.) Only the pursuit of these two – everything lovely and love itself – whatever it takes, and even in the face of bereavement, can be meaningful loyalty.

I loved StJohn partly because his acceptance of me enveloped my difficulty of living with myself. I don't think he even knew of it – the disappointment, unrealised hopes (though many were realised), my social inadequacy. It was all irrelevant within the warming activity of himself and the project. In the same way perhaps I ignored his moods, the occasionally revealed slab of stone. Perhaps I only came to partially understanding it when learning more about his father. And now I have to seek out a different garment to hold myself together.

It was the undeniable need that brought about the purchase of this house; and as it would have been impossible for me at the time to search for myself, I can only be grateful that it was found for me. And if sometimes I feel in a foreign land, and scream inwardly – well, so do many others, and there are a great many blessings to count.

I have a spare bedroom for the first time. On a shelf is a row of the first, and progressive, pots that StJohn made at Camberwell (our second wasted try at life). In my room is a row of little magazines (*The Countryman*) containing pieces I wrote that virtually wrote themselves – about some of the best moments at The Mill, from those years that he faced, started and worked through for my sake as well as his own. I pick lettuces and beans and turnips and tomatoes from the few square feet of ground tucked around the house, and sometimes lean back in a reclining chair to watch the twilight filter through the tall trees at the back – ash and sycamore – in that transformation that ever holds its magic for me. And lacking a party straw to draw the air from my beans before freezing, I use my beautiful silver maté *bombilla*.

So I find myself in moments of stillness or creativity, sweeter far for the richness of the life that preceded it, but sweet also for themselves.

And there are these amazing adults, our children, who somehow, all devoid of silver spoons, pushed their way through the opposing branches we allowed across their paths – and with their lovable partners and offspring.

Sometimes, if spring sunshine pours in warm through my windows, a breath of that other place courses through me – that world of green trees and space – and I am altogether lost within my own longing and the rain of my love in that so-sweet lost place.

Yet my dozens of exercise-book diaries express a fifty-fifty mix of pure enjoyment with anxieties and anguish, every month unrolling with agonising problems followed by rewards and delights. We might have been more useful to the children and others doing almost anything else, and StJohn, throughout, intermittently talked about moving, yet to have shared Earth's bliss and furies is worth more than any wealth could be, and the work we did there was repaid.

And if I should become aware far down my road of the advancing shadow of the cuckoo, I trust I would have the wit and courage to forestall it with finality.

I have never been so free. And with the freedom ideas drop into my mind like ripe apples – sometimes poems, sometimes essays involving contented hours in the library. The history was put into my hand. Liking or disliking my surroundings is not relevant. I can utilise what I find and what I can experience – words, a few vegetables, sunshine, quiet, music, warmth, amidst huge gratitude for all who have helped me in so many ways – and my children, and their children, who forgive, and visit me.

I walk down the hill, in spring, passing celandines and primroses and periwinkles, to a sheltered bus stop – my route to books. Or up the lane to a track where in summer I can pick blackberries, perhaps to freeze, or just enjoy. I can look over the outstretched fields – spaces that thirteen generations of Gervis forbears looked over, rode their horses over – and I am content with those spaces, under the wide sky.

The End

234

Many Thanks

Life has given me all that I ever loved.

I rolled in the dew, that sunny early morning
In the wild part of my friend's garden,
When we were small, and ecstatic for the gold and silver
On the grass and the buttercups.

I ran down the hill in the wind on the Common
Early, no one else there.
Danced to music by myself
For the joy, the rhythm, the tune,
The freedom of unwatched movement.

And read, silently to myself
Or aloud with delight, poems repeated, repeated,
Or newly found, or newly understood.
Mastered the climbing of an awkward tree,
Needing that step, that grip,
Stretching courage.

Practised, over and over and over,
Phrase by slow phrase, a small piece of piano music
That eluded me – the notes reluctant
To bridge that gap between desire and ability,
Stumbling between steady trickle and flow
Of tune as it should be, chord as supposed to sound,
Again, and again (Don't slump, don't slump—
Try, try) until sometimes
The sequence and my fingers knew each other—
The sounds at last belonging to the music,
Not just to me.

In sudden shameful greed – school tea.
The bliss of butter, new bread, strawberry jam,
Milk and honey.
The beach, lying drying, waves lapping,
Overspread with warmth, the body full-stretched,
Each limb in utter peace.

And later – so much later—
Bliss of desiring and being desired.
Of being complete with one another.
Of tipping two basketfuls of thoughts,
Wishes, bubbling creative visions
Into one heap of fullness of days,
Years, and doing.

Dawning responses in the infant face.
The answering smile in shine of the eyes.
The hands patting each other,
Tiny feet joyously kicking the air.
To the talking, the sharing of stories and poems,
And trees, flowers, outspread grass.
Challenge of rain, snow trodden, stamped
Under little boots.

Till ongoing questions, plans, disconnect—

To what? What is best?
Queries – and guilt uppermost.
Chasms opened in certainties, needs unfulfilled.
Light cast back—
Back along lines that had seemed complete,
Revealing spaces, rents unmended.

Then recompense unthought
Arriving as sudden gifts
On the doorstep of my age, they come:
The light in the eyes, the kindness.
They are here – and theirs, not mine, yet mine.
Pain dropped to fade along the way.
And *we* are whole again.
The words spin for me – the notes at last
Play themselves.

Acknowledgements

1. Photographs and reported account taken from the *Sunday Telegraph* magazine of the crating-up and transport of Cleopatra's Needle, in 1877.

2. 'Mrs Bull's Adventures on the Way to England', an account handwritten by Mary Anne Bull in 1891.

3. Stories and comments about the Alderson family, gathered and written down by Christine Alderson (later Mrs William Rose) and Dorothy Backhouse.

4. An account written by Dr Henry Gervis of Brighton, describing his experience in the First World War.

5. *Alexandria, City of Memory* by Michael Haag.

6. *Gallipoli* by Henry Broadbent.

7. *Fighting for the Bucks* by E. J. Hounslow.

8. Chief of the Arab Scouts" by Hugo Backhouse.

9. Being unable to find a version of *Chief of the Arab Scout*" in English but in possession of it in Swedish, Lesley Evans translated it on her computer and printed it out for me. I am deeply grateful.

10. *Among the Gauchos* by Hugo Backhouse.

11. Shipping, census, polo records, and parts of family trees, gathered by Joanna Backhouse and Laura McNeil.

12. StJohn Backhouse, who passed on stories of his childhood, and enough of his creative and outdoor spirit to enable thirty-eight years of rural

living, providing inspiration for many articles of mine published in *The Countryman* magazine.

13. To our children, endowed with difficult transitions, a difficult father and imperfect mother.

14. To their ever developing gifts, strengths and affection, and that of their families.

15. To the staff of Barnstaple Library, ever patient in finding books and facts for this computer-illiterate.

16. To Rob Palmer, who lent me books and helped me align the military record of Hugh (Hugo) Backhouse, which I obtained from the Archive Department, with other records.

17. To my youngest son, Hugo, who photographed photos and some objects for transfer to computer.

18. To Tricia Simms who transferred my story, much of it from my handwriting, to her computer, to send forward. I am grateful for her patience and kindness.